Love In The Shadows

JulieAnn Platz

AmErica House
Baltimore

Copyright 2000 by Julie Ann Platz.

All rights reserved. No part of this book may be reproduced in any form without written permission from the publishers, except by a reviewer who may quote brief passages in a review to be printed in a newspaper or magazine.

First printing

This is a fiction novel. Names, places, characters and incidents are fiction.

ISBN: 1-58851-668-7
PUBLISHED BY AMERICA HOUSE BOOK PUBLISHERS
www.publishamerica.com
Baltimore

Printed in the United States of America

Dedication:

For Steve,
my high school sweetheart.
Walk with me, my love,
and close the door behind us.
Look not upon yesterday
and the places we've been,
but for tomorrow and the
possibilities of where we
can go together.

Chapter 1

    Jenny stood up from where she knelt in the dirt and brushed the moist earth from her rolled-up baggy blue overalls. The soil that felt cool to the bottoms of her bare feet earlier in the day had grown hot from the afternoon sun. She brushed the stray hairs that fell from her blond pony tail away from her face with the back of her hand, as she squinted in the sunlight with pale blue eyes. With the last of the potatoes harvested, she gathered her gardening tools and began walking toward the old storage shed that her father built when she was a small child. Across the yard, a red corvette slowly rolled up the driveway, catching her attention immediately. Hurriedly, she put the tools in the dark shed and closed the door behind her. Her heart beat rapidly as she peered out the dirty window of the shed. She wiped the window clean with the sleeve of her shirt and peered out through the small, clean spot. She watched with anticipation as the handsome visitor left his fancy car and strolled confidently toward the old farmhouse.
    The visitor knocked once and entered, ducking through the low frame. He was more handsome than she remembered and had grown quite tall since she saw him last. Jenny tapped the dusty window ledge nervously, contemplating what to do. She couldn't let him see her this way. Her clothes were a mess, her hair was tangled, and her feet were filthy. She glanced furtively toward the house, opened the shed door, and slipped behind the building without being noticed. Quickly, she headed toward the grassy spot by the creek and planted herself on a huge boulder a short distance from the murky water's edge.
    A mallard glided across the ploughed field on the other side of the creek, discreetly lowering itself to the surface of the water. Jenny watched as the mallard put its webbed feet in front of its body, grasping the rapid ripples in the water created by the fall breeze as it blew through the meadow. The mallard closed his wings and gently settled atop the water's surface, bobbing along with the gentle rush of the water. He dived his head under the dirty water searching for tiny fish. Jenny watched diligently as the duck's tail flipped straight up in the air as it dived. The bird reminded Jenny of the way the Titanic looked in the movie as it bobbed above the ocean waves before diving to the bottom of the mucky ocean floor. Within seconds, the duck had a

mouthful of food. He puffed his belly, stretched his gallant wings and, flapping them rapidly, he flew off above the treetops. It was time for the birds to fly south for the winter and Jenny would miss them fervently until their return again in the spring.

Jenny felt her belly and wondered about the life that nestled safely inside. She and Gregg had made love only once but she missed her last period and she knew she must be pregnant. The home pregnancy test she used a week ago turned a light shade of pink. Even with the newest forms of technology, the home pregnancy tests were not proven to be one hundred percent accurate. Although the results were questionable, Jenny knew in her heart it was true. She would like to have given the test a little more time to soak but she nervously disposed of the box and its contents as her brother Jason beat on the bathroom door, urging her to hurry for church.

Gregg, the father of Jenny's baby, was average height with sandy blonde hair. He was very handsome and had the deepest blue eyes that Jenny had ever seen. They reminded her of the ocean. He was strong, respectful, and worked very hard. Gregg was a couple years older than Jenny and she loved his maturity. That was what attracted her to him in the beginning. He was very shy and came from a rather wealthy family. His father worked at the bank and his mother volunteered for a lot of committees and was active in their church. His mother was very strict and cold, so different than Gregg. There was talk about town that she was mentally ill, but Jenny knew it was just small town gossip. She had been through much trauma when Gregg had a drunk driving accident several months earlier that nearly killed him.

Gregg's relationship with his mother wasn't a pleasant one and Jenny did know Gregg had a fight with his mother the night of the accident. Gregg had asked her to go to a party that night. They were both very serious about their relationship and they were becoming more than just friends. Jenny remembered how she prepared for their first lovemaking. She visited the doctor and asked for birth control. She purchased condoms and was physically prepared for that special occasion. Nothing could have prepared her for what happened next. They both drank too much at the party and, after harsh words that night, they parted in anger. The next thing she remembered was that

Gregg's car was found in a ravine a short distance from her home and that he was in the hospital in a coma.

Gregg's parents blamed her for the accident and refused to let Jenny see him in the hospital. How could she have let their son drive drunk? Jenny blamed Gregg's mother because she knew that she had a fight with Gregg before he picked her up for the party. Gregg and his mother fought a lot and she thought he drank to cover the pain that his mother caused in his life. Jenny knew that his mother was very protective of Gregg and criticized every girl he dated, even Jenny. The night of Gregg's accident, she forbade him to date Jenny. Gregg left his home in angry fury and that was the last time he returned for a long, long time.

After months of fighting and pleading with Gregg's parents, they finally agreed to let her visit Gregg in the hospital. Gregg's mother spent a long time in psychiatric therapy, but Jenny found the strength to go on for Gregg's sake. After Jenny was allowed to finally see Gregg, he began to show signs of movement and one miraculous day, he woke up. After the accident that nearly left him paralyzed, she stood by him and never gave up hope that he would recover from the coma that he had been in for months. She helped him with his therapy and eventually he recovered, except for a slight hint of a limp in his left leg and a scar beneath his left eye.

During the comatose period, Jenny's love only grew for the blonde-haired man that stole her heart. After he recovered, she vowed that she would stay with him as long as he would have her. They did make beautiful love one starlit night after Gregg proposed to her. Afterward, they both agreed that the next time they made love would be as man and wife.

Jenny grew anxious to tell Gregg about her pregnancy. She wanted to wait until he was through with all his tests before she announced it to him. He seemed preoccupied with everything that was going on lately and, although Gregg could be impatient and selfish at times, he was an honorable man and Jenny felt lucky to be loved by him.

Jenny was lost in her daydream when John Hawkins rushed up behind her and frightened her. She had not expected him to find her hiding at the water's edge. Jenny stepped down off the sparkling boulder as he strode across the meadow to greet her. Across the field, a train whistle blew, drowning out the sound of his words as he called to her. She watched with a quickened heartbeat, taking in the sight of his dark tanned skin, black hair and pearly white smile. He was dressed in simple faded blue jeans and a white cotton shirt. His cowboy boots made a whispering sound as he swished through the tall grass. In a few long strides, he was in front of her, scooping her up in his arms like he had always done when they were kids. He flung her gently over his shoulder and spun her several times until she was dizzy.

"Put me down," she cried as she pounded on his back with her balled up fists. He spun her one more time before he set her down on her dirty bare feet.

"You're a lot heavier since the last time I did that," he said laughing at her disoriented state. When she regained the sense of the grass below her feet, she became angry with him.

"I hate it when you do that to me!" She plunged her hands deep into her pockets. "Don't ever do it again!" she snapped. She stood still before him a while before the sickly dizzy feeling totally left her. It seemed like a long time before the trees stopped spinning. She stood there looking at him sheepishly. When they were kids, he was a lot bigger than she. He would pick her up on his shoulders and spin her as he had just done. She hated it then and she hated it now.

"You're still a peanut," he said through twinkling dark eyes. He pulled her to him in a tight hug, squashing her arms between them. She hated it when he called her Peanut. He pulled her hands from her pockets and held her away from him. "How have you been, Peanut?"

"My name is Jenny," she corrected between clenched teeth.

"Oh! That's still a thorn in your side, is it?"

Jenny pulled her hands away and stuck them back in her pockets. She looked down at the lush green grass. He bent his knees to look into her face. He reached up and brushed the blond strays from her face tucking them behind her ears.

"You still have freckles. I thought you would outgrow those," he said pressing his finger to the tip of her nose.

"What brings you back to Chesterfield?" she asked in a scrutinizing glare.

"I missed my little Peanut. Why else would I come back?" John could never give Jenny a straight answer. That was another thing that really irritated her. She crossed her arms over her chest and glared at him as she always did when he teased her. She could see his body had grown but his demeanor hadn't. He still knew how to get under her skin. She studied him, tracing his dark eyebrows, his jaw line and tantalizing lips that parted slightly hinting at straight white teeth.

"What has really brought you here?" she demanded.

He stuck his hands in his pocket. "A business proposition," he said slyly. Jenny narrowed her eyes on his. She knew he wasn't going to tell her the reason for being in Chesterfield. He was still the mysterious person she remembered from her childhood.

Chapter 2

John Hawkins came into her life when she was just thirteen years old. Aunt Jeanine adopted John when he was four years old. Aunt Jeanine was her mother's only sister and whom Jenny was named after. Jenny preferred being called Jenny, but her birth name was given as Jennifer Jeanine Elerose. Aunt Jeanine lost her husband when he was killed during a flying lesson in Montana. The engine on his personal aircraft stopped, leaving Uncle Joe falling to his fate. That same dreadful day, his body was recovered from his plane that crashed into Flathead Lake.

John was a rambunctious teenager and Aunt Jeanine felt she could not give John the proper care and attention he needed while she grieved for her husband. After sixteen years, Aunt Jeanine was forced to find a job to support herself and John. That meant leaving him alone most of the time. Jeanine felt he would be better off with someone who could continue to teach him family values. At age fifteen, John was sent to live with Jenny's family. Good looks, a mischievous personality, and raging hormones were all wrapped into one frightened teenager.

Jenny had met John only once before when she was about five years old. She remembered her family taking a vacation to Montana and staying two whole weeks. Being only five, she didn't remember much of John except that he was a wild boy and did things her own mother would frown upon. She remembered how he used the couch cushions as a trampoline, stacking them on top of each other. His mother would tell him to stop, but he would just jump higher.

When John moved in with Jenny's family, he came with only a small tattered suitcase of clothes, a football his father had given him, and a broken heart. For the first few weeks John didn't speak to anyone. He shared a room with Jenny's brother, Scott. He used the floor and a sleeping bag for a bed until her mother could purchase one for him. He would sit in the dark in the bedroom with his feet on the wall and stare at the ceiling. There he lay hugging his football until dinner was ready. Then he would eat in silence and retreat to his room again. Scott reported daily to his mother telling her how he heard him whimper during the night.

LOVE IN THE SHADOWS

Jenny felt sorry for him and eventually worked up the courage to enter his room and lay down next to him. He didn't look at her when she entered or when she lay down beside him. She lay there in the darkness with the shade pulled staring at the ceiling, wondering what was going through his mind. Jenny felt confident that John would be offered a good home and she was certainly going to make sure he did his share of the chores. There was no way she was going to let him get by without helping out around the house. Jenny was a fairness freak and wasn't happy until she spoke her piece. When he didn't speak she said to him,

"I don't know what you are going through, but I know that you will like it here. Mom and Dad are good parents and they will treat you fairly as long as you show them respect. As long as you are here you will be expected to accept your share of responsibility, though." Jenny waited fifteen minutes for a sign that he had heard her. When she didn't, she left the room and closed the door behind her.

Jenny remembered a particular day in early spring several years earlier when she sat on the grassy edge of the creek that flowed past the farmhouse. The sun was high in the afternoon sky and birds chirped happily as they discreetly carried grass and twigs to the tops of the trees. The water was dangerously high that spring and the gushing water chiseled away the banks of the creek leaving steep embankments that declined to the water below. She sat on the edge of the bank dangling her bare feet over the edge. In one hand she held a chocolate chip cookie. In the other, she held a fishing rod. Her braided pigtails lay flat against her back as John stood behind a tree and watched her. He sneaked up behind her and yanked her pigtails as hard as he could. Jenny screamed in pain, letting go of her cherished fishing rod. She put her hands to the base of her pigtails, watching in horror as her cherished rod slid down the steep embankment, disappearing into the dark murky water below.

"You creep," she screamed. "That was my magic fishing rod!" John howled with laughter as he yanked on her other pigtail. "Ow!" she screamed again. Jenny raced to her feet, chasing John through the meadow barefoot. "I'm going to catch you one day, you creep," Jenny promised. She weaved in and out of trees until she was breathless. Unable to catch him, she sat down on a fallen log and cried.

That afternoon, Jenny ran home crying to her mother, who showed little interest in her story. She entered the stone walled basement through the open cellar door where her mother was washing eggs to take to town to sell at the local supermarket. The room was dark and made Jenny feel claustrophobic. She kept her eye on a hole dug deep in the wall near the ceiling. When she was little, her brothers told her that monsters came out of the hole at night and danced in the dark. She never saw any monsters and she made sure she was never alone in the room, especially in the dark.

"I'm sure he didn't mean it, Jenny," her mother suggested after she told her mother the story of her fishing rod. "Now help me dry these eggs and put them into cartons. I will be taking them into town this afternoon. I need you to stay here with John so he is not home alone. I will only be gone for an hour or so." Having to stay home upset Jenny. It was a treat when she would get to go into town with her mother on a Saturday. It was fun quality time spent alone with her mother. Her favorite part was that she got to pick out one box of expensive cereal and one special treat for the week. Her younger brother usually rode in the tractor with her dad or went along on errands with him. He was only ten and whined a lot. Jenny was glad to get away from him for those few precious hours on Saturday. It was the only time besides her fishing excursions that John or Jason couldn't follow her everywhere she went.

The egg washer was like a miniature washing machine. It was round like the size of a metal garbage can cover and was about six inches high. Her mother filled the machine with warm soapy water and plugged it in. The machine gently agitated the eggs. When they were clean, she would unplug the cord and dry them before putting them into crates for the market. One of Jenny's favorite chores was to help her mother with the egg machine. Jenny dried the brown eggs and filled a carton with them. She carried them to the table to be put into a larger box, all the while chattering continuously. The carton filled with eggs slipped from her hands and fell to the floor. Yellow egg yolk splashed everywhere. Jenny knew her mother would be heart broken and she squeezed her eyes shut as her mother's voice pierced through the sound of silence.

"Oh Jenny! We can't afford to be dropping eggs like that!" her mother scolded. "Run along now and check on your little brother." Jenny felt awful knowing she had disappointed her mother and ruined her opportunity to put away a little extra spending money for herself.

Tears couldn't fix the broken eggs and tears couldn't fix her broken heart over her fishing rod. The fishing rod that was now lost forever. It was a special gift that Scott had given to her on her fifth birthday. Scott was her favorite sibling. He always let her tag along with him. He told her the rod was magic and if she learned to use it right, she would always catch fish with it. He promised to teach her one day when the weather warmed. Scott honored his promise and just as he assured her, she always caught fish with it. Scott and Jenny spent many hours on the edge of the creek catching bullheads, rainbow trout and crayfish. The crayfish were fun to catch and more fun to dangle from the end of the fishing line. As Scott approached his teenage years, he lost interest in fishing days at the creek with Jenny. He turned his mind instead, to pretty girls and motorcycles…and drinking. So until the day John made her drop her rod, Jenny sat by herself on lazy weekends in the summer with her magic fishing rod and her favorite chocolate chip cookies.

At the dinner table everyone was assigned a seat. Whichever seat was designated as yours when you graduated from a high chair was yours until you left the nest. John was assigned a seat next to Jenny. Of course, this added fuel to the fire. Before John came to live with them, everyone fit around the table perfectly. Her mother and father sat on each end and she and Jason sat on one side with Scott and her older brother Jake on the other. Jenny now sat between John and Jason, leaving little elbow room. At each meal, John would kick her under the table or pinch her legs. She would cry out in pain, only to have her mother or father ask her to mind her manners and be quiet. It didn't seem to bother anyone that John was causing the trouble. Her parents chose to ignore it for their own reasons she would learn about later.

After John grew accustomed to living on the farm, he was assigned chores like everybody else. He was expected to dry the dishes and take out the garbage, in addition to other outside chores. He rarely did any of the work expected of him, leaving it for Jenny or Jason to do. Soon they became like siblings, fighting over everything. Fistfights were almost a daily occurrence. Jenny's brothers had taught her well and she won a few of the battles. Because John was so much bigger than she, Jenny was usually the one that went crying to her mother.

John was the one that first taught Jenny about taking risks. One day he decided to pester her at the creek. He did his usual number, sneaking up on her and scaring the wits from her. He teased and taunted her and poked fun about her bare feet and skinny legs. He dared her to go skinny-dipping and he threatened to remove all his clothes and dive into the creek. He removed his shirt and began to unbutton his jeans when Jenny gasped and turned away from him. A few minutes later she heard a splash and turned to see him chest deep in the cool water. He taunted her to come into the water and when she refused, he threatened to come out of the water stark naked. She removed her cutoff shorts and t-shirt leaving on her training bra and panties. He laughed wickedly as she neared the water's edge.

"You have to take it all off, he teased. Just like I did. Do you want me to tell all your friends at school that you are a chicken wiener?" Jenny had a lot of pride and she didn't want anyone to think she was chicken about anything. Being or acting tough was how she protected her delicate heart. She was a very sensitive person but she rarely let anyone close to her know what she held in her heart.

Jenny pondered his temptation and knew full well that he would do just that. She wanted to beat him at his own game just once. She knew he didn't think she would do it and she set her mind to prove him wrong.

"You have to turn around then," she suggested falling for his trick. She removed the rest of her clothes and waded into the water staying below the surface a good distance away from John. He stared at her glistening body in the early evening sun, stunned that she did what he dared of her. Seeing she was completely nude, he quickly swam to the grassy bank and climbed out, underwear in tact. He grabbed her clothes and ran toward the farm leaving Jenny angry and alone in the creek. She waited for nearly a half hour for him to return with her clothes. As dusk neared she climbed out of the water and sneaked through the trees wearing nothing.

In the meantime, John had put on his clothes and climbed a large oak tree on the edge of the farm. He waited as Jenny passed through, getting a good look at her young blossoming body. That was his first experience with lust. As she passed beneath the old oak tree, he dropped her clothes next to her. Smiling wickedly, he watched her gather them as she screamed at him. She disappeared into the trees to dress in privacy. When they returned to the farm that evening, her mother inquired suspiciously about their wet hair. John snickered as Jenny made up a story about how she tried to walk across the creek on a log and lost her balance and fell into the creek below. Her mother looked to John for confirmation of the bewildering story. John nodded, scrambling off to take a shower. John would never let Jenny forget that she had fallen for his cruel trick.

From that day forward, John became her worst enemy. Little did she know that John held a secret love for her in his heart. When it came to the point of receiving punishment for fighting, Jenny usually got all the blame. Being a demanding teenager herself, she finally cried to her parents about the way things had changed in the household. It wasn't until her parents sat down with her and explained the details of John's life that Jenny understood why he was treated differently. Her parents told her how he was abandoned when he was four years old. He was found in a vacant house, starving and dirty before Jeanine and Joe adopted him. Jenny's mother told her that Aunt Jeanine didn't want John to come back to Montana. Because Jeanine couldn't handle the rambunctious teenager, Jenny's life would be hell for the next three years.

John was enrolled in the Chesterfield high school and each summer, went back to his mother for three weeks. During his stay with his mother, Aunt Jeanine complained that John was a hellion and out of control. The police arrested John for vandalizing neighborhood buildings twice in three weeks. Jenny's mother agreed to let him stay at the farm until he became an adult. Then he could decide where he wanted to live. After graduation, John left the farm and no one heard from him until a year later when he showed up on Jeanine's doorstep looking for help in the search for his real parents.

Chapter 3

"Come back to the house with me. I have a gift for you," he said looking at her with his dark twinkling eyes. His eyes still held mischief like they did when he was a teenager. As they walked side by side, Jenny looked down at her bare feet. She wondered what he thought of her now, all grown up. It angered her that he made fun of her freckles. She remembered how he used to tease her about them when she was younger.

"What are those brown spots on your face?" he asked her one day. "They look like ant poop," he told her. "And why don't you ever wear shoes? A proper lady wears shoes on her feet. Can't you afford them or what?"

John's words were cruel and she realized they still bothered her today, three years later. The freckles on Jenny's face still remained, even at age nineteen. She tried to keep up with his large stride so he wouldn't notice her bare feet. John kept his gaze straight ahead as he spoke.

"I see you still go barefoot. Hasn't anybody ever taught you how to dress like a lady?" he said escorting her by the elbow. Jenny pulled her elbow from his grasp, keeping time with his stride.

"Don't you ever stop criticizing people? You still haven't told me why you're here. Why have you come back after all these years?"

"I told you, it's business," he said in a cold, low voice. Jenny shivered at his words but continued on toward the house with him beside her.

The farmyard covered a vast area, decorated with dense trees on every side. Lilac bushes lined the driveway and large willow trees occupied the yard reaching upward and outward as their graceful branches gently swept the earth below. A white wire fence enclosed the house offsetting it from the buildings that surrounded it. A section of plush grass encompassed the house separated from the fence by blooming petunias and geraniums on one side. A yellow rose bush overwhelmed the fence on the other side of the house and a small gate kept the dogs and other stray animals from upsetting the beautiful grounds. The black shutters next to the windows looked freshly painted as he glanced to the window of his old room.

"The old place hadn't changed a bit since I left three years ago," he commented lazily. The scent of his after-shave smelled as though it were freshly applied only moments before. When they reached the gate, he opened it and motioned for her to enter first.

"Hmph, I see your manners have improved somewhat," she muttered under her breath. Without a word, John continued to follow her up the walk into the old farmhouse. Jenny disappeared for a little while and when she came back to the kitchen, she was clean and had straightened her hair. By now it was dinnertime and, as always, her mother had a delicious meal waiting when they arrived. John didn't take his place like he had done when he was a teenager living under their roof. Instead, he seated himself across the table from Jenny. His legs stretched across the floor and his stocking feet brushed against hers. At one time, his touch could have intimidated her, but not tonight. She didn't move her bare feet when he began to massage the top of her left foot with the bottom of his own. She felt heat rush to her face, hoping no one noticed the intensity in her facial color.

The kitchen was large with cupboards lining one entire wall. The table sat in the center of the room like an island, separating it from the appliances that surrounded it. Above the table hung a cheap but beautiful chandelier. From the table it looked real, but John knew it wasn't. He remembered swinging from it when he was a teenager, pulling the electrical cord from the ceiling where it hung. Plaster fell from the ceiling as he watched Mrs. Elerose stand in the midst of the mess with her mouth agape. Then darkness fell over the kitchen. He could still see the rough texture where the plaster had been repaired. Mrs. Elerose grounded him for two weeks. It didn't matter anyway. He preferred to stay on the farm and tease Jenny.

"Oh John, I'm so glad you found Jenny. I'm sure you two have a lot to talk about," her mother said welcoming them to the table. John winked at Jenny as he took in her true beauty. He always thought she was pretty. He felt ashamed for all the mean things he did to her when he was a young teenager. He was embarrassed by his lust for her since the day he dared her to skinny dip and didn't know how to hide it. So he did it by making her think he hated her. Back then she was more like a bothersome sister to him than a friend. He was glad she wasn't his sister. He remembered lying in bed at night thinking impure thoughts as she lay sleeping across the hall. She would never know the number of nights he lay awake wondering what she was dreaming. He wished for the day when they could become civilized friends.

"Where are you staying while you are in town?" her mother asked breaking the awkward silence.

"I planned on staying at the motel on the edge of town until my business is taken care of," he replied not making eye contact with her. But John remembered the kindness of the Elerose family and he knew Mrs. Elerose would never allow him to stay in the grubby hotel in town.

Mrs. Elerose was a short plump lady with leathery wrinkled skin around her deep-set eyes. She wore her soft white hair in a bun at the top of her head and it was unusual to see her without an apron tied around her waist. The softness in her hair matched her personality. And she was known around the town as being a kind, quiet, Christian woman who treated each of her friends like cherished Christmas ornaments with love and respect. Mrs. Elerose's life was a difficult one, raising five children of her own besides John. She was a child during the Great Depression, surviving years of anguish and poverty. The lines around her eyes reminded John of years of hardship each time he looked at her. She never complained when things got tough, but did her best to make everyone else happy.

Just as he thought, Mrs. Elerose gasped. "I will not allow you to stay in such a place. You will stay right here with us until your business is finished. Scott's room is empty now. You are welcome to have your old room back. We're so glad to see you John. We were worried when you left. No one heard from you for months!" Jenny's eyes turned toward her mother in surprise.

"I didn't know you heard from him at all, mother," she said in a snarl tone. "Why didn't you tell me?"

Jenny didn't know why she cared that her mother didn't tell her about John. In an awkward sort of way she cared about John a lot. After all he had lived with them for three event filled summers. Jenny was taken aback by her own anger toward her mother now but it was too late to cover her feelings.

"Jenny, I knew how you felt about everything." She glanced at John wondering if she should save the conversation until they had privacy. John caught her glance. He held up his hands.

"It's okay, Rose. Go on. Tell her."

By then, Jake, her father and Jason had joined the dinner table. Her mother's eyes saddened as she continued. "I knew how you felt about John coming to live with us," she said glancing around the table. "I know you sacrificed a lot when we accepted John into our family. I just thought you were still bitter about it."

Jenny lowered her eyes in embarrassment. She realized she had been selfish. She felt guilty for wanting to be put first in her family. It wasn't until John left that she realized how much she really did like having him around. She missed how he teased her. She missed his twinkling dark eyes and his howling laughter. She missed the daring things he taught her. Jenny had seen the compassionate side of him a few times. She remembered times when he teased her to the point of tears, he would take her into his arms and hold her and apologize for being so mean. He apologized for making Jenny's life miserable. He told her that one day soon, he would disappear. It came as no surprise to her when he finally did leave the farm. When John left, a piece of her went with him. She missed him terribly, but as time went on the feelings she had for him slowly dissipated. She was no longer willing to take risky chances. Yes, John was a good influence on her once, but here he was three years later back in her life again. What could possibly have brought him back to Chesterfield? Jenny let out a sigh realizing he would be sharing living space with her once again. It would be difficult to ignore him this time.

Jenny lost her appetite as she watched John inhale the roast beef dinner her mother prepared. He was licking his fingers when he noticed Jenny was watching him from across the table. He began to seductively lick each one clean as everyone else quietly chewed the contents on their dinner plate. Her father looked up from his plate and witnessed John teasing Jenny. His eyes flashed to Jenny's reddening face. Mr. Elerose cleared his throat, breaking the silence around the dinner table.

"Yummy, yummy. That was delicious Rose," Dave complimented his wife. She smiled in return, quietly capturing her husband's wink. Dave was tall and lean with light brown curly hair and light blue eyes. He reminded Jenny of an overgrown schoolboy from the olden days wearing his suspenders and lace up boots. He was a strong Christian like her mother but was more aggressive in speaking his piece when something was on his mind. He was an easygoing man and hid his age well behind his schoolboy appearance.

"Well," her father said to John. "Would you join me for the news?" Then turning to Jake and Jason he said, "Time to get those cows milked boys." Rose stood and began helping Jenny clear the dishes.

"I'll help tonight Mrs. Elerose," he said ignoring her father's request.

"I'll let you only if you call me Rose," she teased. She handed him a flowered dishtowel and left him alone in the kitchen with Jenny. She joined her husband for the six o'clock news as she always did each night after dinner. Jenny cleared the table and filled the kitchen sink with hot soapy water. She tried not to notice how handsome John was. She felt uncomfortable knowing his eyes studied her body the whole time. She moved busily about the kitchen trying not to let it bother her. The dishes were almost finished and she couldn't stand the quietness any longer.

"What was that all about?"

"What was what all about?" he asked pretending to be ignorant.

"You know, under the table?" she said meeting his dark eyes.

"Oh that, I just wanted to know if I could get under your skin like I used to," he said smiling back at her. She glanced at him sideways catching his wink. She threw the soapy dishcloth at him barely missing his face. She ran to her room, slammed the door and flopped down on her bed. She lay there deciding what to wear for her meeting with Rachael. Choosing a loose fitting pair of jeans and a red blouse, she tossed them on her bed and reached for her robe. She showered quickly, stepping out into the chilly bathroom to dry her changing body. She hung a towel across the doorknob on the bathroom door, remembering the times she would catch John Hawkins spying through the keyhole as she dressed or undressed behind the closed door. She laughed aloud remembering how she poked a toothpick through the keyhole one time, poking his nose and barely missing his eye. He ran from the hall howling like a wolf in the night. It didn't take long to catch onto his pranks and she learned to play a few too.

Jenny finished tying her robe and opened the squeaky bathroom door. She let out a small scream when she found John on the other side. He stood there leaning against the wall smiling. She pushed the strands of wet hair from her face.

"I see you haven't changed a bit! Still spying on innocent young woman are you Mr. Hawkins?" she sneered.

He held up his hands taking in the sight of the beauty before him. She tightened the white terry cloth robe around her waist. The top gaped open leaving enough space for John to get a close look at the prize inside. She caught him staring as she pulled the top closed with her hand.

"I didn't peek, honest," he said laughing wildly and I'm not so sure you're innocent yourself. He noticed how she stared at him and studied him she thought he wasn't. He knew there was an attraction between them lying quietly waiting to be sprung to life.

"Liar," she teased.

She went to her room and slammed the door in his face, turning the lock in the gold knob. She leaned against it holding her hand to her chest. It irritated her that he was here. Everything was going so well. She hoped he didn't plan on staying for more than a few days. She would be able to avoid him while at work and she would think of an excuse to avoid him the rest of his stay. She lay down on her pink flowered bedspread thinking about Gregg. She missed him dearly the last few days. She recounted the accident that occurred only two years earlier and now he had gone to Baldwin to a fancy clinic for psychological testing of the impact of comas on mature brain cells. Doctors all over the country heard about Gregg's miraculous recovery and Gregg agreed to allow them to do a few more tests to help find answers regarding brain activity after a lengthy coma. She hoped he wouldn't let them use him as a guinea pig for fear of what might happen to his future.

She massaged her belly, remembering the agreement she and Gregg had made. They only made love once and had agreed to wait until they were married before they did again. It was a difficult challenge to stop her body from doing what her heart wanted most.

She heard the loud engine of John's corvette and went to her window and separated the pink flowered curtain that matched her bedspread. He caught her watching, and waved as he sped out the driveway. She dressed quickly and drove to Chesterfield to meet Rachael at the bowling alley.

Chapter 4

John pushed open the door of the Ox Yoke Saloon, entering a fog of cigarette smoke and loud country music. His mood had darkened since leaving the Elerose farm. His cowboy boots tapped the wooden floor as he strode across the room and found a stool at the end of the bar. The room smelled of sweat and a freshly smoked cigar. A luscious young woman bounced over to him showing more cleavage than she should have.

"Whiskey, straight up," he growled taking in the sight of her round bosom. She smiled a crooked smile and sloppily filled a shot glass not taking her eyes off him. He looked rugged and handsome and rich, just the type she was looking for to sweep her off her feet. John studied her body. She seemed very young and her hair was curly and bouncy just above her shoulders. She wore bright red lipstick and licked her lips frequently in a slow seductive manner.

"Suzie Cauwer is the name, what's yours?"

"John, John Hawkins," he replied lazily. "What's a pretty young thing like you doing in a dirty place like this?" he asked twisting his head.

"A lady's gotta do what a lady's gotta do," Suzie laughed coming around the bar to stand close to him. She let her hand trace over his arm, noticing the bare finger on his left hand. She ran her hand up his shoulder as she rubbed her breasts against his back.

"You look sooo tense." She traced up his shoulders, squeezing the muscles on each side of his neck. He rotated his head enjoying the wonderful sensation she was giving him. She moved her hands down his back along his sides and to the front of his chest. She pressed her breasts to his back massaging his hardening nipples through his western shirt. The clientele in the bar was all men and he noticed everyone staring at him as Suzie worked her trick. She continued to unbutton his shirt baring his full chest of hair and taut nipples.

"Can't we go someplace more private?" he asked her uncomfortably, hiding disgust he was feeling for the young hooker. He swung around to face her and she moved in between his knees placing her large breasts against his partially bare chest.

LOVE IN THE SHADOWS

"I'm working now, but you can meet me at about ten o'clock outside honey." Every man in the saloon was snickering and John felt the tingle in his pants more acutely as Suzie rested her hands on his thighs just inches away.

"That'll be a promise I know I can keep," he lied brushing his lips against her cheek. He stuffed a twenty-dollar bill between her breasts and gently pushed her away. She followed him out the door as he made his way awkwardly to his corvette. He leaned against the car to compose himself when Suzie appeared before him. John noticed Jenny crossing the street out of the corner of his eye. Suzie stepped forward to massage his chest. John caught her perverse hands and held them away from him.

"What time do you get off work?" he asked slyly.

"Ten o'clock sweetheart," Suzie replied huskily.

"Why don't we continue this at ten o'clock then," he said as his eyes followed the gentle sway of Jenny's body a short distance away. Jenny cautiously glanced his way before entering the bowling alley just as the saloon door swung open and a gruff old man with missing teeth hollered out.

"Suzie, there's customers waitin." Suzie backed away from John and blew him a kiss before she disappeared into the dark, dirty saloon.

John couldn't wait to get away from her. She was a bar whore just like his mother had been and he felt sickened as he thought of what his mother must have looked like when she was younger. He leaned against his corvette to compose himself, digging in his pants to adjust what Suzie had gotten out of place. He needed to get away from the farm and away from Jenny. Seeing her after so many years brought back all the feelings he had for her when he left. He had no idea he'd run into Suzie Cauwer. He thought he remembered the name. Now he knew who she was. She was the daughter of the most indecent woman in town. John hated women who sold their bodies and had no intention of going back to meet her at ten o'clock.

Jenny found a table inside the bowling alley and sat down facing the bowling lanes. It was empty except for an older woman behind the counter who busied herself with a copy of Soap Opera Update. Seeing John outside with Suzie sickened her. She had no idea he entertained himself with that type of woman, but remembering him as a lustful teenager made her realize it was probably right up his alley. She waited for fifteen minutes before the door opened and shed light on a young woman with auburn curly hair. Jenny jumped from her chair and ran to the door to greet Rachael. It had been so many months since she had seen her good friend from high school. The two girls hugged before holding each other at arms length.

"Rachael, you're still too skinny," Jenny teased. "It's good to see you."

"And you still look good in your favorite color." Rachael laughed. Jenny ordered two Root beers, one for Rachael and one for herself. Rachael looked at Jenny excitedly squeezing her arm.

"You said in your last letter that Gregg is doing well. I can't tell you how happy I am for you. It's a miracle isn't it? Where is he anyway? I thought he would be with you," Rachael said. Her eyes glimpsed around the room.

"He went to The Mayo Clinic for more tests," she said looking over the rim of her Root beer mug. Rachael looked worried.

"Is something wrong?"

"No, it's nothing like that. He has agreed to help the doctors with research. He will undergo tests for the next week while they study his brain, that's all. He'll be back Saturday."

"Well," Rachael said raising her eyebrows high. "Is everything working like normal?" Jenny blushed and looked away. Rachael always had to be the one to bring up the personal questions.

"Well?"

Jenny didn't know how to answer. She was caught off guard with a question that demanded an isolated answer. She didn't want to tell Rachael that she and Gregg made love and she was now pregnant with his child. Rachael could never keep a secret in high school and she doubted if she could now. She hadn't even told Gregg yet.

John spent the last twenty minutes cruising Main Street of Chesterfield and he had enough. He parked his corvette on the opposite side of the street from the bowling alley. He watched the old building hoping he would see her come out. The outside of the building was covered with climbing ivy giving it a dumpy look. From what he remembered, the place was dumpy in the inside. A window reflected beautiful light as the setting sun sprayed hues of purple across the western sky. He climbed out of the corvette and crossed the narrow street. He took a deep breath of cool evening air before entering the bowling alley. He recognized her immediately. She was in deep conversation with a curly hair woman who looked anorexic. As John approached the table, Jenny looked upset with the woman across from her. Jenny looked up in surprise thankful that his rude interruption rescued her from the scrutiny of Rachael's questions. Rachael studied the man as Jenny introduced him.

"Rachael, this is John Hawkins. He is my... cousin." John looked surprised that she had introduced him as such. After all, they weren't really related.

"John, this is Rachael, my best friend from high school." John took Rachael's hand in his. It didn't surprise Jenny when he gently bent his head and kissed it.

"A pleasure to meet you ma'am. May I sit down?"

"Don't you have some place to be? Like maybe next door?" Rachael gazed at John taking in the sight of his suntanned skin, his dark eyes and dark hair. His arms and broad shoulders hinted at years of laborious work. Rachael was surprised at how rudely Jenny spoke to him.

"Oh Jenny, let him join us," she pleaded amused by his handsome appearance.

It still angered Jenny that he left three years ago with out a word to anyone. Then he had the nerve to come back and expect everyone to welcome him with open arms. Now he was here ruining her reunion with Rachael. It was the same as it was when he came to live with them. He was always the center of attention. He always interrupted her plans, her conversations, and her life. She felt robbed of a childhood that would have been much happier had he not come to live with them. Instead she felt ignored for three years because John needed the most love and attention. Her parents took the love she was supposed to get and gave it to John. It wasn't fair then and it wasn't fair now. He was back in Chesterfield, back in her home and back in the middle of a conversation with a friend she hadn't seen in months and he was still annoying.

John sat between them and did most of the talking. He spoke intensely with Rachael who listened eagerly to his stories, some true, some made up. Jenny wasn't sure who he was trying to impress more, Rachael or herself. He talked of a fast life in Texas working as a hired hand on a cattle ranch. He talked of parties and women and rodeos and fights, all of which of course he was the winner. He looked at Jenny checking her attentiveness from time to time. Nothing he talked about seemed to interest her. Seeing the discomfort he caused her, he excused himself.

"Miss Rachael," he said taking her hand again. He brushed his lips gently across the back of her hand. "It has been a pleasure meeting you." He smiled and winked.

"The same to you," Rachael said in a half dazed voice. After he left them, Rachael leaned across the table, whispering loudly.

"Jenny, he is adorable. You never told me you had a cousin as handsome as he is." Jenny cocked her head to the side meeting Rachael's eyes. Jenny felt a tiny stab of jealousy, but brushed it aside quickly.

"Have you found a nice guy yet Rachael?"

"No, but I think the possibility just walked out that door!" Jenny didn't want Rachael hooked up with someone like John Hawkins. He was a womanizer and he was as unsettled as he ever was.

"I don't think you want to get mixed up with him. He's an outlaw Rachael. He's the love 'em and leave 'em type."

"Oh?" Rachael pondered the idea and knew Jenny was a good judge of character.

"How's mother?"

"I haven't seen her much. I do know her heart was broke when you went to live with your dad. Justin doesn't stop by for coffee much anymore so I don't hear much about her. Doesn't she know you're here?"

"I wanted to surprise her. That's why we're meeting here and not at the house. I wanted to see you first Jenny. I have missed your friendship. You look well and I'm glad your relationship worked out for you. How's the new job?"

"It really isn't new anymore, I've been at the hospital since July but each day is a different tragedy for somebody else. I float between the hospital and clinic so I'm on the move all the time. I see a lot of people coming into the emergency room. There are a lot of accidents down on Highway 52. A lot of little kids come in with broken arms, legs what ever."

"It sounds exciting!"

"What about you Rachael?" Jenny asked nodding her head toward her friend.

"Well, I'm living with Dad. It's tough though, he's got a new woman and I feel in the way all the time. I don't know how long I can stick it out with him. School is going okay. I've got most of my required courses out of the way. I'm working toward a degree in human relations." Rachael laughed. "With the way my love life is going maybe it's not the field for me."

"Why do you say that?" Jenny asked sympathetically.

"My relationships with men always seem to end in disaster. In one year, I have fallen in love with a man only to find out he's married. I've been mistaken for a prostitute and landed in jail over night. I have been dumped by an older guy when he finds out I'm only nineteen and living with my dad. There are no decent guys left out there for me." Jenny watched Rachael empathetically.

"Oh yes there is! You just haven't found him yet."

Rachael looked at her watch realizing it was almost ten o'clock. "Where has the time gone? I wanted to get to mothers before ten. She'll probably be in bed by now."

"When are you going back to Utah?"

"Sometime next week. Tuesday or Wednesday. We'll get together again before then, I promise," she said sliding out of her seat. Rachael put five dollars on the table and left the bowling alley. Jenny watched her curly auburn hair bounce as she neared the door. Rachael seemed cheerful but Jenny could sense sadness in her eyes. She felt sorry for her knowing she still hadn't found her place in life. Jenny sat alone at the table pondering the issue. She definitely did not want Rachael mixed up with someone like John. A few minutes later, Jenny opened the door of the bowling alley and stepped into the chilly night air. She wished she had brought a jacket. It was almost November and no snow had fallen. She could hear a lone Canadian goose cry out in the night confused by the unseasonable warmth. It was late for them to still be here but she knew that with the first glitter of a snowflake, they would head for their winter home in the south.

Chapter 5

Chesterfield was a small town buried deep in the heart of farm country. It was a town where everyone knew every body else and gossip spread like wild fire. In the past few years, newcomers were a frequent happening in the small town. Drifters came and went faster than a flooding river but not without being noticed by most town folk. She wondered how long it would take for people to find out that John was in town and expected people to be asking her about him before long. Jenny glanced toward the saloon where she had seen Suzie drooling on John's chest. She wondered if he was going to meet her at ten o'clock like she heard him say. She thought she should warn John about Suzie, but after what she witnessed tonight, she thought they were a perfect couple. She tried to fool herself by thinking she didn't care about Mr. John Hawkins. Somewhere deep inside her heart, she still cared for John.

Feeling bad about the way she acted, she decided to wait for him and apologize. By ten thirty he had not arrived. She saw Suzie pacing in and out of the saloon and at ten thirty Suzie walked alone down the street toward her apartment. Jenny started the engine and drove back to the farm. John's car was not there when she arrived. Feeling more tired than usual, she slipped into her pajamas and climbed into bed. She fell asleep and dreamed about the life she would have with Gregg.

Jenny awoke around two in the morning when she felt heavy arms flung over her body.

"Gregg," she said groggily. I'm glad you're here." She rolled over and settled into the curve of his body and went back to sleep. She felt a tug on her earlobe that sent a chill through her body. She nestled closer to him. Then she felt hands on her body. First he massaged her hip, her waist and then his hands moved around to her chest. She rolled over on her back and when she smelled cigarette smoke and whiskey her eyes flew open!

"Gregg?" She tried to sit up but his strong arms bound her to the bed.

"Ah my sweet innocent Jenny," came a voice as hands continued to massage her breasts.

Jenny, fully awake now reached over to turn on the small lamp beside her bed. She gasped and pulled the blanket to her chin. The lamp lit up her face in the darkness creating a silhouette on the wall behind her. The room was small with cape cod style slanted walls that met the ceiling three feet off the floor forming a peak in the center of the room. It always reminded Jenny of a teepee.

"I'll bet you're still that sweet virgin girl I left behind," John said in a slurred whisper.

"John Hawkins, what are you doing in my bed?" she whispered loud and stern.

"Come here my sweet," he said moving lazily across the bed. Jenny moved out of the bed and stood beside it as John fell to the floor. She stood with her hands on her hips pursing her lips together like a scolding schoolteacher.

"You're drunk aren't you?" She helped him to his feet, noticing he was fully clothed. "You're room is next door Mr. Hawkins. Or have you forgotten?" She held him by the back of his shirt and showed him to Scott's old room.

"Oh I haven't forgotten anything my sweet, sweet Jenny," he said in slurred speech reaching for her again. She opened his bedroom door and helped him to the bed. He fell down on the bed and sprawled across the bedspread. He lay there half asleep as she helped him remove his boots. She put them down on the floor next to the bed and studied him before she closed the door and walked quietly back to her room. She hoped her parents hadn't heard the commotion.

The next day Jenny decided to go about her business as usual. She doubted John would remember the incident from a few hours earlier. She arose early so she could get chores finished before church. She removed her thin cotton pajama gown when a nauseating feeling came over her. She covered her mouth with her hand and rushed to the bathroom. She flipped up the toilet lid and knelt down before vomiting violently into the bowl. Her body shivered on the cold floor. The act of vomiting left Jenny feeling exhausted. She flushed and went to the sink to wash her face. When she stood up next to the toilet she caught a glimpse of movement in the mirror. She turned to look at the doorway, tiptoeing on the creaky floor. She peered down the hallway seeing nothing but the rays of the early morning sun shining in through the window at the top of the stairs. She quietly closed the door and finished her personal hygiene. She pulled her hair back in a long braid and put on baggy overalls. She rolled them up and went barefoot down to the kitchen to help her mother with breakfast.

"How is Rachael?" her mother asked.

"Oh you know the same old Rachael. She hasn't changed." Jenny seemed preoccupied.

"What was the noise in your room last night? Do you still sleepwalk?" Jenny nervously dropped the egg she had been cracking into the bowl of raw eggs.

"I uh, I bumped into my dresser on my way to the bathroom. A few things fell off my dresser."

"Is anything broken?"

"What? Uh, nothing." Jenny had three porcelain dolls on her dresser that once belonged to her mother when she was a child. They were kind of ugly but Jenny loved them just the same.

"You look a little peeked this morning, are you okay?" Rose felt Jenny's forehead with the back of her hand. She was glad she washed her face and removed the sweat that gathered there after she vomited.

"Yea, I'm just a little worn out that's all."

"Have you heard from Gregg?"

"No, he said he would call tonight?"

"Do you miss him?"

Jenny wondered what all the questions were about. "Yes, I do."

"You know, John felt bad about last night."

"Mom, I don't want to get into that. What does he want anyway?"

"He said a business proposition has brought him to town."

"Yea, I don't believe him either," Jenny grumbled.

"Why not?"

"Because John has always been a good story teller and he still is a story teller!" Just then John came into the kitchen scratching his head. He heard Jenny's comment. He met her icy gaze. She looked away in embarrassment. His hair was a mess and it looked like his facial hair grew one quarter of an inch over night. He had on clean clothes and smelled of mint mouthwash. She noticed he was barefoot as he took a cup from the cupboard and filled it with coffee. He chose to sit in his old spot at the table so he could watch Jenny move about the kitchen. He noticed the lack of color on her face and after seeing her vomit, wondered if she were ill.

"Are you going to join us for mass, John?" her mother questioned.

"No, I'm not much of a churchgoer anymore." She looked away in disappointment wiping her hands on her apron.

"How's your mother?"

"She got a promotion at the factory about three months ago. She works in the office now. Some type of customer service job I guess." Rose looked up in surprise. She wondered why Jeanine didn't mention the promotion the last time they spoke on the phone.

"What type of job do you have John?" Rose asked. Jenny continued to ignore John, mixing the eggs and frying them in the pan. Soon, the kitchen was overwhelmed with a wonderful aroma of food, just as it has always been. John cleared his throat.

"I buy and sell real estate," was the only answer he gave. Jenny wondered about the story of the ranch that he told Rachael about last night. She wondered which story was true.

After mass, Jenny slipped back into her overalls and over coat and went out into the barn to feed the calves. Scott was helping the Johnson's and was over there everyday since Gregg had gone to Rochester. Jake was on the tractor feeding the steers when she crossed the yard to the barn. Inside, the air was frosty and steam rolled from the warm manure into the dim light. The young calves snorted and their hot breath dissipated into the air like a steamboat. They kicked their hind legs in delight as she neared their eating area. She crawled up into the hayloft to get down a bale of hay for their feeding. She reached the loft and sat down on a bale to think. She wondered how long it would be before anyone noticed her growing abdomen.

She and Gregg originally decided to wait until the next fall to get married. She always dreamed of a garden wedding and would be planting peach gladiolus bulbs to use as cut flowers for the wedding. The wedding would take place at the Johnson farm, a few miles down the road. Jenny felt overwhelmed by everything that happened in the last two years. Everything seemed to be going too fast. She put her head in her hands and began to sob. She wondered how Gregg would feel about being a father. She wondered how they would support a family on their minimal income. She knew farming was only a money flow and it would be years before they would have a real income. She wondered if she could continue working after the birth of the baby. The thoughts startled her and she sobbed louder. John entered the barn and heard her sobbing in the hayloft. He quietly climbed the wooden ladder and sat down on the hay next to her. He studied her frame for a long time. She did not look at up him.

"Hey, Peanut, what's wrong?" he asked putting his hand on her back. She wondered if he remembered what he had done last night. How would she ask him if he remembered coming to her bed. It didn't even matter if he did. Her life was in turmoil and nothing John said or did could change that.

"You're certainly not mad at me about last night are you?" he asked sarcastically. Jenny looked up at him in surprise. He did remember. She became angry then. What right did he have to sneak in her room and try to take advantage of her in her parent's home?

"Exactly what did you think you were doing?" She pushed him off the bale and began to wrestle with him. She wanted to fight like they fought when they were kids. She sat on him and lifted her hand up in the air to get up the power to send a good punch into his solar plexus. He grabbed her wrist and rolled over on top of her. She lay beneath him breathing heavily from her effort.

"I'm sorry I ruined your reunion with Rachael last night. I didn't know it was a reunion or anything. Your mom told me you haven't see her in a while."

Jenny realized he was talking about his interruption at the bowling alley.

"That's not what I'm upset about," she snapped at him trying to free her wrists. "What were you doing in my room last night?" He lay on top of her squashing the breath from her body. He didn't remember going into her room.

"What are you talking about?" he growled.

"You came into my room last night. You were drunk."

He thought about the incident of the night before. He didn't remember much. He was very surprised to find himself in his old bed when he woke this morning. He freed her hands.

I ended up going to a more respectable bar in Prairieville after I left the bowling alley. I overstayed my welcome and got into a fistfight with some guy for taking his parking spot. The guy swung at me just as I ducked." John scratched his head remembering that part about the evening. After that everything was blank. Drunkenly, he found his way into his car and tore out of the parking lot at closing time.

"I think you are making this up!" she snapped. Jenny swung at him missing his nose by half an inch. She dropped a punch on his left cheek.

"Ow, that hurt." He grabbed her wrists again. "You are a feisty one aren't you? You always were."

"I always wanted to do that. That's for all the rotten things you've done to me when we were kids." She wrestled her hand free and planted another punch on his left cheek.

"And that's for leaving without saying good bye." He studied her angry face for a moment and began laughing hysterically.

"You are pretty when you're mad." He bent down to kiss her pursed lips. Jenny was astonished at the softness of his lips. He had never kissed her before. He let her wrists go and took her face in his hands, still kissing her lips. He adjusted his body careful not to crush the breath from her. She relaxed her tense lips and the kiss seemed like it lasted for minutes. Jenny didn't protest but wrapped her arms around his neck forgetting her surroundings and everything that happened over the last year. They both heard a giggle and looked up soon enough to see Jason's head disappear down the hay barn hole. John released Jenny and stood up reaching for her hand and helped her to her feet. She brushed the hay chaff from her over coat and sat down on a bale.

"Why did you kiss me?" she asked taken aback by his actions.

"I've always wanted to, I just thought the time was right," he said plopping on a bale beside her.

"Where have you been for the last three years?" She lowered her voice to a serious tone.

"I left to find my real parents. It took more than two years but I found them." He put his face in his hands. "The funny part is they are married to each other. It was the last thing I ever expected." John spit into the hay chaff. "They live in Texas and they are filthy rich." He threw his head back laughing wildly. "They inherited a lump of money from my grandmother's death several years ago. My mother is a high-class lady of the evening if you know what I mean. I found out that my real name is John Olson. Did you know my birthday is in August, not June?" Jenny didn't care when his birthday was. All she could think of was how it must have felt to come face to face with the people that abandoned him when he was four years old. She held her hand to her mouth as he unveiled the news. Her eyes held a look of disbelief.

"How did you find them?"

"I started with newspaper clippings from when I was found in the abandoned building."

"Wait a minute, how did you know you were abandoned? Mom said no one ever told you about that."

"I overheard her telling you Jenny. I was listening around the corner that night you were upset with me for taking your clothes. I heard everything. I know you hated me. I didn't mean to make your life miserable. I couldn't wait to find my real parents. I hate them for what they did to me. I was an inconvenience for them so they left me. I told them I was going to make them pay for what they did. They gave me money and bought me that car. My father even got me a job but I blew that too. I never did what was expected of me. I was lazy, rarely showing up for work. When I did, I was hung over or high on something. I've led a fast life Jenny. You have no idea what I've been through the past few years. It was all too much for me to manage." John sighed heavily. "I've bounced from job to job, getting in trouble for drugs."

There was more to his story than what he shared with Jenny. He didn't have the heart to tell her how he would get high and then use women for sexual pleasure. He couldn't count the number of women that fell for his one-night stands. With the money he got from his parents, he could buy any number of them. Most of them were bar whores only doing their jobs and supplying him with drugs, but nonetheless it helped to ease the pain he felt since the dis natural birth parents.

"Are you high now?"

John laughed. "No, I'm not high Jenny. I'm clean now. It took six months, but I'm fine."

"You're not in real estate are you?"

He let out another long sigh. "No, I'm not."

"Then why are you here?" John stuck his hands in his jacket pocket and sat silent for a long time.

"I came back for you." Jenny couldn't believe what she was hearing. Then she started to protest. John held up his hands.

"Don't say anything, just let me explain." He put his finger over her soft lips to quiet her.

"I've never belonged anywhere Jenny. Here I am, twenty-one years old and I don't know where I belong. Your parents were great. I can't believe they took me in and put up with my crap for three years." He reached over and took her hand in his. Jenny looked at him bewildered by his confession. "You were even better. You were there for me Jenny. I still remember when I first came to your farm. You were the one who talked to me. You were the one who cared about me. You came into my room and lay down next to me and tried to make me feel welcome. You were the one who put up with all my teasing and pranks. You were the one who deserved your parent's love. I know I took all that away from you. When I left, part of me stayed with you here. The best part of me stayed with you. I loved you for what you did." John put his hands in his face. Jenny put her hand on his shoulder. Visions of the awful things he had done clouded his mind.

"I'm sorry that your life has ended up like this John, but did you expect me to just sit around and wait for you while you were gone? I was sixteen years old. I thought you hated me the way you picked on me?"

"I was in love with you Jenny. I just didn't know how to show it. No one has ever showed me how to display love. Not until I came here."

"I have moved on with my life John. I think you better do the same. I want you to find a hotel… tonight!" She stood and swatted the back of her clothes with her hands to clear the hay chaff. He reached for her and caught her hand.

"Do you really mean that Jenny?" His pleading eyes bore into hers. She paused for a short time.

"Yes, I do. I have chores to do."

She turned and climbed down the ladder leaving John in the dark hayloft.

Late that afternoon, John packed his suitcase and left the farm. Since Chesterfield was the only place he ever felt happy, he decided to stay and find a job in the surrounding area. After two weeks of searching he was hired on as a bricklayer for a small company just outside of Baldwin. Baldwin was a busy town larger than Chesterfield. He stayed in the cheapest hotel he could find for a while before saving enough to rent an apartment on the west side of Baldwin. He hadn't seen Jenny during that time. He wanted to show her that he could turn his life around and that he was able to settle down. He knew she would be proud of him.

Chapter 6

Christmas was a special time for Jenny. She felt happier than she had ever been. No one heard from John Hawkins and everyone assumed he went back to Texas or Montana. Jenny was disappointed when Gregg did not present her with a ring at Christmas time. Gregg did indeed ask her to marry him in the heat of passion the one night they spent together beneath the golden moon. Each time Jenny brought up the subject of marriage, wedding plans and children, Gregg could talk of nothing but his miraculous recovery. At first Jenny understood his excitement. She was excited for him too but wished they could put the past behind them and move on with the wedding plans. Gregg became obsessed with the miracle and she was afraid that catering to area newspapers and radio stations would only harm him.

Jenny grew more nervous after each week that passed. She still hadn't told Gregg she was pregnant. When she mentioned children, he would tell her that there would be plenty of time for little Johnson's, and that it wasn't something one rushed into. After taking a shower she paced in front of the mirror deciding what to do. She could not keep the secret much longer. Soon she would need maternity clothes and she could no longer hide the growing child inside her.

"I love you little one she whispered," tapping her stomach lightly. After she said that she felt foolish for speaking to someone who couldn't hear and to someone whom she could not see. It just didn't seem real. A knock sounded on her door.

"What do you want?" she yelled a little more angrily than she would have liked to.

"There's someone here to see you," Jason called with his newly deepened voice.

Thinking it was Gregg, she fumbled with the buttons on her flannel shirt, leaving it hang outside her jeans for comfort. She rushed down the stairs and stepped into the kitchen, thinking how happy she was that Gregg had come. The smile faded from her lips when she saw it was John Hawkins. He had been talking with her parents, telling them about his new job and that he planned to stay in the area. He told them about finding his real parents and that he was not in real estate. Jenny would be proud of him for telling them the truth. Her mother just invited him to stay for dinner when Jenny walked in to the kitchen. John stood in the doorway holding his over coat. His hair was dampened by snowflakes and he seemed thinner than when she saw him last.

"Hi, Jenny," he said. His eyes roamed her body. "It's great to see you." She flushed as she watched his eyes, embarrassed that he was so bold in front of her parents.

"You look good too John, how are you?"

"Will you take a walk with me?" Jenny nodded and put on her overcoat as he held his arm out for her. They stepped out into the heavy wet February snowflakes that melted when they touched the ground. The snow that covered the earth for a month had melted, giving way to an early spring. They walked down the road to the place where the creek crossed the road, arm in arm.

"You look more beautiful now than I have ever seen you look." He smiled down at her sincerely, but knowing how John seemed to always woo the women, she brushed off his comment.

"What brings you to the farm John?"

"I came to tell you that I have a steady job." He glanced at her to see if she was taking an interest in what he was telling her. She continued to look straight ahead.

"That's wonderful. Are you still clean?"

"I'm still clean," he stated offhandedly. He pinched his black eyebrows together as he spoke. "I plan to stay in the area."

She raised her eyebrow. "Where are you living?"

"I got a place on the edge of Rochester. It's small but it serves me just fine."

"Jeanine was asking about you, don't you think it's time you call her?"

John remained silent and then after a moment of thinking about Jeanine whom he hadn't spoken to in two years he balled his hands into fists blurting out words of anger.

"Jeanine gave me up Jenny. She didn't want me. I'm surprised she even cared to ask!"

"She loved you John. She just didn't know how to deal with a high strung teenager."

"It killed her to have me visit in the summer!" he snapped.

"I know, it must have been hard for you. But it was hard for her too."

"Damn you! Why are you always defending everybody except me?" He stopped walking and turned to her. "I'm the victim here. I'm the one that was left abandoned. I was the one forced to live with stranger after stranger. I was abandoned three times Jenny. My birth mother abandoned me. Then, I was abandoned by Joe and finally by Jeanine. Am I going to be abandoned by you too?"

"I'm not the one that left three years ago!" she screamed. Jenny turned and stormed angrily back to the house. By the time she reached the house she was feeling silly for screaming. She felt out of control and broke into tears. The last weeks had raked havoc on her emotional system. She dried her tears and went into the kitchen.

"Dinner's ready," her mother sang out as she entered. "Where's John?" she asked holding a plate of hot biscuits.

"He's right behind me. I'll go wash up."

John and Jenny sat opposite sides of the table from each other as they had done the first time John came back. John didn't try to play with her feet this time and she stared down at her steaming chicken soup, never once looking up. John watched Jenny over the rim of his bowl. He noticed a sadness that had overcome her since his last visit and he wondered how he could soften her feelings for him. Jason glanced back and forth from John to Jenny, carefully watching their behavior. The table was quiet except for the sounds of slurping soup. Nothing could prepare anyone for the shocking comment that Jason blurted out into the silence.

"Are you in love with John?" Jason asked suddenly, nudging her under the table. Jenny took her fork and pierced it into Jason's thigh. He let out a loud cry as three pair of eyes riveted on her face. John sat emotionless wondering what she was going to say. The boy had a lot of nerve but had grown up a lot and John was fond of his boldness. He did feel sorry for Jason though. He knew that the boy would be a victim of Jenny's venomous anger.

"No, Jason, I'm not!"

He inched his chair away from her. "Then why were you kissing him in the hay loft?" he asked innocently.

Jenny's eyes shot toward John. He smiled and continued sipping his soup. The boy had totally destroyed his chance of redemption and

John guessed he was still naïve about the way things worked between men and women. John broke the thick silence.

"This soup is fantastic Rose. I always liked your soup." Rose nodded, as she wondered what Jason was referring to.

"Jason, why don't you begin your homework?" Rose suggested.

"Yes, ma'am."

Jason nudged Jenny one more time before he left the table. Jenny's father took his eyes off her and wiped his mouth with the napkin. He shoved his chair away from the table.

"John, please join me for the news." This time John followed Jenny's father to the family room. He did not bring up the subject that Jason just referred to and John was relieved.

Rose was silent for a long time during the dishes.

"Jenny, have you told John you are getting married in the fall?" Jenny looked at her mother in surprise.

"I think I mentioned it, yes." She continued to dry the dishes hoping her mother would drop the subject.

"Are you in love with John?" She dared to ask. Jenny felt like shriveling into a tiny ball.

"That's a silly question mom. I am marrying Gregg. We haven't been through this much together for nothing. Besides, I don't see what concern it is of his."

Jenny's mother wondered if what she said was true. She knew John cared for Jenny. After all, she was the one he came back to see. She noticed how he looked at her. How could he not have feelings for her after spending three years in the same house with her? At one time, they fought like siblings. She hoped her daughter had the sense to make the right decision. Jenny carried a pile of her mother's Corel dishes to the cupboard and began to pack them, trying to hide her face from her mother's view.

Rose opened her mouth to speak, but decided to wait. She felt something was going on between Jenny and John. She knew John wasn't in real estate and she knew he had not been in contact with Jeanine. Jeanine had not gotten a promotion at the factory where she worked since Joe died. Jenny finished packing away the dishes and ran off to her room.

Gregg was coming tonight and she had hoped John would be gone before then. She turned on the shower and pushed the curtain aside climbing in to the hot steam. She stood leisurely letting the hot water run over her body. Her stomach was quite swollen and she decided she must tell Gregg tonight. The morning sickness she had encountered earlier had reversed. Instead of feeling ill in the mornings, she was getting ill at the end of the day, especially after a big meal like tonight. She dried her body, changed into her white robe and wrapped her long wet hair in a towel. She turned off the light and peered out the window. John's car was still in front of the house. She wondered what John and her father were discussing in the family room. She barely made it to her room before she had the feeling to vomit and ran toward the bathroom.

Before John left he made an excuse to go upstairs by telling Jenny's parents he forgot some items during his last stay. John climbed the stairs quietly two by two. As he passed the bathroom door, he heard someone vomiting within and decided to wait. He made his way to Jenny's room stopping by the door before entering. His eyes wandered over her personal things, seeing it wasn't much different than he remembered. The room resembled more of a child's nursery than that of an adult woman. The old porcelain dolls her mother gave her were still displayed on her dresser. He remembered the day her mother gave them to her. She was upset because no one remembered her birthday. She blamed John that day, and felt that no one loved her since John came to live with them. Poor kid, he thought. She deserved so much better. And so did he. John picked up her pillow from her bed and brought it to his nose. He breathed in the scent of her and lay down on the bed still hugging her pillow. In a few minutes he was sound asleep.

Chapter 7

Jenny brushed her teeth using mouthwash afterward to remove the rancid taste she had grown accustomed to. She turned out the light and walked down the hall to her room. John's big body lay sprawled across her bed as he lay with her pillow on top of him. She watched him in the dim light. She noticed his shallow breathing, studying the dark features of his face. She wondered what he dreamed as he lay there. Her heart went out to him as she thought about the reason for his return. Had he expected her to sit around and wait for him after he left? Did he think her world stopped when he packed his bags?

Her life had changed so much since he left. She had been through some tragic times, maturing along the way. She was no longer the ugly teenager he flung on his back and spun in circles. She was no longer the naïve girl he played so many rotten tricks on. She felt sorry for him, not having a mother or father who cared about him. It was bad enough that his birth parents abandoned him, but his adoptive mother did too. Jenny wished she could back up the calendar and start over with John. She knew that under all the pranks and orneriness, there was a beautiful heart waiting to be loved. She sat next to him on the bed tracing his lips with her finger as he slept.

She whispered softly, "I know you cared for me but I was jealous of you. I didn't mean to say some of the rude things I said. I hope some day you forgive me. I am so sorry, John." She sighed deeply and seeing no harm in showing her feelings to a childhood friend, she bent down and gently kissed his cheek. She held her face close to his listening to the sound of his breathing. She lay her head on his chest and listened to his heart tell its story. She loved listening to the sound of a man's heart. She remembered when she was a very small child she would lay down and rest with her dad on the living room floor. She loved to cuddle next to him with her head on his chest listening to the echoing within. Her dad's heart seemed to tell a story of hard labor and tiredness. When she listened to Gregg's heart it spoke of struggling and pain. John's heart told a story of sadness and fear. She knew what the sadness might be, but what about the fear? She pulled away from John as his arms closed around her. He pulled her tightly to him rolling over and wrapping his legs over the top of her pinning her beneath him. The pillow fell to the hard wood floor. John began to snore loudly.

"John," she said aloud. She shook him. No response. "John, wake up!"

John stirred snuggling his chin next to her shoulder. He mumbled in his sleep, tightening his grip. What kind of predicament did I get myself into? She wondered. Gregg would be expected any minute. He had grown accustomed to finding his way to her room if she weren't down stairs. John loosened his grip letting his arm fall down around her waist. His eyes fluttered open as he lay there enjoying the warmth of her body next to his. He put his hand gently on her stomach feeling the small mound underneath her robe. When he opened his eyes fully, her robe was agape giving way to creamy white skin and young breasts that had matured since the last time he saw them. He began to massage her stomach in a circular motion. It made her skin shiver but she couldn't think about that now. She pushed his hand away.

"John, thank god you're awake. You have to get out of here." He didn't respond. He moved his hand upward pushing aside her white robe. Reaching for her breasts he lifted himself up bringing his lips to her own. He covered each breast with one large hand and applied gentle pressure while brushing his hands upward. Everything in her body tingled and she could feel his maleness against her leg. "John," she tried to speak but he quieted her with his gentle kiss. A soft moan escaped his lips and his hand moved back down to her belly where he continued to massage. She could feel her body respond to his gentle touch. She knew she must stop him before things got out of hand. For a long time she had wondered what it would be like to kiss the wild teenage boy he had been. Now all her wonders were answered. John made things exciting. He always did the unexpected thing. He always made her feel mischievous about the things he dared of her. Having him in her room, in her arms and in her bed excited her now. He stopped kissing her, still feeling her rounded stomach inside her robe.

"Who's bastard are you carrying?" he asked solemnly. His eyes bore into hers in the dimness of the light. Jenny removed her arms from around his neck and pulled her robe together in an attempt to hide what was conceivably present in her womb. Jenny could not find the words to answer. A tear rolled down the side of her cheek. He pulled her hands away from her robe.

"Who has done this to you?" he demanded through gritted teeth.

"I don't owe you any explanations," she replied through her own clenched teeth, trying to pull the robe tightly over her. John scooped her into his arms pulling her close against his chest.

"Please, Jenny, talk to me about this." Her soft whimpers were muffled against his chest as he held his hand to her naked abdomen. "It's okay Peanut. Shhhh."

Gregg entered the farmhouse like any other member of the family. Upon seeing the kitchen deserted, he climbed the stairs to Jenny's room. In his arms he carried six white roses and six red roses. He took one last sniff before he reached her doorway. His mouth dropped open in awe when he saw her nearly naked as she lay cradled in the arms of a stranger. He had one arm around her back and his other hand caressed her stomach inside her robe. Her legs extended straight behind the man as his large hands splayed across her abdomen.

Gregg gasped noticing how the man's fingers spread across her stomach almost reaching her soft downy pubic hairs. Her head was buried in the guy's shoulder and she seemed to be enjoying the massage this stranger was giving her. His heart felt like it had been pierced with a dagger. All the blood in his body rushed to his face. The muscle in his jaw tensed as he clenched his teeth. Gregg stood inches inside the doorway. When he spoke, it was just above a whisper.

"I can see you won't be needing these." He tossed the roses angrily into a nearby armchair and disappeared down the stairs.

"Oh my gosh! Gregg, please wait! It's not what you think!" She flew out of John's arms and ran to the door but it was too late. He saw what he saw and there was no convincing him any differently. Gregg strode through the kitchen nearly knocking Rose off her feet. He sped out of the farmyard leaving tire tracks in the mushy gravel. Jenny watched him leave through the upstairs window. Tears streamed down her cheeks as she clutched her robe. She turned to John who had a stunned look on his face.

"This is all your fault! Get out of this house! Get out! You have been nothing but trouble for me since you came here!"

"Was that the father?" John asked. His voice a low tone as he clenched her shoulders. Jenny was sobbing violently now and she felt disgusted with herself as his presence reminded her of what she was doing when Gregg arrived. Jenny pointed to the stairs. Through clenched teeth she ordered John out of the house. He held her tightly by the shoulders and looked into her teary eyes.

"Does the father know you're expecting?" John demanded to know but Jenny would not answer.

Rose glanced out the window and saw John's car still parked outside. She heard shouting and went to the bottom of the stairs.

"Jenny? Is everything all right?" John removed his hands from her shoulders and stuck them in his pocket. He never took his gaze off Jenny. Jenny struggled to dry the tears from her eyes and to right her robe. Her mother called again.

"Jenny?"

"Yes, mother," she replied in a trembling voice.

"Is everything okay?" John reached out to touch her cheek.

"I'll be in touch," he said before walking to the top of the stairs.

"Everything is fine Rose. There's just been a little misunderstanding. I'll be leaving now." He began to descend the stairs and met Rose below. He gently touched her shoulder as he passed. Her eyes held a questioning look. Jenny was certainly going to have a lot of explaining to do. John wasn't finished with her yet. He wanted to know who the father of her child was. In all the years he knew her he never guessed her to be irresponsible and careless. There was no ring on her finger and he knew the baby was illegitimate. There was no doubt about it.

Rose climbed the stairs to Jenny's room. Jenny had gone inside and closed the door. She picked up the armful of roses and sat down on the bed, rocking as she cried. With a gentle knock, the door pushed open. Rose peered inside seeing Jenny cradling the roses in her arms. She went to the side of her bed. Jenny did not look up at Rose, only stared at the worn wooden floor as she rocked.

"Jenny, I must know what is going on between you and John. Has he hurt you?"

Jenny's lips trembled as she began to cry even harder. Her mother took hold of her shoulders to stop her from rocking.

"Has John hurt you?" she demanded in a stern voice. Jenny shook her head.

"Then what? What is going on? I saw Gregg leave the house like a mad man. Have you broken off the engagement?" Jenny wiped the tears from her cheek. She looked painfully at her mother.

"What engagement? Look at my finger. Do you see a ring?" She held her hand up to her mother.

"I don't understand."

"Gregg asked me to marry him, yes! He has not made it official! It has been months and he has not spoken of a ring. We have not discussed a wedding date! Whenever I bring it up, he talks of nothing but the research study of his brain! Are we engaged?" Jenny threw her hands up in the air in a questioning gesture. Her mother sat, listening quietly to Jenny's confusing concern. Rose thought that the wedding day was set for the coming fall.

"Those are issues you need to work out with Gregg. You need to be open about what you want. Gregg's recovery was a miracle and I think he is still dealing with the shock himself. You can't expect him not to be excited about it."

"Am I being selfish mother?"

"No, I just think you need to be honest with Gregg by telling him what you want. Good communication is going to very important if you want to have a good marriage. Your father and I don't keep any secrets from each other." Rose stroked her daughter's hair.

"Let's turn to what John wants from you. I suspect something happened between you two since his return. I know it's none of my business. You are an independent woman, but I need to know if he is hurting you in any way. If he is, he will not be allowed in this house again." Jenny felt like a hypocrite. She wanted to be in John's arms tonight just as much as he wanted to be in hers. She felt confused about what was right and what felt good.

John caused her so much pain over the years yet she liked having him around. There were so many times when they were teenagers that he had stuck up for her and he was around for her when she was feeling sad. He protected her from bullies in school, more than he should have. He was like a big brother only a little different. She didn't know how to explain it. She knew that his presence was comforting to her.

He always seemed to be in the wrong place at the wrong time. Had he come back for her sooner, or had he asked her to wait when he left, things would be different. But he didn't come back sooner and he didn't ask her to wait. She had no idea he even cared for her at all.

"Every thing's fine. It was just a misunderstanding, that's all. I will get dressed and go see Gregg tonight." Jenny felt horrible for lying but she needed to protect her secret until Gregg knew he was going to be a father. Jenny knew that everything was not all right. She was pregnant, frightened that Gregg would change his mind about the wedding and afraid that she had feelings for the wrong man. No! Everything was not all right. Rose hugged Jenny and closed the door quietly behind her.

It was almost nine o'clock before Jenny quit crying. She lay on her bed trying to figure things out. She got up and dressed in loose fitting sweat pants. She carried the beautiful roses to the kitchen to put them in water before she stepped out into the chilly evening. The raw wind stung her face as she made her way across the muddy yard to her car. She cursed the ground under her feet as she climbed into her car bringing the mud in with her feet. She drove to Chesterfield, crossing the bridge where Gregg's car was found the night of his accident a year and a half ago. It still gave her goose bumps to cross that spot. She pulled her car up in front of his parent's house.

The house was brightly lit as she scanned the front of the house. Gregg's car was parked across the street. She unbuckled her seatbelt and nervously walked up the path and climbed the stairs to the wooden porch. Seeing a shadow of a person through the curtain, she tapped lightly on the glass door. She could hear shuffling inside the house and finally the door opened. Jenny met Gregg face to face. His eyes held a grim stare.

"I see you decided to put some clothes on." Gregg knew his piercing words hurt her by the look on her face. "Look, what ever it is you have come to tell me I don't want to hear it." He began to close the door in her face.

"Gregg, please let me explain." She reached for his arm and pulled him as he was turning around. He looked down disgustingly at her hand.

"Please, don't touch me. I know what I saw."

"Gregg, you don't understand!"

"I understand perfectly. So what is this guy to you? Soul mate? Pity companion? Lover? All of the above?" Gregg was seething inside and the muscles in his jaw flexed as he spoke. The whites of his eyes seemed enlarged as he spoke to her through clenched teeth.

"What has it been Jenny, five months since we've been engaged? Is he some side dish for you while I remain celibate and faithful to you during our engagement period? I thought we were doing the right thing here! I thought I was doing right by you!"

"Will you be quiet while I explain?" She shook violently, not from the chill of the wind but because of the anger caused by Gregg's accusations.

"You don't need to explain. Just leave," he said quietly. "I have nothing more to say." There was no reasoning with Gregg. He wasn't going to listen. Jenny decided to let him cool off before trying the conversation again. She left in tears as a chilly rain began to pound the pavement. Gregg went to his room and slammed the door. He reached into his pocket for the box that held the tiny gold engagement ring and flung it at the wall. It hit Jenny's graduation picture, which fell to the floor shattering the glass in the frame. It shattered like the dreams they shared together.

Now he knew why she was acting strange. She had been acting distant for some weeks and it all seemed to fit. It was easy to understand now. She had another lover. It was a simple explanation, yet not quite so simple to accept. Why didn't I see it? She seemed nervous and fidgety like something else was on her mind. Now he knew that something was actually somebody. He thought Jenny was different than most women. He thought he knew her. Fooling around with another guy was the last thing he thought she would do. What nerve it took to do it right in her parents' own house! Didn't she remember he was coming tonight? God how he missed her while he was away. All he wanted to do was hold her in his arms. Couldn't she at least do it discretely? She knew he had access to her parent's home any time he pleased. Perhaps she planned it that way. Perhaps she planned to let me catch her with another man. It was probably easier than telling me face to face.

Gregg thought that during his coma, a lot probably happened that he was unaware of. He remembered a man named Gary who Jenny spoke frequently of. He realized there was a lot about her that he probably didn't know. It was better that he found out now before the plans for the wedding were well under way. He had already gone ahead and chose a date for their wedding without Jenny knowing. It was to be the fourth Saturday in August, a full moon. He knew how much Jenny loved the full moon. He wanted it to be a gift for her. He wanted to give her the moon on their wedding night. It would also be the right time to harvest the peach gladiolus that his grandmother so laboriously planted just for that occasion.

For a week Jenny tried continuously to contact Gregg, but each time he refused her phone calls. Each time the door was slammed in her face. For weeks she penned him letters, each he shredded before even opening them. In her letters she explained her relationship with John and how he was trying to comfort her when he found out she was pregnant that night in her room. She explained that John was like a brother to her and that he lived with her family for three years. She also wrote to him that the baby was due to arrive in early July. Upon hearing no response, the time neared for her to tell her parents about the baby. Rose held her in her arms afterward. Jenny sobbed, telling them how Gregg wanted no part of her or the baby. He didn't even acknowledge her phone calls or numerous letters. She knew she was on her own. Her parents were disappointed but not that upset. They were very concerned that she was single and concerned about Gregg's lack of responsibility for his role in the events that lay ahead.

Since the confrontation with Gregg, John made a habit of stopping by the farm. At first his visits were unwanted and mostly unexpected. Jenny's parents greeted him coldly sensing he was part of the reason Gregg and Jenny were no longer together. They made it a purpose to make sure John and Jenny were not left alone together. One beautiful sunny Saturday afternoon John dropped by the farm while Jenny's parents were in town selling eggs. They walked to the creek and sat side by side on the tile above the creek watching the spring floodwaters fight its way through the tile. John took Jenny's hand and squeezed it gently. He brought her hand to his lips blowing her fingers in a gesture to keep them warm.

"Who is the father of your baby?" John asked. He knew the guys name was Gregg but John wanted to know more about the guy that dumped her like a rock.

"Why does it matter to you John? He left me because of you, because of what he saw going on between us. It's because of you that Gregg is not with me. He won't listen to my explanation. He won't answer my calls. He won't answer my letters." Her voice escalated as she explained her situation to John. "And because of you my baby does not have a father!"

"Damn you woman, why do you always blame me for your short comings? Not everything that has happened here is my fault," he said trying not to get her upset. "I didn't get you pregnant and you were the one who kissed me first. What was I supposed to think when I woke up and found you kissing me?" He remembered how she was dressed and added, "Let alone half naked. What is a guy to do?"

The words stung Jenny's heart like a blow with his fist. It was the cold hard truth and John put it to her bluntly. "A gentleman would have left." She began to cry making him feel like a creep for hurting her. He put his arm around her and tried to comfort her. The air felt damp as they sat huddled together on top of the tile.

"That's not fair John. I kissed you as a friend, not a lover!" John pinched his eyebrows together.

"How was I supposed to know that?" he said throwing his hands up. "I didn't know you were seeing anyone. You wanted that kiss just as much as I did. Admit it to yourself for cripes sakes!"

"Okay I did!" She said shaking her fists and screaming at him. "I did! Does that make me a bad person?"

"No," he said in a quieter voice. "It just makes you a human being with very bad timing." Neither of them spoke for a long time. They sat side by side silently watching the turbulent water gush under the tile. After an uncomfortable silence, John spoke.

"Did it ever occur to you that if he really loved you he would have given you a chance to explain yourself?" Jenny did not answer. She had been fighting the same voice in her conscious for weeks.

"Does any one besides me know you are pregnant?"

Jenny smiled at John as she sat next to him dressed in a warm zippered jersey. The sleeves were rolled down and she pulled the hood over her head to keep the spring breeze from chilling her body. She didn't even bother to try and hide her pregnancy any more.

"My family knows. Gregg knows. I can't give up hope that he will change his mind. I just can't," she said tossing her head into her hands.

"I'm so sorry Peanut. I promise I won't make any more advances toward you. I want you to be happy. I want you to be able to work this out with Gregg." He brushed her bangs from her eyes.

"He has no idea what he is turning his back on. Just remember one thing. If it weren't for this guy, I would be romancing you. You wouldn't even be able to say no. If you ever change your mind…"

She smiled at his sweet gesture putting her finger to his lips to silence him. He hugged her pulling her close to him. "I promise I won't interfere unless you ask me to, okay?" His words sounded reassuring but in his heart John hoped that Gregg would stay out of Jenny's life permanently. He knew that Gregg's absence would make it easier for him to become more involved in Jenny's life. Since finding his real parents, he needed a family more than ever. He wanted Jenny to provide him with that. It didn't matter that she was carrying some one else's kid. He had Jenny and everything was going according to his plan.

Chapter 8

The shock of Gregg's rejection lingered for weeks. Eventually Jenny became numb and once again became accustomed to being alone. After all, that's what she was since Gregg's accident. Alone. The feel of John's comforting arms around her made her feel safe. It made John sick to think that a man could father a child and just walk away without another thought about it. He knew one day when he was a father himself that things would be different. He hated his parents for what they did to him. He hated the bastard that left Jenny pregnant and alone. He felt sorry for her and responsible for Gregg's rejection of her. He knew that he should give Jenny time to work things out with Gregg before trying to win her heart. He owed her that much for all the pain he caused in her life. He pretended to support her decision to try to reach Gregg through weekly letters.

"Did you love him?" he asked her on another day as they walked by the creek together. The sun was high in the afternoon sky but the raw wind blew swirls of dust across the fields like miniature cyclones. The cattle were turned out to the pasture to chew the succulent grass and clover growing in thick cover.

She looked sadly up at John. Her bottom lip quivered when she answered. "I still do."

"What are you going to do?"

"Nothing."

"Nothing?"

"Next week I'm moving into an apartment in town. The stress is too much for me here. I want to be settled and comfortable before…" She looked down at her stomach putting her hands on top of John's.

"Before what?"

"Before July when the baby arrives." John's eyes grew wide.

"Oh! It's sooner than I thought. Have you been to the doctor yet?" Jenny didn't answer. John stopped walking and turned to face her.

"Okay, Monday I am making you an appointment and we are going to get you in for a visit." Forgetting his promise to her, he immediately began to take control of her situation.

Jenny raised her eyebrow. "We?"

"I am going with you. There is no reason a woman should have to do this alone." He took her hand.

"Come, let's get you out of this chilly air." He took her hand and pulled her close to him. She felt relieved about John's offer and wondered why he would want to accept the responsibility of someone else's pregnant ex-girl friend.

"What are you going to do, about the baby I mean? You are going to keep it right?" He put his right hand on her stomach as they walked back to the house. "After all, it's part of you isn't it?" Jenny was uncertain what to do. She knew that having an abortion was out of the question. She could never take another human life. She was raised to believe that God takes part in the conception of new life. She chose to take the risk of getting pregnant. She thought about all the people in the world who couldn't have children. She thought that God devised His plan that way so all the abandoned children in the world would have someone to adopt them. Jenny felt she was allowed to get pregnant for a reason other than her lack of responsibility to have protected sex. Having a deep respect for life, she knew she didn't have a right to take away what God had allowed. She was already into the second trimester of her pregnancy and the sickness was finally easing.

John noticed the absence of Mr. and Mrs. Elerose's warmth toward him and he accepted their anger. Jenny listened to her father's advice asking her to live under his roof, providing the support she would need once the baby arrived. Jenny loved her parents for offering their support and, feeling like she betrayed them, she decided it was best for her to live on her own. Her parents weren't getting any younger and it would be a big stress on them to have a baby in the house. She couldn't expect them to raise the child while she worked at the hospital.

Within a week, Jenny moved into a small apartment on Main Street. It was dull and inexpensive but provided her with the essentials for raising a child. The park was right out her back door and she knew she would visit frequently with the bundle of joy she carried within. She knew that if she couldn't have Gregg in her life, at least she would have something that was a part of him. She wondered what the child would look like as she pictured a little blond boy with bright blue eyes. She wondered how she would ever tell him about his daddy. She felt compassionate toward John, knowing that her baby was abandoned, like John had been so many years ago.

John was there to help her the day she moved. It was a rainy day and he graciously carried her things into the apartment and put them where she requested. He insisted she stay out of the way and wouldn't let her lift a finger during the moving process. Jenny never complained about the mud he dragged into the apartment nor did she complain when he dropped her box of dishes, breaking all but three plates. John scheduled an appointment for Jenny seeking her permission to accompany her into the examination room. She nervously granted him permission wishing she had had the courage to ask him to wait outside in the waiting room. Her nurse's name was Kathy. The same nurse that was so kind to Jenny while Gregg was in the hospital.

Kathy watched John questionably while she took Jenny's blood pressure, temperature and pulse. He seemed nervous and out of place but she shrugged off her dubious feelings of him and turned her attention back to Jenny. Kathy was a small woman who had dark eyes and short brown bouncy hair that swung as she walked. Jenny didn't know that much about her except that she had two small boys of her own and that she met her husband at a college party while he was attending the police academy. They were married immediately after college and decided to have children right away. Kathy continued to be keenly aware of John's presence. He had an awkward air about him that she couldn't explain. Being married to a police officer taught her to be skeptical of everyone she met. She could have sworn she had seen a picture of him before. Shrugging off her skepticism, she concerned herself with the comfort of her patient.

"You can wait outside Mr.?"

"Hawkins, John Hawkins." He held out his hand to her.

"Pleased to meet you." Kathy returned his greeting graciously noticing his dark eyes and straight white teeth.

"I'd like to stay if you don't mind." Kathy looked at Jenny raising her brow.

"It's okay, he can stay," Jenny said smiling at John. Kathy cleared her throat.

"All right, then, please change into this gown and Dr. Skoblik will be in after a few minutes." She tossed Jenny the skimpy white gown with blue polka dots on it before leaving the room. She grasped the gown to her chest and stared at him. Her face reddened when he did not leave the room.

"Well! I'm not about to undress in front of you!" she snapped.

John smiled at Jenny as he walked toward the door. He opened it and turned around sticking his head in.

"It's not like I haven't seen you naked before," he teased. She threw the gown at him as he closed the door. The gown fell to the floor. When she was dressed in the blue gown she cracked the door and motioned for John to enter. Holding the back of the thin gown closed, she climbed up on the table and covered herself modestly with the cloth provided. John went to her side and held her hand as she lay waiting. He looked into her blue eyes thinking how beautiful she seemed. Just as beautiful as the first day he met her.

"Nervous?"

Jenny nodded. Her bottom lip trembled as she squeezed his hand tightly. In a few minutes Dr. Skoblik entered.

"Hello Ms. Elerose," he said taking her hand.

He looked at John who stood next to Jenny still holding her hand.

"And you must be the proud father," he said reaching out to John. The smile faded from John's lips and his face grew white.

"My name is John."

"Well, John, thank you for coming with this lovely young lady today." Jenny worked under Dr. Skoblik several times and he knew she wasn't married. She blushed as she watched the expression on John's face. He did nothing to correct Dr. Skoblik's understanding that he was not the father. Dr. Skoblik thoroughly explained what he was going to do. He lifted her gown and spread gel on her stomach. John moved closer to the middle of the table to get a better look. Dr. Skoblik listened with the stethoscope moving it around her abdomen. In a moment he was able to locate a heart beat. He turned up the sound on the stethoscope for both John and Jenny to hear. A tear slid down Jenny's cheeks as the life inside became real to her. All those weeks she wondered about the tiny life inside. The baby didn't seem real until she heard its beating heart. A bond formed that day. It was a bond that would grow stronger with each passing day.

Dr. Skoblik continued with a breast exam, lifting and feeling for lumps. He chatted calmly to John telling him what good work Jenny did and how proud he was to have her on his team. John caught a glimpse of her bare breast, a stout nipple and turned around in embarrassment to find a chair. The hair stood on his arms as he watched the doctor's hands artistically move over her breasts during the examination.

A brief moment of jealously swept over him as he watched the doctor's skillful hands. He wondered about the passion she shared with the man who impregnated her. Picturing them lying together in the heat of passion angered him and he wondered what kind of man would turn his back on a beautiful woman and child. What kind of man wouldn't give her the benefit of doubt or the chance to explain? Jenny turned into a wonderful woman and he wished she wouldn't have been so bitter toward him. He had not known she was in love with someone else the night he climbed the stairs to her room. He had no intention of screwing up a life she was building with someone else. He wanted to ask her forgiveness for all the terrible things he had done.

He recalled that night as he sat there waiting for the examination to end. He suspected she was pregnant when he stayed at the farm the first time. Hearing her vomit that night proved him right. Why had she climbed in bed with me as I lay sleeping? He thought she enjoyed his caress and his kiss. He knew he should have gotten in contact with her after he left years ago, but he made bad choices and he would have to live with the consequences. He remembered how full of anger he was toward his adoptive mother when he learned she didn't want him to return to Montana. He was even more furious when he found his real parents and how filthy rich they were.

They made him, gave birth to him and tossed him away like a used piece of paper. He knew Jenny was bitter about him living at the farm. He wished he had been nicer to her. It wasn't his fault that he had to live with them. The Eleroses were the only real parents he ever had. Joe was John's adoptive father and Joe loved him like his own son but after he was gone the Elerose family was all he had. If it had not been for them, he probably would have ended up on the street. John wished he was the father of Jenny's baby. He knew he would be a good father one day and he would succeed in taking care of his wife and their baby. It was exciting to be able to hear the heartbeat and he wondered if it was a girl or boy. Dr. Skoblik shook his shoulder when the examination was over, snapping him out of his daydream.

"Congratulations," the doctor said. "It sounds like you have a healthy beater. I'd like to see her back once a month until she grows closer to delivery. Then we'll increase the visits. Have you considered parenting classes or Lamaze?" Dr. Skoblik looked questioningly at Jenny and then John. John's mouth fell open. He didn't know how to answer and felt relieved when Jenny spoke up.

"What do you offer for parenting classes?"

"Dr. Skoblik reached in a drawer with his long skinny fingers and pulled out some pamphlets. It is all explained in here. He handed her a blue piece of paper. This is the schedule for Lamaze classes. Read it over and call the number at the bottom if you plan to attend. Since this is your first birth, I strongly recommend the Lamaze classes. You will be taught breathing and relaxation techniques, which can help tremendously during the labor process. John, we recommend you attend also. Child birth is a joint venture from start to finish." The color drained from John's face and he stood speechless, staring at Jenny. Jenny noticed his discomfort and promptly thanked the doctor for his care. The doctor excused himself from the small cold room. John followed him out the door allowing Jenny to dress in privacy. John drove Jenny back to her apartment in silence with the apprehension of the doctor's visit behind them.

"Thank you for that." She leaned over and kissed him softly on the cheek. "You don't have to pretend you are the father though. Everyone knows you're not." Her words stung like a bee bite. A lousy mood overcame him as he sat in the exam room watching the doctor invade Jenny's body like a bomb squad invading a building, combing each article as if it were fragile.

"I know, I just thought it would be awkward to explain. I'll call you," he said leaning over to push open the door for her. Jenny climbed out of the car and walked alone into her tiny two-bedroom apartment.

Chapter 9

Jenny notified her supervisor of her pregnancy the same day of her checkup. She was able to hide it under her baggy smocks and elastic pants. She planned to work up to the day she gave birth. A lot of preparation had to be done before the arrival of the baby. She was looking forward to garage sales and freshening up the apartment. Her landlord agreed to let her paint the room that she would turn into a nursery. He even agreed to pay for the materials. It was late in her pregnancy when she decided it was time to do the painting. John was coming around more often helping her with household chores. His presence was a constant reminder of the reason there would be no wedding in the fall and she felt that if Gregg truly loved her he would have given her a chance to explain what he saw that night in her bedroom. Jenny put her anger aside and focused on the upcoming birth. Jenny was growing fond of John, seeking his friendship when she felt lonely.

The frequent movement in her womb never let her forget that she was faced with a future of enormous responsibility. At times it overwhelmed her and she would break down in tears. She would fall apart in the emergency room with a life hanging in shreds on the operating table, in the shower with the size of her womb evident and in the very own privacy of her lonely bedroom where Gregg belonged. She felt foolish for her own gullibility when she fully gave herself to Gregg. But she trusted him with her body, her soul and her heart. The security she felt in his arms disappeared with her virginity never to be recovered again. Now she suffered the consequences of her decisions and her vulnerability leaving her alone and afraid of what lay ahead.

She felt punished for showing affection for John, affection she denied him as a young teenager. Affection she held locked in her heart for fear of being rejected. Now here she was living the reality of her fears. It probably did look peculiar to Gregg as he stood there with an arm full of roses. How it must have hurt him to see her dressed in a disheveled robe in the arms of a stranger in her bed. She laughed at the image it must have created and the impossibility of the awful mishaps tossed into the path of her life's journey but she trusted God and knew there was a reason for all that took place.

Each month that passed became more difficult for Jenny. Her feet swelled, her back hurt and most of all the pain in her heart grew worse. John was a great companion when he was around. He would make her sit on the couch with her feet up and rub them for her. He ran for groceries, he straightened up the apartment and more importantly he provided her with company. A gentle knock sounded at the door as she sat alone in her apartment. Jenny wiped her tears with the maternity top her sister in law had given her. She opened the door for Shari who stood there holding a hot steamy pizza smiling a smile that hid the pain of losing a child herself. Shari was medium height with black hair and dark eyes to match. Her shoulder length bouncy hair was always perfectly styled and curved around her face framing it like a picture. Her teeth were perfectly straight behind thin pink lips. She was sweet natured and always seemed to know what feelings Jenny was fighting. Her daughter was born full term but only lived for a few short hours due to unimaginable complications in the growth of the child's brain.

"I always had the craving for pizza when I was pregnant. I know how much you love pizza. Can I tempt you to join me?"

Jenny took the pizza from Shari and placed it on the kitchen counter. Shari noticed the redness of Jenny's eyes and the wet spot on her top.

"Those maternity tops make great tear dryers don't they? I've used it for that a few times myself."

Jenny removed plates from the cupboard and set them aside. She walked over to Shari, fell into her arms and wept.

"Let it out Jenny. I always felt better after a good hard cry." Shari patted her sister-in-law's back, as a tear slid down her own cheek. Not for Jenny, but for her own sadness of a child lost but still loved. Shari was gracious in helping Jenny with the preparations for the birth. She passed along all her parenting books that she had collected during her own short pregnancy. Scott was a recovering alcoholic, but he handled the death of their daughter with all the strength he could muster. Jenny was the one who helped Scott realize his drinking was a problem and was there for him when he decided to quit. Gregg's grandfather had helped too by offering Scott a job at their farm while Gregg lay in a coma in the hospital. Even though Gregg recovered, he was still promised a full time job there.

"Does Scott say? How is Gregg?"

Shari rubbed Jenny's arm letting go of the embrace.

"He's hurting too Jenny. Scott says he barely speaks anymore. Scott gave his notice last week." Jenny's eyes met Shari's.

"What do you mean? Is Scott out of a job? Is it all because of me?"

"No, it's nothing like that. Your dad has decided to start integrating Scott's responsibilities on his own farm. It's a good time and a good opportunity for Scott right now. Since I am working, Scott can take the time to learn more about the purchasing and operations of your dad's farm. We'll survive. Gregg is running his grandfathers farm alone now."

"So this isn't a result of Gregg and me breaking up?"

"No, your dad decided it could take months to teach Scott all there is to know. He is anxious to retire. It is perfect timing really. What better place to learn than right there on the farm he will be working." Shari smiled a genuine smile showing Jenny she was happier than she had been in months.

"I want to thank you for everything you have done for me. I don't know where I would be without you," Jenny said in a croaking voice.

"I'm happy to do it. I wish my parents had been as supportive as yours. At least they didn't kick you out," Shari responded in a sad voice.

"I know it's not what my parents wanted but I couldn't dump my problems on them. Dad isn't getting any younger and mom certainly doesn't want to start raising kids all over again. Besides," she said looking down at her oversized belly. "It's my responsibility, not theirs."

"I know, I just want you to know you don't have to do it alone." Shari squeezed her shoulder. Jenny took the plates and dished up the pizza motioning for Shari to follow her to the living room just around the corner.

"Has John been around?" Shari asked opening her eyes wide for a huge bite of pizza.

"He comes by on weekends. The weeks get pretty long for me. Gregg…" Jenny took a deep, shaky breath.

"Gregg used to fill so much of my time. Now the evening hours drift by in slow motion the way it seems. Is Scott staying sober?" Shari put her pizza down brushing back her black hair from her face.

"Thanks to you he is. We're going to wait for a year or two before we try to have any more children. We want to do it right this time." Jenny looked down at her pizza. Shari meant no harm in her comment but Jenny couldn't help but feel her criticism.

"Unlike me right?"

"That's not what I meant." Shari said apologetically.

"It's just that everything was wrong all at the same time. I was fighting with my parents. Scott was drinking heavily. I was pregnant and had nowhere to turn. I was kicked out of my home. Thanks to my sister and to you for helping, Scott and I were able to get things straightened out." Shari let out a heavy sigh. The room fell silent as the two women munched their pizza. Jenny set her plate down, her pizza only half eaten.

"Things aren't exactly great for me right now Shari," she said almost tearfully. Gregg wants no part of this baby or me for that matter. He thinks I am sleeping with John."

"What happened with you two anyway?"

"I don't know. I thought everything was going great until John showed up. He figured out that I was pregnant and he was comforting me. That's all. I hugged him because I felt rotten for all the terrible things I said to him when I was a kid. One thing led to another and that's when Gregg appeared in my bedroom doorway."

Shari gasped. "What was John doing in your bedroom?"

"I don't know. He was sleeping on my bed when I got out of the shower. He wanted to talk to me about something I guess."

"So, I don't understand why Gregg would be upset about you giving John a hug." Shari scrunched up her nose as she questioned Jenny. Jenny's face was beet red and Shari noticed. Shari's actions froze in space as Jenny explained.

"I was dressed only in a robe and it was half undone. I just got out of the shower. John was…was rubbing my bare belly when Gregg walked in with an armful of roses."

Shari put her hand over her mouth. "Oh my gosh! Now I understand! I guess it would look bad. You half dressed and all." Shari was embarrassed for asking.

"It doesn't matter now, it's behind me. Gregg refuses to listen to my side of the story. He doesn't want any part of me, or our child. My child." Jenny looked down and patted her stomach.

"It's just me and you kid," she said talking to the child she was carrying.

"What about you and John? You said he visits frequently."

"John and I are just friends. It was what I hoped we could have been when we were kids. He knows that I love Gregg and that I still do. When he came back to the farm, he tried to seduce me. He told me that he came back for me. I had no idea he even cared about me."

"Does that change anything?"

"No, it just complicates things."

"What do you mean by that?"

Jenny let out a sigh. "It means that I secretly had feelings for John. I had a lot of anger toward him when he lived with us, but I liked him. A lot. He was exciting, funny and daring." She looked up at Shari and smiled. "And handsome."

Shari giggled. "You can say that again. So you are saying you have feelings for John then?"

"I do, but I don't. I mean I let John make advances toward me only because I was trying to figure out if I was making the right decision where Gregg was concerned. I needed to know if I was ready to be committed to him for the rest of my life or if there is someone else out there for me. I was trying to figure out what I wanted and when John came back, I felt unsure about what I wanted. He turned my head. You could think of it as an experiment. I did nothing wrong. I didn't cheat on Gregg."

"But do you think you could have given in to John's advances?"

"No, I know in my heart I wouldn't have let it go that far. It was exciting to be in John's arms but I think it was more of a fairytale feeling. I got caught in a fairytale. Now I'm paying the price and so is this baby." A loud knock sounded at the door.

"That's probably John right now," Jenny said with a little more excitement than she had wanted. Shari raised a brow. She started to get up from the couch.

"You stay right there, I'll get the door. A pregnant lady needs to stay off her feet."

Shari opened the door for John as he carried an armload of paint rollers, paper towel, plastic protectors and paint cans. He smiled at her through gritted teeth as he dropped one of the bags to the floor before setting them down on the kitchen table.

"Hi, Shari. Is Jenny here?"

Jenny got up from the sofa and waddled into the kitchen holding her back.

"Is everything all right?"

Jenny nodded. "We were just sharing a pizza. There's some left. Want some?"

"I'll go get the rest of the supplies and then I'll join you."

"I'd better be going too Jenny. Scott will be home soon."

"You don't have to go just because I'm here Shari," he said winking.

"I know, but it's getting late." She hugged Jenny and patted her stomach. "I'll call you next week. Maybe we can do this again."

John brought in the rest of the supplies and set them down on the kitchen table. He looked at Jenny noticing the size of her girth. She grew tremendously in the past few weeks.

"How was your doctor appointment Monday?"

"Just fine," Jenny lied. John looked at her in surprise searching her tired blue eyes. Jenny noticed his look of concern.

"You look a little tired. Are you feeling better?"

"Yea, I'm fine. Here, have some." She handed him the pizza box. He reached in and picked up a slice with his big hands and ate it in two gulps. She went to the refrigerator and handed him a Root beer.

"Thanks, I hope you are eating better than this during the week," he said referring to the size she had become in just a few short weeks. His statement came across as an insult to her.

"Rest assured, I am not feeding my child pop and pizza for dinner every night," she growled.

"I didn't say that you were. Just forget it. I'll get started on the baby's room."

John was surprised when he opened the door of the tiny bedroom. The cheap pine woodwork was already covered with tape and the worn brown carpet was covered with plastic her dad gave her. All the tedious work was finished. He turned to face her, angry that she worked so hard.

"You were always one to get your work done weren't you?" Instead of lecturing her he smiled and turned away from her and began to set up the ladder.

"I couldn't sleep last night so I figured I'd give you a hand. I do appreciate you helping me like this."

He didn't answer but went straight to work. She watched him pour the paint into the pan and dip the roller into the creamy yellow liquid. She watched the muscles ripple on the backs of his arms as he spread the paint across the walls like artwork. The smell was intoxicating and she closed the door, leaving John to his work. She checked on him from time to time supplying him with a fresh glass of ice water. The whole apartment smelled of fresh paint. Her excitement grew as his progress became evident. It was eleven o'clock that night when he finally finished.

"Hey, Peanut," his holler came loud and excited. "Come look at your baby's room!" Jenny put down the book she was reading and waddled to the bedroom. Her eyes widened when she entered the room. Outside the night was dark and the windows reflected the light from the objects inside the room. She took in the sight of the brightness of the walls. It livened up the room tremendously. Her eyes roamed the walls stopping when she met John's eyes. He stood before her naked from the waist up. Sweat formed at the top of his lip as he stood smiling at her.

"Well, little mama. What do you think?" he said taking her into his arms. His skin was damp and his armpits smelled like yesterday's socks.

She giggled as he danced around the room with her. "I think it's beautiful. Thank you so much."

"Thank you for letting me help you." They stopped dancing and stood inches apart. Their eyes held each other's for a long time before

Jenny pushed away. She reached for a wet cloth from the top step of the ladder and holding his chin between her fingers, she brought the cloth to his face wiping the paint from below his left eye.

"Your hair is full of paint too. You are welcome to take a shower before you leave." John lifted up his arms revealing the paint on the back of his elbows as a whiff of the odor escaped his hair covered pits.

"Pew, I guess that would be a good idea. I want to give it one more coat, but I am kind of exhausted to work any more tonight," he explained looking for an excuse to go home and get high.

"I thought you were finished?"

"The room hasn't been painted in several years. See here," he said pointing to patches on the wall. "You can still see the old blue that it used to be. It definitely needs one more coat. It's really late," he said digging in his pants pocket for his watch. He turned the watch over.

"It's almost midnight. I'll take a shower and be on my way. I'll be back at seven tomorrow morning."

"John," she said touching his arm. "Why don't you just stay here tonight? I have a rollaway bed. All I need to do is find the sheets for it. It hasn't been used since I graduated college," she called over her shoulder. "Then I can throw your clothes in the washer and you'll be ready for another day." John followed Jenny to the hall by the bathroom. "Towels and washcloths are next to the sink. Everything else is on the shower ledge." She didn't give him a chance to say no. She pushed him inside the door and closed it behind her. "Hand me your clothes so I can wash them right away, please." John smiled as he undid his belt. She was just as bossy now as he remembered her as a child.

The scent in the bathroom smelled of fresh strawberries. The room was decorated simply, in pink toilet accessories. The walls were bare. He removed the rug from the edge of the tub and laid it on the chilly tile floor. He dug in the cupboard for a towel big enough to wrap around his waist. Having no luck, he wrapped the towel and held it shut with one hand. He started the water and picked up his clothes holding them out to her through the opening in the door. She gasped taking in the sight of his near nakedness. He smiled at her, his dark eyes twinkling. She turned away in embarrassment. He laughed aloud closing the door. Jenny stood in the hallway for a minute before going across the hall to the laundry room. The bathroom door opened and out flew a pair of white briefs. She bent down and picked them up between her thumb and forefinger in a disgusted gesture.

"I never did like washing men's underwear," she grumbled under her breath. John took a leisurely shower toying with the idea of Jenny's offer. It was a dangerous offer and he wondered if she realized how difficult it would be for him to lay in the next room while she slept. How would he resist the urge to creep into her bed at night and make wild ravishing love with her? It would be just as difficult than his need for a hit tonight. He shook his head realizing her naïve mannerism, and knew he couldn't take advantage of her delicate condition.

"Oh Jenny, my sweet innocent child. What am I going to do with you?" he whispered as the water glistened over his muscular chest. His body reacted to the impure thoughts that filled his mind. "I was a fool for leaving you. Why couldn't I have been satisfied with the family I was given? Why did I have to open up an ugly past? What have I done?" He grasped the wall of the shower for support as he broke into tears of guilt.

John decided the day he left the farm that his past needed closure. He asked himself so many times why his parents abandoned him. When he heard Rose tell Jenny that Jeanine didn't want him back he was determined to fill a void in his life by finding out why he was unwanted. Now that he knew, it didn't make any difference at all. He wasted three years he could have spent with Jenny. John turned off the shower and stepped out into the chilly room. He reached for the undersized towel and dried himself. Wiping the steamed up mirror with his towel, he studied his face wishing he could at least shave. He hadn't shaved the day before and he hated the feel of wiry hair on his face. He found a comb and combed his hair to the side wringing water droplets from the dark wisps. He laughed aloud realizing he had no clothes to put on. Noticing a white robe hanging on the back of the door, he reached for it and tied it around his waist. The sleeves were too short and it didn't cover much below his thighs. The scent of her lingered on the cloth as he became aroused again.

"I can't do this," he said pacing in front of the mirror. "This robe hides nothing," he growled. He sat down on the lid of the toilet as a knock came at the door forcing him to jump off the seat.

"Is everything all right in there?" Jenny leaned against the door trying to hear his grumbling better.

"Yea," he replied in a squeaky voice pulling the belt of the robe tight cursing his body for reacting out of lust.

"What?"

"I said, I'll be out in a minute."

During the time John was in the shower Jenny prepared the rollaway bed taking care to tuck in the crisp yellow sheets neatly. She spread a blue knit blanket, filled the pillowcase and tossed it at the head of the bed. Exhausted, she picked up her book and continued to read. After what seemed like an hour, the bathroom door opened and John stepped out looking like a bishop from the medieval. Jenny roared with laughter, letting herself fall backward onto the couch. John's face reddened as he stood looking down at his ridiculous outfit.

"You're the one who wanted to wash my clothes. I don't think this is so funny." After a minute, John joined in the laughter until tears streamed down both their faces. It felt good to laugh as she dried the tears from her face. John sat down on the couch pulling the robe down around his thighs. Jenny retrieved the blanket she had spread and covered his lap. He held out his arms to her taking her hand as she reached for him. They sat together in the silence of the night snuggled together on the sofa.

"Have you spoken with Gregg?" he asked squeezing her shoulder. Jenny shook her head too tired to speak.

"Are you tired?"

"Yes, it has been a long day for me. I should get to bed."

"We both should." Neither of them made the effort to move as they enjoyed the pleasure of feeling safe and comfortable. John began to nod off and he caught himself.

"Hey," he shook her shoulders. "Are you awake?"

He shook her again hearing a light purr under his chin. John quietly slid off the couch and went to Jenny's bedroom. He turned on the lamp near her bed and looked around the room. Her room was tiny with dull beige walls, which lacked decoration. He pulled back the pink flowered bedspread he remembered from her room at the farm. Before leaving the room he fluffed the pillow and pulled the shade. He walked back to the living room and carefully picked her up in his arms. Her head rested on his chest as he carried her to her bed. Laying her on the mattress he pulled the covers up to her chin. He sat down next to her on the bed kissing her forehead. He studied her facial features bending down to brush his lips against hers. It was tempting to climb in next to her, tempting to take her into his arms and hold her tight. Kissing her softly one more time he turned off the lamp.

"Until morning my sweet," he whispered.

Chapter 10

Jenny was a complicated person when she was a child. She was still a complicated person with a complex life ahead of her. She was brave for what she was going through alone and he admired her for her strength. John locked the apartment door and tossed the robe he was wearing on the couch before climbing into the roll away bed. It was nearly morning when he finally put her out of his mind and went to sleep. He was awakened at ten o'clock by the smell of fried bacon. He lay on the bed enjoying the warm sunshine radiating through the crack between the curtain panels. Jenny peeked around the corner for the fourth time wondering how long he was going to sleep. He caught her watching him. The blanket fell to his waist as he rolled over and leaned on his elbow, showing off a thick mat of dark chest hair. He patted the spot next to him.

"I have this spot all warmed up for you. I dare you to join me," he said in a deep, tantalizing voice.

"I'm not going to fall for that one Mr. Hawkins," she giggled. She reached for the clothes that she dried and neatly folded, tossing them to the brown armchair across the room. She gathered her robe from the couch.

"And I dare you to rise from that bed and fetch your clothes," she said with a mischievous grin. John held her daring stare, his face reddening. He paused for a minute before slowly tossing the covers across the bed. Jenny lowered her eyes to his groin as he climbed out of bed. She gasped at the fullness of him and raised her eyes to meet his stare.

"You're playing with fire little girl," he said chasing her from the room. Jenny giggled like a schoolgirl ducking into the kitchen to the smell of burning bacon. With shaking hands she turned off the burner and removed the pan from the stove. She opened a window to let the smoke and smell escape. In minutes John came to the kitchen wearing only his jeans.

"It looks like I've burned our breakfast," she said in disappointment.

"Why don't we go down to George's? I've heard they have fantastic hash browns," John suggested.

"I'll be ready in five minutes." She dashed into the bathroom and closed the door.

George's was a tiny restaurant just off Main Street that catered to retirees and gossipers. They chose a booth along a wall lined with shelves of antique coffee cups and sat down. The smell in the restaurant was invigorating. Jenny ordered a ham and cheese omelet with hash browns and orange juice. John chose a larger meal consisting of three eggs over easy, hash browns, and four slices of bacon, toast and coffee. She watched him in amusement as he gulped his food cleaning his plate before she was half finished.

John waited while Jenny finished her meal. He felt an uneasy stare from across the room. His dark eyes darted toward the booth near the front of the restaurant and met Gregg's icy stare. John wondered when the day would come that he would be face to face with the man that left Jenny alone without giving her a chance to work things out. He felt like a dandy rooster as he sat across from Jenny, proud that he was the one that was in her company. John wondered how Gregg would feel if he knew he spent the night with Jenny and he was tempted to confront the guy and rub it in his face. Jenny noticed the smirk on John's face.

"What's wrong? You look like you've just won one hundred dollars in pull tabs." Jenny craned her neck in the direction John was staring. She too, met Gregg's icy stare. She felt a stab of pain as he stared at her. For a long moment, Gregg's eyes bore into hers. His blonde hair was cut short for the summer that lay ahead and his eyes were the deepest shade of blue against his red shirt. Jenny turned back to the table and set down her fork. She closed her eyes wondering what to do. She hoped neither man would make a scene in the restaurant.

John watched her face grow serious and her lips began to tremble.

"Why don't you finish and we'll get out of here," John suggested.
"I'm finished now. Please get our bill," she said quietly.
Jenny's legs felt weak. It was as though her body wanted to get up and move but her legs wouldn't cooperate. Jenny wished they had chosen a table near the door so they wouldn't have to walk past Gregg's booth. Unfortunately, it was the only way out of the place besides escaping through the kitchen. John went to the counter feeling Gregg's

stare behind him. He paid the bill and returned to the table for Jenny. He held her elbow as she emerged from the booth. With her eyes downcast she walked past the table where Gregg sat idly fuming. She could feel his incriminating eyes on her belly forcing her to keep walking without looking back. The aisles of the restaurant seemed to close in on her. Gregg caught her hand as she passed. He swung her around to meet his ocean blue eyes.

"I can see you and your lover have been busy," he said through clenched teeth. His stare could have melted steel a foot thick. His eyes roamed her body making her feel naked and ashamed. She glanced at the man who sat across the table before turning to leave. The man resembled Gregg in many ways except that his eyes were a shade of light green. His hair was the same light color and his smile was a mirrored reflection of Gregg's. He shot Gregg a disapproving look. Gregg felt foolish for the harsh words he said to her. In some awkward way, he thought the baby Jenny carried must be his. He let go of her wrist. John escorted her by the elbow out of the tiny restaurant and into the fresh sunshine. Jenny let out a sigh of relief, breathing in the country air.

"I'm sorry about that," John said once they were inside his corvette. Jenny made a waving motion in the air.

"It's a small town. It was bound to happen sooner or later."

"You said you told him you were pregnant. Does he know he is the father?"

"I haven't told him in person. He never gave me a chance to say anything. I've written him letters explaining everything. It's all in black and white. That's the only thing I know to do. What more can I say or do to convince him otherwise?" She squinted up at him in the sunshine.

John nodded feeling relieved that Gregg knew he was the father. The man had plenty of time to hash it over and deal with the shock. John felt it was Gregg's loss and that he must be a fool for realizing exactly what he was rejecting. Jenny felt sudden movement in her womb and put her hand across her abdomen. John noticed her quick reaction.

"Are you okay?"

"I just felt the baby kick," Jenny laughed happily. "It was a sharp kick. I wish you could have felt it."

John reached across the seat resting his hand on her stomach. Jenny picked up his hand and moved it to the right location. A wide smile formed on his lips as he felt a tiny jerk under his fingertips.

"Oh," Jenny gasped again. "Now it's over here!" She took his hand and moved it across the left side of her stomach. "Feel here." John did indeed feel the minute movement of the life inside.

"Which do you think is the hands and the feet?"

"I don't know. It must be lying sideways." She put her hands on her stomach and leaned back in the seat smiling all the way back to her apartment.

John held her hand as they walked side by side up the sidewalk. By late that afternoon, the room was finished and the mess was cleaned up. John and Jenny sat on the front steps of the apartment enjoying iced tea. The leaves on the large oak trees that lined the narrow street swayed gently in the afternoon breeze, shading the front of the apartment house. John handed her his glass.

"I'd better be going. Tomorrow is a workday. Five a.m. rolls around pretty fast." He bent down and planted a tender kiss on her cheek. "Take care of that baby," he said pointing to her belly. John scurried off down the sidewalk to his car. He had already been late for work seven times in the few months he worked at the brick company and he didn't want to jeopardize another job because of his tardiness.

Chapter 11

Jenny lay on the cot in the cold exam room at the clinic waiting for Dr. Skoblik. She was concerned about how much weight she gained since her last visit. Kathy entered cheerily and took her vitals. A look of concern crossed her face when she noticed the wait gain and the fluid around her ankles.

"How have you been feeling Jenny?"

"I've been really tired." Jenny pulled the gown up slightly. "Look at the size of my ankles. What are they going to look like by July?"

Kathy patted Jenny's shoulder. "It's very common for pregnant women to have swollen ankles. Try to keep them up as much as possible. I think it's important for you to think about cutting back at work. I'm concerned about your blood pressure."

"Kathy, I can't. I'm living on my own. I need the money. I need the insurance. I can't cut back my hours." Jenny was near tears.

"Have you been feeling the baby move?"

"It moves all the time. I don't get any rest at night. During the day it doesn't bother me because I'm moving around."

"I see," Kathy replied feeling that something was very suspicious about Jenny's pregnancy.

"I'm going to ask the doctor to come in now. Be sure you tell him how you've been feeling." Kathy left the room and met Dr. Skoblik behind the desk.

"Dr? Ms. Elerose is ready in room two. I think there is something going on with her baby. Here's her chart. It could be just a hunch but I think she is carrying twins." Dr. Skoblik looked at Kathy in surprise. She held up her hand. "Don't say anything. I just want you to know, I've been right the last four times." Dr. Skoblik laughed dismissing her suspicion.

"Hello Jenny," Dr. Skoblik said smiling as he entered her room.

"Hi," she replied nervously. She was becoming more uncomfortable with Dr. Skoblik. Over the last few months she was getting to know him on a more personal basis and it was embarrassing that he knew her body better than she did.

"Kathy says you've been pretty uncomfortable. Why don't you lie back and we'll measure you and then we'll have a listen." Dr. Skoblik measured the size of Jenny's abdomen.

"Humph," he said studying the chart. "You've grown quite considerably since last month. Your weight gain has reached thirty pounds. Tell me about your diet?"

"It's nothing out of the ordinary. I don't eat a lot of junk food if that's what you mean," she replied a little more sternly than she wanted to.

"Are you exercising regularly?"

"I exercise every night. I walk when I can but it's getting pretty uncomfortable."

"Let's have a listen, shall we?"

He spread the cold gel on her stomach as she lay there dreading the weeks ahead. What the doctor was saying was that she felt miserable because she got fat. Dr. Skoblik was a tall lanky man with a long narrow face and tiny squinty eyes. He could probably eat a pound of bacon without depositing any fat. Dissecting her weight gain was a blow to her self-esteem, which was already low enough. The doctor continued to listen with the stethoscope. She smiled to herself as she watched his mustache twitch. He moved the stethoscope around her belly with his long fingers making funny faces. She listened carefully to hear the beating heart over the static of the stethoscope. The doctor moved it around more turning down the volume. Shaking his head, he wiped her abdomen and helped her to a sitting position. He knew Kathy had been right. Dr. Skoblik looked at Jenny silently through squinty eyes that made him look like he was always smiling. Jenny felt uncomfortable with the way he was looking at her.

"Is everything all right?"

Dr. Skoblik heard through gossip that Jenny was going through her pregnancy alone. He pulled up a round stool and sat down to face her. "Is the father active in this pregnancy?"

"No, why?" she said holding the paper lap cover tightly.

Dr. Skoblik sighed deeply. "I don't know any easy way to say this but you are carrying twins."

In most situations when he told mothers they were carrying twins, they were ecstatic. Some were shocked but happy. Some were afraid but supported. Some were praying for twins. Jenny's situation was completely different. She was young, alone and pregnant with twins. Jenny's face turned white. She felt like she had been hit in the head with a sledgehammer. The room spun and she felt nauseated. She didn't respond to Dr. Skoblik's revelation. He put his hand on her knee.

"Are you all right? Is there someone you want me to call?"

"Are you sure?" she cried. "There has to be a mistake. I can't be having twins. Oh no." Jenny put her head in her hands. She wept as the doctor spoke to her.

"There are two heart beats present. They are very close but with the measurements and from what you've told me I'm pretty sure. We will schedule an ultra sound for you tomorrow. You can get dressed now." He squeezed her shoulder. "I'll leave you alone." The doctor left the room feeling sorry for the young girl he left behind.

Jenny sat on the cot and stared at the floor. She felt her stomach, which seemed big and ugly to her.

"What am I going to do?" She looked up as though looking up to heaven. "Why am I being punished? Why? This isn't fair," she cried aloud. A light knock sounded on the door. Jenny ignored it. Kathy opened the door quietly and came inside. She walked around to the table and hugged Jenny. Jenny put her head on Kathy's shoulder. She felt exhausted.

"You knew didn't you?" Kathy nodded and stepped away.

"It was just a hunch. I didn't want to say anything till it was confirmed. There's still the ultrasound."

"I hate myself for this," Jenny broke in. "I hate myself for what I have done. These babies don't have a father. They don't deserve this!" Kathy reached out to hold Jenny until she was ready to dry her tears. Kathy took out a box of Kleenex from under the table and handed it to Jenny.

"Here, use these." Jenny blew her nose four times before she spoke again.

"I'll do the ultrasound tomorrow. I have to know for sure."

"Do you want me to come with you?"

Jenny shook her head. "I'd like my sister-in-law to come with me." She and Shari had grown very close in the last months. She was silent for a while. "I'm scared."

Kathy sat down on the stool. "I'm sure you must be. There are people in your life that can help you. Have you thought about moving back home?" Jenny nodded.

"I can't. I can't put this burden on my parents. It's my mistake, not theirs. I have to accept the consequences. It's just that…Twins? I can't believe I'm having twins." And she cried again.

Shari went with her for the ultra sound. She held Jenny's hand as she lay on the table in the dark room. The nurse put a computer screen next to Jenny so she could watch the activity inside her womb. During the ultra sound she squeezed Shari's hand frequently with sweaty palms. Shari stroked Jenny's hair as she lay nervously on the cot. Sweat formed on Jenny's lip as she waited for the process to begin. The probe was inserted and images, unclear at first appeared on the screen. Jenny cried in disbelief when she saw the two tiny forms lay face to face in her womb. A tear rolled down Shari's cheek as she moved closer to get a better view. The nurse leaned toward Jenny. Jenny felt awful for asking Shari to accompany her on such a visit and she realized now how difficult it must be for Shari.

"Jenny?" The nurse called softly over the sheet that covered her knees. She spoke in barely a whisper afraid that a loud voice would disturb the babies' in her womb. Jenny met the nurse's eyes.

"Yes?"

"I'd like you to meet your babies," she said motioning toward the screen.

"There they are Jenny!" Shari exclaimed excitedly. "You have two beautiful babies growing inside you." She held Jenny's hand to her lips as she cried with her sister-in-law. Jenny studied the view through teary eyes. The heads seemed so much larger than the bodies. Jenny clutched her gown with her free hand.

"Why do they have such big heads?" she asked fearfully through trembling lips. "Aren't they normal?"

"It's normal for them to be disproportionate until the last few weeks. Their brain develops before their lungs and so forth." The nurse moved the probe around. "See here, both hearts are beating," she said pointing to the screen. Jenny studied in awe. She couldn't believe what was before her eyes. What a miracle it was to be able to look into a womb and see a baby before you could even touch it.

"If we zoom it in we can tell if they are boys or girls." The nurse moved the probe slightly. Jenny could tell the woman was experienced and she sensed that she loved her job. "Would you like to know the sex of your children?"

The two girls looked at each other. Jenny searched Shari's eyes for the answer.

"It's up to you kid. They're your babies," she said wiping a tear from Jenny's cheek.

Jenny shook her head. "I can't take any more surprises today. Why don't we wait until they are born?" She let out an exhausting sigh. The nurse removed the probe and left Jenny and Shari alone. Jenny lay there quietly not knowing what to do next. She stared at the ceiling absorbing everything that she learned about her pregnancy. "What now, Shari?" Then she began to sob uncontrollably.

"Let's just take one day at a time. At least we know why you have gotten so big. Do you have enough maternity clothes?" Jenny shook her head. She lay there for a little while before she composed herself. Drowning in self-pity was never her game and she wasn't going to start now.

"Can you help me up?" Shari reached for Jenny's hand pulling her up off the cot.

"Are you going to tell Gregg about the twins?"

Jenny shrugged. "I'll write it in my letters. I don't know what good it will do. I just hope he doesn't stop reading them."

Chapter 12

John cradled Jenny in his arms when she told him the news. The shock of it almost knocked him off his feet. Jenny had a knack for finding trouble. This time she hit big. He sat silently pondering her situation for several minutes.

"You know the Northerns would be spawning about now. Why don't we try our hand at fishing in the creek by the farm?"

"I gave up fishing the day you threw my magic rod in the creek," she said sadly.

"I didn't throw your magic rod in the creek, you dropped it!"

"You made me drop it!" she snapped angrily reliving the event like it was just yesterday. She crossed her arms over her chest and sat silently in her seat. John gave her an uncanny smile. Going fishing was a wonderful idea. It had been several weeks since she had visited the farm and she looked forward to seeing her parents. Jenny packed sandwiches and put water in a thermos for the afternoon refreshment. At least that was something she couldn't burn she thought, shoving the sandwiches into a small red cooler.

"I know I'm not as welcome there as I used to be," John said wheeling the red corvette down the last dirt road to the farm.

"Are you sure you want to go?"

John nodded. "I have to if I'm ever going to reconcile with your family."

"It wouldn't be so bad if Jason wouldn't have opened his big mouth." Jenny said sternly.

"Aw, he's just a kid. He was only curious. He wanted to get a rise out of you just like I would have done had I been him. Don't blame him Jenny." John's eyes looked pleading. "He was just trying to figure out why adults do what they do. He was just trying to understand his own adolescence."

"My parents don't blame you. I'm the one that made a mistake."

John's heart sank. He wished she wouldn't refer to the passionate kiss they shared as a mistake. The only mistake here was that the guy she claimed to love, no longer wanted any part of her or the babies. It just didn't make sense.

"Are you sure it was a mistake?" he murmured quietly shutting off the engine. He turned to look at her reddening face. It was her father who startled her when he banged on the window on her side of the car. She turned and smiled as he opened the door for her. She slid from her seat and hugged him tightly.

"It's good to see you Peach. It looks like you've grown since the last time I saw you."

It embarrassed Jenny when everyone discussed her size. She was still uncomfortable about the idea of being pregnant, let alone being twice the size she used to be. He took her by the hand ignoring John who stepped up behind them. Her father put his arm around her and escorted her into the house.

"Look who I found wandering around Rose," he said beaming.

Rose came out of the laundry room carrying a basket of sheets to be pinned on the clothesline outside. She set the basket down on the kitchen table, reaching out to Jenny for a hug. Her gaze swept behind Jenny's head meeting John's sheepish smile.

"Hello Rose, it's nice to see you again."

Mr. Elerose reached out his hand to meet John. He took hold of John's shoulder with his other hand.

"How's the job going son?"

"Just fine thanks," he said wiping his sweaty hand on his pants.

"So are you just out for a Sunday afternoon ride?" Jenny's father asked turning his attention back to his daughter. Rose motioned for them to be seated at the table. She set the basket of sheets on the floor.

"We thought we would try a little fishing down at the creek," John answered.

"Jason caught five Walleye the other night. The rods and tackle box are in the old storage shed on the shelf. You're welcome to use what you need," her father offered.

"Thank you Dave," John replied sincerely. Everyone was quiet for a long time. Rose wished Jenny could stay so they could discuss her situation in detail. Rose wondered how she was feeling and felt awkward discussing their daughter's condition in front of John. Feeling the uneasiness settle over the room, John stood up from his chair and moved behind Jenny to help her up.

"We should get going if we're going to catch anything."

"I wish you could stay longer," Rose suggested. "Have you reconsidered our offer to move back home with us?"

"I have but I have to decline. If I'm going to make a life for my children, I have to do it myself. It's not fair to you and Dad now that you're so close for retirement."

"The door will always be open. I'll visit next week Jenny." She kissed her daughter's head. "Take care of yourself and those babies do you hear me?"

Jenny smiled. "I will mom."

She pecked her dad on the cheek before disappearing through the kitchen door. As they stepped out the front door, Jason was approaching the house.

"Hi! Come to get more stuff?" he asked sticking his hands in his pocket.

"No, we were just visiting." Jason looked docile staring at the shadow on the ground in front of him. He shrugged his shoulders. He missed Jenny terribly and felt she would still be with them if he hadn't opened his big mouth in front of everyone. It was the first time Jenny had seen him in months. Jenny smiled at him as she noticed the fuzz above his upper lip. Seeing him was uncomfortable so she tried to visit during the week when Jason was at school to avoid conflict with him. She still had hard feelings about the way he told everyone that he saw her and John kissing.

"Um, Jen? I'm sorry about everything."

"I know. Forget it okay." She ruffled his hair before waddling over to the old storage shed to fetch the fishing equipment.

John parked the car along the road near the area they would fish. He held the tackle box in one hand and the fishing rods in the other as he followed Jenny to her favorite grassy spot by the creek. It was the same as she always remembered it. She walked over to the fallen log that was pulled near the creek bank several years earlier and sat down. Peering over the edge she saw her reflection staring back at her. She remembered how that used to scare her when she was only a small child until one day her father poked a long branch down into the water so she could see that it was only a reflection and nothing else. John set the equipment down and walked over to where she sat.

"Stay here, I have to get something." John rushed to the car and opened the trunk. He removed the new rod he bought her to replace the one she lost years earlier. He already strung new line and the rod was ready for presentation. He tiptoed up behind her.

"Close your eyes, I have a surprise." She could feel his warm breath on her neck and it made the downy hairs on the back of her neck stand up. She had her hair up in a bun with little wisps of hair dangling at each side of her face. John thought she was even more beautiful with her hair pulled up that way.

Jenny smiled and closed her eyes.

"Can I peek?"

"Not yet." He stood before her and held out the rod. It was the gift he wanted to give her when he first came back to Chesterfield.

"Okay, now you can open them."

Jenny opened her eyes wide and saw John standing there holding the shiny golden rod. It sparkled in the afternoon sun as he held it out to her. She frowned as she recalled that summer day so long ago when she dropped her magic rod.

"Here, give it a try." Jenny took the rod from him as a tear rolled down her cheek. "I couldn't find a magic one so I figured gold would be just as lucky." She went to him and reached her arms around his neck as he lifted her gently off her feet.

"Thank you John. Thank you for everything. Thank you for being here for me," she said between kisses. John held her tight enjoying the warmth of her body. He was glad they were finally becoming friends. A tear escaped his own eyes as he set her back down on the grass. John removed a large pocketknife from his pocket. He made a cut in the sod and removed the top layer of grass. He dug in the dirt below for fat, juicy worms to use for their bait. He prepared her line and tossed it over the edge of the steep bank. Jenny loosened the line and let several feet of the line drift down stream with the current. John sat quiet and still beside her. "Aren't you going to fish?"

"Naw, I never did like fishing much. I prefer to sit and watch a beautiful lady like you do all the angling." John turned to a large oak tree behind them.

"See that tree over there?" Jenny's eyes darted toward the large oak tree that shaded the ground behind them.

"I used to follow you when you would go sneakin' off by yourself. I knew where you liked to sit and I'd give you a head start. I'd walk to that tree and climb it and lay in that crotch over there." He pointed to the split in the tree. A large limb grew off to the right and up a little farther a larger limb stretched off to the left.

"I used to sit up there and watch you. Remember when I hurt my shoulder when I wiped out with your bike?" Jenny nodded. "I didn't wipe out with your bike. I fell asleep in the tree watching you and I fell out." Jenny laughed aloud.

"Oh, Mr. Hawkins you are quite a character. I must admit you always made me laugh… and you still do. What else did you do that I don't know about?" Jenny nudged him in the ribs. John rolled his eyes.

"I can never tell." His dark brown eyes twinkled in the afternoon sun. He smiled wide. Jenny was distracted by a slight tug on the line. She sat straight up in a quick movement.

"I think I have something here!" Jenny felt the jerk again and then her line went tight. She gave the rod a tug and began to reel. The reel worked smoothly and was quiet as she increased the speed at which she reeled. Creek water sprinkled her lap as the end of the rod bent over. The gold specks in the rod's design glittered in the sunlight.

"Keep reeling Jenny! I think it's a Northern!" Jenny screamed in excitement continuing to reel in the fish. The Northern jumped up out of the water before it splashed back into the current. She reeled for a few more minutes before the huge, slithery fish finally lay at her feet.

"Oh my gosh! It's the biggest one I've ever pulled out of here!" John held it up by the mouth carefully removing the hook from the outer lining of the fishes jaw. The worm still dangled from the hook.

"It looks like the rod is magic after all," he said grinning at her proudly.   John held up the fish for her to see. He lifted it up and down. "This thing has to weigh at least eight pounds. Maybe more."

"Let's go show Mom and Dad," she said excited about the fun afternoon.

Jenny gathered her rod, removed the worm from the hook and tossed it over the grassy bank.

"Let me get the tackle box. Oh! I forgot to bring a pail. I might have a box in the trunk." John opened the trunk and found only a paper bag with some rags in it. Under it, lay a small pistol that he purchased in Texas. He pushed the pistol to the back of the trunk to hide it from sight.

"Here, we'll put it in this," he said as he dumped out the rags.

Jenny noticed a quick flash of fear in John's eyes. He smiled quickly and slammed the trunk. Dismissing the hint of fear she saw, she climbed into the car next to him. Jenny put her dad's fishing equipment back in the storage shed and secured the door. She hurried into the kitchen ahead of John. Her mother was in the kitchen seated at the table, paying bills.

"Oh my," Rose said bringing her hands to her cheeks. Dave heard the commotion from the living room and came out to see what was going on. It was already time for the evening news. Dave smiled as he listened to Jenny tell them about the fish and the magic fishing rod. She seemed like a small child telling a story about the tooth fairy.

"I'll clean the fish before we leave. It will be easier to transport. I don't want this thing stinking up your car," she said as she turned to John. "Why don't you join Dad for the news," Jenny suggested moving her eyes to her father.

She held his glance knowing John felt uncomfortable being alone with Dave. The two men went off to the living room finally and left Jenny and Rose alone. Her mother went to the kitchen drawer and drew out a long narrow knife. She handed it to Jenny and dug in another drawer for some newspaper.

"Here, use this. I'll get you a zip lock bag to put it in." Jenny smiled at her mother and took the pile of newspaper from her. There was always a bundle of newspaper on hand at the Elerose house. Jenny remembered how embarrassed it made her feel when her mother would spread it on the floor in the porch to keep the carpet clean. She remembered the first time Gregg saw it and how he smiled when he told her his grandmother used it for the same purpose.

Jenny rinsed the fish in the kitchen sink before laying it on the spread out newspaper. Her mother walked around the other side of the counter and watched Jenny fillet the Northern. Its mouth gaped open as she cut into it with the knife. Her mother studied her face as she struggled to cut through the scale.

"The knife is a little dull. Jason used it to fillet his Walleye. I'll sharpen it before it gets used next time." Jenny didn't make a sound during the process.

"How are you Jenny?" Jenny stopped and looked up at her mother. Her kind eyes seemed to have aged in the few weeks since she left.

"I'm fine mother. The babies are fine." She continued her work. "I saw Gregg a while back," she said feeling her mother's eyes on the top of her head. "He was having breakfast with his brother at George's."

Rose listened quietly. "Did you talk to him?"

"Not really. John..." Jenny stopped in the middle of her sentence. "John and I were together." Rose looked at Jenny in disappointment her shoulders slumped. Jenny felt her mother's eyes on the top of her head again.

"The day John painted the babies' room we went down there for breakfast." Rose felt sorry that Jenny had to be confronted with an awkward meeting.

"Did he say anything about your pregnancy?"

"No, Jenny lied." It wasn't worth the bother of bringing her mother into the problem. Rose touched Jenny's hand lightly. Jenny set the knife down on the counter.

"It hurts mom." Tears filled Jenny's eyes and her lips began to tremble.

"It really hurts." She wiped her tears with the back of her hand.

"Why has he rejected me? Why has he rejected our babies?" She looked into her mother's eyes as though she expected her mother to have the answer.

"I don't know sweet heart. Life can take strange directions. Sometimes there is no answer. Here, let me finish." Rose took the knife and finished cutting out the lungs. When she was finished she had two very large pink fillets. She washed them and handed them to Jenny to put into the bag.

"Has John been around often?" Rose asked raising her eyebrow.

"Not a whole lot," Jenny lied again. "It's funny you know. At one time we were rivals, like brother and sister. Now I think we are becoming friends. It's good between us. We've learned to put the past behind us." Jenny didn't want her mother to know the truth. She didn't want her mother to know that John was coming every weekend since she lived at the apartment or that he called her frequently. She didn't want her mother to know he spent the night on occasion. Even though nothing happened, she knew her mother would only worry. Jenny did put the past behind her. In her heart she learned to forgive John and came to realize that she needed his support. He was a tremendous help to her during her pregnancy and she enjoyed having him visit. Having him around helped ease the pain of Gregg's rejection.

"Do you need anything?"

"No, I hardly unpacked my things from when I went to college. It would be neat to have a clothesline like yours though. I love the smell of spring fresh sheets and towels." Her mother smiled.

"Well, we'll see if Mr. Carter will allow you to put one up. I was referring to things for the babies though. Our crib is still up in your old room. We planned to use it for Scott's baby girl. It's doing no good to just sit there. I want you to have it. Dad and I will bring it in next week."

Jenny put her arm around her mother's shoulder. "Thanks mom."

"Have you decided to take Lamaze classes?"

"Yes, but I think I will wait until the next classes begin in mid June. I'd like to wait 'till… you know, 'till I'm farther along." She was quiet for a while. "What is it like toward the end? How will I know it's time?"

Rose shut off the water and wiped her hands on her apron. She turned to Jenny.

"Well, you will feel discomfort at first. Then it will subside. Your water may break or it may not. That is the surest sign it's time, but it doesn't always happen that way. The discomfort you feel will become frequent and eventually turn to pain. When you start to feel discomfort, keep track of the amount of time in between each pain." She looked sadly at her daughter seeing only fear in her eyes.

"You don't have to do this yourself." Rose took her hand. "I want you to come to me any time you have questions. Are you afraid?"

"Of the birth or my lack of support from a husband? The answer is yes to both."

Jenny took her hands away from her mother's and turned toward the sink in an attempt to hide her trembling lips. "I'm afraid of everything. I'm afraid of the mistakes I've made. I'm afraid of the mistakes I'm going to make in the future. I can't believe I was a fool enough to believe that Gregg really loved me." She put her hands on the sink to brace her body. Her mother touched her shoulder.

"Gregg did love you Jenny. What ever it was that happened between you must have hurt him terribly. I know he still loves you. Maybe he needs more time."

"How do you think he felt when he saw me with John at the restaurant?"

Her mother sighed. "I can't answer that. I only know that he is a fool for ignoring his family. Are you still sending him letters?" Jenny met her mother's eyes.

"How do you know I've been sending him letters?"

"I saw you walk out to that mail box every day like a ritual when you lived at home. I knew who you were sending them to."

"I send him one every week hoping I will get through to him. I'm not going to give up that easily. I'm not going to accept the fact that he just walked away without letting myself be heard."

"You always were a strong one," her mother smiled. "Are you sure you won't stay for dinner?"

"It's been a long day. I'm pooped and John needs to get home. It smells good though, what is it?"

"Beef stew."

"Um, you always were a wonderful cook. I hope I inherited some of that talent." The two women laughed changing the seriousness of their talk. John came out of the living room then. His face was very serious. He clapped his hands together.

"Well, are you ready? It's getting late." Rose handed Jenny the bag of fish.

"Remember, I'll call you next week." Rose kissed Jenny on the cheek. Jenny poked her head in the living room.

"Bye Dad. Thanks for the use of your stuff." She sounded like the little girl she used to be.

Dave followed Jenny and John to the door. He watched them leave from the porch window and waved behind them until they disappeared from sight. "How long till dinner?" he asked Rose.

"About an hour or so. The meat is still tough."

He opened the kitchen junk drawer and dug until he found a file. "I'll be in the basement." Rose smiled thinking about the delightful surprise he was working on.

"Why are you so serious all of a sudden?" Jenny asked.

"Oh, it's nothing."

She flung her hand across the seat and gently hit him on the arm.

"Aw come on, you can tell me," she teased. John was silent for a long time. He thought about the conversation he had with Dave. Dave was adamant about finding out what his intentions were with his daughter. John was taken aback by Dave's abruptness. John could understand though. After all, Dave cared very much about his daughter.

"You came back for my daughter?" John remembered him saying like it was an accusation. John explained that he had no idea that Jenny was engaged and professed his feelings for her to her father. He hadn't wanted to but he was backed in a corner with nowhere to turn.

"Just guy stuff, you know," had added after brief silence.

John was being evasive and Jenny knew something went on between her father and John. He parked the car in front of her apartment and followed her to the door. He carried the little red cooler. She dangled the bag of fish in front of him.

"Do you want to stay for dinner? It's the least I could do for all the painting you've done for me." The offer was tempting and he knew if he didn't leave now, it would be more difficult to leave later.

"No, I better be going now." They stood face to face outside her apartment door. He noticed her disappointed look. He bent down close to her and whispered, "Why don't you put them on for Friday night?" Her eyes lit up at his request and he knew that would satisfy her. "I'll be back to get the rest of my supplies." He took her chin in his hand.

"Until Friday," he said and brushed his lips against hers. He set her magic rod by the door and walked away. For him, Friday seemed so far away.

Chapter 13

With each passing week, Gregg grew more irritated. His parents couldn't have a conversation with him without him blowing up at them. His grandparents noticed his ugliness. Even his brother Brian noticed a significant change in his behavior. Gregg told his parents that he and Jenny had gone their separate ways. He was glad he hadn't told them about their engagement before he planned to give her the ring. It made things easier that they didn't know that he planned to marry Jenny. Not a word was said about her obvious pregnancy.

The stack of letters in Gregg's drawer became a nuisance to look at and a constant reminder of guilt for not letting Jenny speak her piece. He hated the man that took his place and he gritted his teeth when he thought of them together. She even carried this man's child. He picked up handfuls of her unopened letters and stuck them in a plastic bag. He drove to the farm and burned them in the burning barrel behind the barn. He sat down on the grass and watched them burn. He watched as the flames shot high at first and then died down to a low blaze. He brought his knees to his chest and buried his face in his arms. He could not clear the picture of Jenny and the guy whom he thought to be Gary, a friend of Jenny's from college. He cursed her name as the picture of them together burned a permanent memory in his mind while the explanation for everything burned in the barrel. He wondered if the two would marry and he wondered when their child would be born. It was the child that was meant to be his own when the time was right. Gregg decided he would curse women forever and vowed to remain single for the rest of his life.

Suzie Cauwer had heard through bar room gossip that Jenny and Gregg broke up. She was still on the prowl for an honest man who could take care of her and fulfill her need for frequent passion. She dressed in a tight red miniskirt that she usually wore while working at the bar. Purposely forgetting her bra, she pulled her cotton blouse over her head, grabbed her purse and walked out the door. She drove to the farm Gregg was managing for his grandparents and parked in front of the white farmhouse. She stepped out of the car wearing red high-heeled pumps. A moving van was parked near the front door. Rusty, the dog ran up to her yelping and barking. He frightened her and she backed away. Mr. Johnson came to the screen door.

LOVE IN THE SHADOWS

"May I help you miss?" Mr. Johnson took in the sight of her body and shook his head in disgust.

"Kind of a chilly day for such a skimpy outfit."

"I'm looking for Gregg Johnson," she said as she kicked at the dog.

"He's in the field, down yonder. I don't reckon there is something I can do for you?"

"Not in the least," she said tossing her head back in a wicked laugh. She opened the door to her car kicking the dog away again before she climbed in. Laughing wickedly, she tore out of the driveway down the dusty gravel road. She pulled her car to the side of the road when she spotted the tractor nearing the end of the row. Squinting in the sunlight, she could see that Gregg was behind the wheel. She left the car, straightened her skirt and hair before she walked out to meet him. Her high heels dug deeply into the rough ground as she struggled to walk in the ploughed dirt. Gregg stopped the tractor as a whirl of dust showered over them. Suzie couldn't figure out why anyone would want to work in such a dirty job. She coughed and swallowed hard eating dust as she did so. Gregg climbed down out of the tractor. His eyes roamed over her body and stopped at her large breasts that spilled over the top of her tight fitting blouse. He bowed his head in a greeting gesture.

"Good afternoon," she said smiling to him. Her voice was soft and sweet inviting trouble. His eyes didn't meet her when she spoke but continued to be fixated on the top of her breasts. Gregg studied her body, thinking she was plumper now than she was in high school. He could smell the heavy scent of her perfume as it mingled with the scent of the fresh country air.

"What do you want?" he asked huskily.

"I've come to give my condolences," she replied swinging her full bust in front of him. Her nipples were pointed and straining through her cotton shirt and it would be hard for any man not to stare.

"Condolences?" he asked as he wiped his face with the back of his hand.

"I heard you and Jenny broke up. I was just wondering if you needed any comforting?" She giggled as she swung her chest in front of him. Gregg's eyes bore into hers. It angered him to think she could stand there and laugh in his face about it.

"I heard she left you for some handsome cattle rancher. Is that true?"

Gregg gritted his teeth.

"I don't care what you heard." He grabbed her by the back of the hair forcing her lips to his, bruising them as he pressed them to her. He smelled of whiskey and it looked like he hadn't shaved in days. He released her and shoved her away from him. "Is that what you came for you whore?" Suzie looked at him in disgust. She put her hands on her lips and stared at him in bewilderment.

"You're definitely not the warm sweet guy I remember from high school!" she screamed at him. "What has she done to you Greggie pooh?" she said running one finger along his unshaved cheek while her other hand found its way to his crotch. Gregg tore at his shirt and threw it to the ground. He lunged forward and pushed Suzie roughly against the tractor tire as he ripped at her blouse with his filthy hands. His hands left fingerprints on her clean white blouse. She became frightened and wondered what had turned him into such a mad man. In high school, every girl drooled at the sight of him and it was no secret that he was bred from high society manners. Suzie wanted to be in control of the situation. It was always the way it worked at the bar.

Now Gregg was in control and she wanted him to stop. He lifted her skirt, finding bare buttocks beneath. He grabbed her wrists grinding his firm groin against her hips. Suzie's face turned from a look of surprise to one of fear. Her goal today was to tease Gregg with her body. She wanted him to come to her on his own but not like this. He wasn't playing the game the way he was supposed to. Gregg tugged at her blouse until her breasts were bared above the neckline. He squeezed them roughly and Suzie cried out in pain.

"What's the matter? Don't you like to be forced upon? Huh whore? Isn't that what you are? You are going to get what you came for. Isn't that what you do to men? Force yourself upon them? I hate women like you!" Gregg forced his lips over her left nipple biting down hard. Suzie brought up her knee and jabbed it into his groin. Gregg let go of Suzie and fell to his knees in pain. She kicked him in the back with her shoe and sent him head first into the plough ground. Tears streamed down her dirty face as she ran to her car. She left her shoes behind in the dirt. Suzie sighed in disgust as she stepped on the gas and sped away.

After a long while, Gregg staggered to the tractor and reached for the bottle of whiskey he carried to ease his heartache. He drove the tractor back to the farm and parked it next to the barn. Then he climbed in to his truck and drove recklessly to the Elerose farm. He was tempted to walk right in but he knocked on the screen door instead. Rose wiped her hands on her apron and opened the door. Her mouth dropped open when she saw it was Gregg. He looked a fright as she took in the sight of him and the liquor was strongly evident on his breath.

"Where is Jenny?" he demanded roughly.

Rose put her hand to her chest, as a worried expression enveloped her face. "Oh, Gregg, she doesn't live here anymore!"

"Is she living with Gary already?"

Rose looked confused. "Who's Gary?"

"Don't play games with me Mrs. Elerose. Gary! The lover? The father of that bastard she is carrying!" he said thrusting his fist firmly into his own stomach.

"I think you better leave Gregg." Rose began to close the door in his face but he pushed the door open forcefully with his hand.

"I'm not leaving until you tell me where she is!" he shouted angrily.

"I told you she's not here." Dave came up from the basement then.

"What's going on Rose?" He asked as he came face to face with Gregg. "You!" he said pointing to Gregg, "have caused my daughter enough pain. I don't want you in this house!" Dave gritted his teeth as he spoke. His face was set in anger.

Gregg waved his hand in front of Mr. Elerose.

"What is he babbling about? What pain have I caused your precious daughter? I'm not the one who got caught in bed with Gary."

Dave and Rose looked at each other in confusion. In unison they said, "Who's Gary?"

"Don't tell me you don't know who Gary is? For heaven's sake, he was right here under your own roof doing who knows what with your daughter." Gregg pointed upward toward Jenny's bedroom.

"You know what? She deserved to get pregnant! I hope she's happy." Gregg muttered and turned to leave but not before Dave grabbed his shoulder and spun him around. He pushed Gregg into the kitchen and pulled out a chair.

"Sit down," Dave demanded shoving him into a chair. Dave's hands trembled in anger as he settled Gregg into his seat. "You're not leaving until I find out who Gary is." Dave pulled a chair out for himself across the table from Gregg. His breathing was heavy and his face was red from anger.

"Rose, get him some coffee please," he asked in a softer voice. "He's not leaving until he comes to his senses." Dave could smell the liquor on Gregg's breath and the sight of his unkempt body sickened him. "Look at yourself. You look like a bum. What has happened to you?" Rose fetched the coffee and set it in front of Gregg. Dave leaned close to his face.

"Drink," he ordered, pointing to the cup. Gregg took a sip of the hot coffee and burnt his lips. Coffee spilled over his hand as he set the cup quickly down on the table spilling more as he did so. Dave ignored his cussing.

"Now, explain to me who Gary is," Dave said through gritted teeth. Jenny never mentioned a guy named Gary. Both Rose and Dave were confused.

"Gary is your daughter's lover!" he said sarcastically. "I caught them in bed together in her room shortly after we were engaged. I knew something was going on with her. She talked about him nonstop. They even created a baby for heaven's sake!" Rose and Dave exchanged looks.

"Son, there is no Gary in Jenny's life. I can guarantee that," Dave said in a quiet, confused voice. Dave studied Gregg's dirty appearance. "I don't know who Gary could possibly be, but I do know that he is not the father of her child. You are!" Dave jabbed a finger into Gregg's chest. His eyes bulged out as he did so. Gregg sat back in the chair like he had been slapped across the face. Then his face turned white as snow. He remembered the evening he and Jenny made love. It was the most beautiful thing he had ever shared with another human being. He remembered laughing about using protection and in the end went without it. Could it possibly be, he wondered?

"How can you possibly know that?" he accused Dave, narrowing his eyes on the tall man across from him.

"It's what Jenny tells us. She wouldn't lie about a thing like that!"

"Then who's the guy I caught her in bed with?" Gregg was exaggerating a little. But from what he saw, he knew no different. Dave looked at Gregg in disbelief. "For heaven's sake she was lying half naked on her bed upstairs and that guy had his hands all over her!" he cried. "Would you think any different had you found them like that? His hands were all over her man I'm telling you that's what I saw!" Dave and Rose sat silently searching each other's eyes. Gregg put his head in his hands and let out a deep sigh. He took another deep breath before he spoke another word. "I loved her so much. Why did she do that to me? Why?" Rose put her hand on his shoulder. "My life has been hell since she betrayed me! How can you defend her? She is carrying his child! Isn't that proof enough?"

Rose remembered the day Gregg stormed out of the house. She remembered John being there and that John told her there was a misunderstanding. Then there was Jason's comment about the two of them kissing in the hay barn.

"Dave can I see you in the living room?" Dave followed his wife into the living room while Gregg laid his head on the kitchen table. A headache had begun to form above his eyebrows.

"Do you remember that day when I told you Gregg stormed out of the house? John went upstairs to get something he left behind. He was still here after Gregg left. Do you suppose it is true? Do you suppose Jenny is pregnant with John's child?"

"I suppose anything is possible Rose," he said tossing his hands in the air. Rose thought for a while. Dave stood silently with his chin in his hand like he always did when he was deep in thought.

"No, it can't be. According to Jenny she is due the first week in July. John didn't get here until the end of October. Rose counted on her fingers. Jenny would have already been a few weeks pregnant. Rose put her hand to her forehead. "This is one awful mess," she mumbled. Dave walked back into the kitchen.

"Come." He grabbed Gregg by the back of the shirt. "I'm taking you home." Dave drove Gregg to Chesterfield and showed him where his daughter now lived. A few moments later he pulled his car in front of Gregg's home and turned to him. "Listen carefully," I want you to get yourself cleaned up and sobered up. I want you to go to my daughter and tell her what you just told me. John is not the father of her baby you are!" he snapped. "Now get out!"

"Wait a minute. Who's John?"

"John is her step brother." Dave pulled out his wallet and opened a plastic fold out with shaking hands. He held it in front of Gregg. "Is this the guy you saw in Jenny's room?" The picture was the last one taken of John. It was his graduation picture but he still looked the same. Gregg nodded.

"That's the guy."

"This is John Hawkins." Gregg was silent as he stared at the picture. His head was throbbing now and he wanted nothing more than to go to sleep.

"How does he fit into all this?"

Dave motioned for Gregg to get out. "That my son is exactly what you're going to find out!"

Lamaze classes began in early June and as Jenny had come to accept, John was there, supporting her through it all. They sat side by side on the floor of the gymnasium surrounded by fifteen other mothers with the fathers or supporters. Jenny learned from the first class that only eight of the women were actually married. There were two young girls who couldn't have been more than fifteen or sixteen. Both looked ready to deliver any day. They looked so young and frightened. One of the girls came with her mother, and one of the girls came alone.

Jenny felt happy that John was there for her. He was so sweet and kind and never demanded anything from her in return. She wondered where their relationship was going and where it would lead once her babies were born. During the Lamaze practice John held a pillow behind Jenny's back and helped her lean forward as she practiced the breathing exercises. He nuzzled his chin close to her neck and provided words of encouragement to her. He counted for her and breathed with her taking his role as her coach seriously. When the practice was over John leaned against the wall and pulled Jenny to his chest. She sat between his legs and listened to the instructor explain the birthing procedure. John massaged her abdomen tenderly and tuned out the words of the coach entirely.

Jenny was extremely uncomfortable as she worked on her feet most of the day. But she continued on trying to prove that she could handle the pressures alone. She took the fish out of the freezer to thaw remembering that John promised to come for dinner. She opened the living room window and let the cool evening breeze blow through the curtains. Then she sat down on the couch to elevate her feet. When John knocked she was surprised that he bothered. Lately he had been letting himself in and she didn't mind. She sat with her back to the door and hollered for him to come in. She heard the door open and close quietly. Gregg didn't speak but just stood there inside the room and looked around. The tiny apartment was spotless and smelled clean and fresh.

"I have the fish thawing. I hope you're hungry. There's enough there to feed an army...John?" When he didn't answer, she stood and turned to face him. Her heart leapt into her throat when she saw that it was Gregg.

"Were you expecting someone else?" he asked in a cold low tone. He had a lazy venomous look on his face. He was dressed in tight fitting jeans and a white polo shirt, which exposed dark curly chest hair. The sight of him took her breath away.

Jenny clutched her chest, nearly losing her balance. Her legs trembled, as she stood quietly not answering his question. Gregg didn't smile but continued to stand by the door. His eyes journeyed over her body settling on the huge hump below her enlarged breasts. Gregg looked troubled as he stood with his arms across his chest. His arms and face were already tanned from the early summer sun. Jenny couldn't feel her legs and began to wonder if she should sit back down. When she opened her mouth to speak, nothing came out.

Gregg came closer and Jenny could feel his breath on her face. "Whom are you expecting?" he demanded through clenched teeth. Jenny still didn't answer.

"Are you expecting your lover?" He asked cocking his head to the side. Jenny shook her head and continued to tremble. "Did you know you were pregnant with my child before you slept with him? Or were you sleeping with him before we made love?"

Jenny glared at Gregg with wide, frightened eyes as he made his cruel accusations. She let him speak his mind before she exploded. His insults hurt her and she was ready to fire back. When Gregg finished speaking his face was red and he was breathing heavily. "How do you even know who the father of that baby is?" he said pointing to her stomach. Jenny looked down at her growing mound.

"Because you're the only man I've ever had sex with," she said quietly.

"Ha," he said making her jump. She felt his saliva land on her cheek. " Then what was this guy doing on your bed with his hands on your body?" Jenny glared at him then. Her own anger grew intense.

"After all the letters I sent you explaining our situation you still don't understand? John and I are friends. That is true. We are not lovers in any way shape or form. Nor have we ever been." Gregg laughed wickedly in her face.

"Do you expect me to believe that after what I saw with my own eyes?" The veins in Gregg's neck were straining through his skin.

"You can believe what you want. I, I don't know what else to say or do to convince you otherwise." She started backing away from him to give herself some room.

The door opened and John walked in with twelve red roses in one hand and a bottle of non-alcoholic wine in the other. He stood inside the door, his mouth agape first looking at Jenny then at Gregg and back at Jenny again.

Gregg pulled his hands to fists at his sides. "Well, if it isn't interesting meeting you here!" he snarled.

John ignored his sneer and spoke directly to her. "Jenny, is everything okay here?"

Gregg turned to Jenny who was still speechless. "So, if you're not lovers, how do you explain wine and roses? Tsk, tsk, tsk. It's not looking good for you here Jen." Gregg was amused and was taking advantage of the situation. "Perhaps your good friend here can explain it," he said motioning to John. John set the wine and roses down on the kitchen table.

LOVE IN THE SHADOWS

"Maybe I should leave you two alone so you can talk this through."

"Not so fast lover boy." Gregg walked over to John who appeared to be quite taller than he was. He grabbed John by the shirt and pulled him closer. "Please do come in and stay. Humor me about your so-called friendship." John took a few steps and stood behind Jenny. He put his hands on her shoulders as if to protect her.

"Please don't do this Gregg. Can't you just accept the truth?" Jenny begged.

"Exactly what is the truth? So far I've heard a rumor that you are carrying my child. I've heard that you two are just friends," he said wiggling his finger at the two. "Yet my eyes see something totally different." John couldn't stand to have Gregg make a fool of Jenny any longer. He knew he had to preoccupy himself with something before he reached for Gregg and choked the life out of him.

"You should get off your feet," he said looking down at Jenny's swollen bare feet. He motioned to the couch and followed her there. She sat down while John retrieved a pillow from her room. She leaned forward and allowed him to tuck it in behind her back. He lifted her legs and swung them up onto the couch. Then he turned to Gregg who had moved in front of them. His face held an angry jealous glare.

"Listen here you no good for nothing bum." The muscles in Gregg's jaw tightened as he stood there listening to John's insults. "I've been here for Jenny through morning sickness, evening sickness, loneliness and heartache. I've cared for her, worried about her, held her and comforted her. I've gone to doctor visits with her and did everything with her that you should have done." He shoved a finger into Gregg's chest. Gregg was growing more furious as he listened to John. Partly because he didn't like people telling him what he should do and partly because he knew John was right. "I've even loved her," he added.

"Have you slept in her bed then too?" John glared at Gregg. Both stood with clenched fists ready to rip at each other while Jenny sat on the couch and cried.

"Stop! Both of you, stop it!" she shouted.

"Have you?" Gregg asked again ignoring Jenny's request. Gregg's voice was escalating. John kept his voice calm.

"I've wanted to and I should have, but I haven't." John boasted. "I've taken over all the responsibility that should have been yours. You gave it up. You denied her. Not me," he said shoving a finger at Gregg again.

"I'll take responsibility for the brat all right, but not until a paternity test proves I'm the father."

Gregg's hateful words stabbed her heart. He was acting like it was a bother, some kind of chore to be a father. Jenny became furious at the two men as they stood and argued over her. They treated her like a piece of equipment to be used and maintained.

"What gives you the right to come here and demand anything after all this time? If you wanted to be so responsible, why did you run off on her? You didn't even give her a chance to defend herself. You ignored all her letters from day one."

"What claim do you have on my fiancée? That is what she was you know. Did she tell you before you bedded her that we were engaged?"

John looked at Jenny. He had no idea at the time they were engaged. The look on her face was one of hurt and anger.

"I didn't think so." Gregg turned toward the door to leave.

"She never wore a ring." John said in an undertone. Gregg stopped in his tracks.

"I didn't think a ring should have made any difference." Jenny stood up between the two men.

"What do you intend to do now?" John asked hoping Gregg would turn his back and walk out the door.

"Talk to me when the paternity test can be scheduled. I'm available any time. The sooner the better. What are your plans?" Gregg asked sarcastically.

John studied Gregg's face. He had one chance to claim Jenny as his own and the chance was now. John worried that Jenny might accept Gregg back into her life. He couldn't let that happen.

"I plan to make her my wife...if she'll have me," he said offhandedly challenging Gregg's icy stare. The room was suddenly quiet. Outside, a car horn sounded and screeching tires could be heard. Birds chirped happily outside the window. The world inside her tiny apartment seemed to stop while everything outside continued spinning like a child's toy top. No one moved until Jenny finally spoke.

"I think you should both leave," she said barely above a whisper. She passed between the two men and went to her bedroom and closed the door with a slam. Jenny thought she was handling things pretty well until now. She couldn't believe what John just told Gregg. She felt like her life was in a glass ball and she was looking in from the outside. She had no control. It had been seven months since Gregg was an active part in her life. She accepted the fact that Gregg wasn't going to be part of her children's life. She let John into her heart keeping him at a safe distance but silently hoping one day they could be more than friends. She let him comfort her, take care of her, guard her from loneliness and more importantly, she accepted his full support. It was more than Gregg had ever done for her, she thought as she lay down on her bed. She put pillows under her large stomach and drifted off to exhausted sleep.

Only a couple more weeks and her physical discomfort would be over. The hospital regulations allowed her twelve weeks maternity leave and she had planned to take advantage of it all. John opened the bedroom door and peered into her room.

"Jenny, are you all right?" John's voice startled her from her sleep.

"Get out," she said quietly. "Leave me alone."

John knew he was out place when he told Gregg he planned to marry her. He didn't even know how Jenny felt about it. Now at least she knew how he felt about her.

"I'll be back tomorrow after you've had a chance to rest." She did not answer. He came closer to her bed. She lay with her back to him and refused to look at him. "Is there anything I can do before I go?" Jenny still did not answer. John sat down on the bed and rubbed her arm. "I'm sorry Peanut. I didn't plan on you finding out this way. I do love you Jenny." He massaged the side of her stomach and it tingled her skin.

"I love what's in here. It's a part of you and I want it all to myself. Is that so wrong? I knew from the first day I left the farm that I had to have you. But I had a past I needed to figure out first and I got myself in a lot of trouble along the way. I've spent some time in jail for drugs but I'm clean Jenny and I'm sorry it took so long. I couldn't contact you and ask you to wait for me until I could get out of jail. I knew what your answer would be. I couldn't tell you I was a drug addict. What picture would that have painted for you? I knew you had set high standards for yourself and I wanted to get my life cleaned up before I came for you. I had feelings for you when I left and I still do, only these feelings are stronger than they've ever been. I don't have much to offer you and two babies, but I have a steady job and contrary to what you thought of me as a teenager, I am a good worker." Jenny did not respond to John but listened with her heart. He bent over to kiss her cheek and then he left her alone. "I'll be back tomorrow." He closed the door and left quietly.

Chapter 14

John needed a hit. His stash that he brought with him was gone. The money that he got from his real parents was used to purchase several ounces of the drugs. It was completely spent. He paced in his small apartment and stuck his trembling hands into his pockets. He dialed the number for his sponsor once and got the answering machine. He dialed again and again, slamming the receiver down hard on the base. He wanted to speak to her so badly, but given his situation, he couldn't let her know where he was. He left the apartment and jumped into his corvette. He drove madly to the west end of town where he heard from a guy at work that he could buy cocaine. All he had to do was use a special knock and the seller would know he was legit.

He circled the block three times before he decided to go in. He parked in the alley behind the ram-shacked house. The back steps led to an apartment on the top floor. The steps were wooden and mostly rotten as he climbed slowly toward the top. He knocked on the door using the pattern he was taught. After a few minutes the door opened and a small Mexican child came to the door. John peered inside the dark apartment scanning the room in disbelief. A baby was crying in a distant room and a woman lay naked except for her underwear, passed out on the floor. A white male appeared behind the child with a beer bottle in one hand and a joint in the other. The child was filthy and appeared to be about three years old. He was dressed in a cloth diaper without any covering. He was holding a ragged looking teddy bear. The room was covered with garbage and empty McDonalds cartons.

"My mommy is sick," the child said in a sad slow voice. The man behind him kicked the child in the rump, which forced the child to fall forward.

"Shut up, you little bastard!" The man bellowed. "What do you want," he asked, nodding his head toward John. John scratched his head. The sight of the apartment and the way the man treated the child sickened him. He wanted to turn and run.

"Uh, I'm looking for a friend of mine. His name is Joe Baure. He gave me this address." John trembled and hoped the man hadn't heard him use the secret knock.

"There ain't no Joe Baure at this address," the man growled. "Haven't I seen you around before?" he asked shoving the beer bottle toward him.

"No, I'm new in town. Just arrived today. Thanks." John turned and began to descend the stairs. His heart beat wildly as he made his escape.

"Hey wait a minute. You knew the knock!" the man shouted after him. John increased speed taking the steps two at a time. John knew that if he were ever arrested, he would spend the rest of his days in prison. The man was too intoxicated or high to be able to catch him anyway. His heart didn't slow down until he was nearly to Chesterfield. He parked his car in front of Jenny's apartment. The sky was dark and the wind died down, creating a peaceful feeling in the atmosphere. John tried the knob but the door was locked. He banged on the door several times. Jenny refused to answer.

"Jenny, are you in there?" John ran to the back of the apartment and peered in the window. The living room was dark. John banged on the window. He knew she had to be inside. Her car was parked out front.

"Jenny!" Jenny was startled as she listened to John run around outside like a mad man. She went to the front door and leaned her head against the door listening for the sound of his car. She jumped backward when he pounded as hard as he could with his fist on the other side. The door actually moved as she backed away from it. She held her hand to her back and pressed where it ached. It wasn't enough pain to be concerned about, just a dull steady discomfort that eased when she soaked in the tub.

"Jenny, I know you're in there! Please let me in! I need you!" Jenny's heart pounded as she listened to him holler. She wondered if he was high. He certainly acted like it.

"Damn it let me in!" John felt out of control. The tips of his fingers felt like his nerves were growing out the ends. He kicked at her door and then turned to walk away.

"I'll let you in if you calm down." Her voice sounded tiny from the other side of the door. John stopped and turned toward the front door. A dent appeared where he kicked with his boot.

"Jenny, I need a hit!" he cried aloud. "I need somebody to talk to!" She slowly opened the door for him. Tears streamed down his cheeks and his eyes looked wild. He reached for her and she stepped away from him afraid of what he might do.

"It's all right. I'm not going to hurt you," he said reaching for her. She backed into her apartment and he reached for her again. This time she let him touch her. He took her into his arms and held her close against his chest. He sobbed heavily swaying back and forth with her.

"I called my sponsor but she didn't answer. I need someone to talk me out of needing a hit. I need it bad Jenny. You don't know how bad I need it." He let go of her then and began to pace like a mad man.

She went to sit on the sofa. He knelt before her and hugged her stomach. He put his head there and sobbed. She stroked his head like a small child who needed comforting. "I almost did it." He wiped his eyes with the back of his hand. "I almost bought some coke tonight."

Jenny bent down and kissed the top of his head. "What stopped you?" she whispered.

"You should have seen it. A little kid answered the door in a dirty cloth diaper. His hair was all stringy. His mother was passed out on the dirty floor and the guy was loaded. He kicked the child out of his way. He was only about three years old. There was garbage everywhere. I could hear a baby crying in the back room. It was a sight to see. I felt so sorry for the kids. It reminded me of where I used to live when I was a small child. I remembered Jenny. It was awful. Is this the way I want to live? Do I want a junkie wife and neglected babies? Do I want to lie around all day strung out on drugs not knowing if it's morning or evening?" I don't want to sit around wondering when I'll get caught and arrested. John sat back on his haunches looking up at her with a sincere expression. His breathing slowed. "That isn't what I want at all. I want us to be a family. You and me and these two precious lives," he said rubbing her stomach. "Will you be a family with me?"

Jenny studied John's wild eyes. Finally she asked, "What happens when we argue and you need drugs? Where does that leave me, and two children? Have you ever thought of that?"

"I've been clean for five months," he lied. With support from people who care about me I can beat this thing. I'm like an alcoholic.

I'll always be recovering. The temptation will always be there, taunting me Jenny. You can help me be strong. Together we can beat it but I need you to help me through it."

"You told me a long time ago you were clean. You lied to me. How can I trust that what you're telling me now is true?" John knew Jenny was right. She was so damned right all the time. It was like she had her life all figured out and he hated that.

"Let me show you. Give me time to prove it to you." Jenny looked sadly into John's eyes and then she looked away.

"I don't have time John. These two are due to arrive in another month. They need a father. They need someone to guide them and be there for them. Are you telling me you will be there for them? How do I know you won't take off again like you did three years ago? I can't go through this again. You've lost parents but I've lost people too. I've lost Gregg twice. Once, when he was in a coma, and now again. I can't lose you too. I don't think I could live through it again."

"Jenny, I've been here for you since the day I came back to tell you I've cleaned up my life. I've helped you through your first doctor visits. I've helped you fix this place up. I've been here, supporting you through Lamaze classes. Isn't that enough proof?"

Jenny clasped her fingers together. Tears lined the red lids of her eyes.

"I'm scared John. I really am. And do you know what? It's all my fault. It's my fault because I trusted one man too much. I reached for the first sign of love and I grabbed it. Before I met Gregg I was afraid I'd never feel it. I fell hard and fast not thinking it would ever turn out this way. I opened my heart to him for the biggest fall of my life. I can't rush into it like I did in the past. I'm not going to fall that easily the second time around."

John grasped Jenny's hands. "Why don't we take it one day at a time," she said. He searched her face looking for the answer he wanted to hear. Jenny bent down hugging his head into her lap. John wept as she held him.

"I need to know if I can come to you when I have the urge to snort." He looked up at her. "Will you be here for me?" Jenny answered his question with her own question. Something that bothered her since John and Gregg argued in her apartment.

"Did you mean it when you said you loved me?"

John reached up to Jenny and put his big arms around her. He cradled her swollen body in his embrace and kissed her cheekbone. I've loved you since the day you lay down with me on the floor of your brothers' room. I was fifteen years old. You were the only one who cared about me. I know you care about me now. I know you cared when I left. It was hard for me too, but don't you see? I had to do it. I had to find out who I was. Until I did that I couldn't give myself fully to anybody. I want to give myself to you. Will you have me Jenny? Will you accept me for who I am?"

"Who you are doesn't bother me. I don't care if you are the Prince of Egypt." Jenny rubbed her hand through John's thick jet-black hair like a mother would do to her little boy.

"I do care for you. A lot. I'm thankful that you are here and for all the help you have given me, but I can't help but think what my life would be like if you wouldn't have come back."

John sat back on his haunches. "But I did come back and we can't change that fact can we? I didn't mean for any of this to happen. I did mean for us to happen but not like this. I didn't mean to ruin your relationship with Gregg. That's not what I came to do. I came back thinking you'd still be the same sweet Jenny I left behind. I was wrong to think that you'd sit around and wait for the day I walked back into your life and I realize that now. I can't change what has happened but I can change what happens from this day forward." Jenny smiled for the first time that day. John looked deeply into her soft blue eyes.

"I want to kiss you," he said holding his lips just inches from hers. When she did not protest he leaned closer covering her lips with his own. Jenny responded fervently allowing John to explore her mouth with his tongue. It was several minutes before they parted.

"I want you Jenny. I can't wait until the babies are born. I need to have you now."

Jenny felt awkward about her size and did not feel even a bit sexy. She couldn't imagine anyone wanting to make love to a woman who resembled a watermelon. Early on in her pregnancy her doctor told her that she could continue sexual relations as long as it was comfortable for her. Jenny studied John's face as a tantalizing grin crossed his lips. She stood, took his hand and silently led him to her bedroom. At the bed, he sat down and watched her turn on the dim lamp. She stood before him then and he began to move his hands up her blouse to reach for her bra clasp. Gently he unhooked it and slid his hands around to the front of her body to feel her engorged breasts. He moved his hands down to her waist, edging down her elastic pants until they were on a heap on the floor. She stepped back and removed her blouse. Then she stood naked before him. She knew it was wrong but she was tired of being alone, tired of being perfect and she longed to be in someone's arms. Why couldn't it be John? She had come to trust him. To hell with doing what was right.

"You're even more beautiful naked," he said scanning her body as he slowly unbuttoned his shirt. His eyes never left hers. Fully nude, he laid his clothes neatly on the chair beside her bed and turned to her. He gently took her into his arms and he could feel her tremble beneath his touch.

"Are you sure this is what you want my sweet?"

"Yes, oh yes," she whispered hoarsely as he planted kisses on her neck. She forgot about the dull ache in her spine that made her uncomfortable earlier. He picked her up and turned to lay her down on the bed. He climbed in beside her and propped himself up on his elbow and began to massage her breasts. She ran her fingers through his thick black hair as he lay beside her. He worshipped her body with his hands and lips until she arched and writhed beneath his touch. Pictures of Gregg flashed through her mind and in her heart—she knew she was making love to Gregg. If John knew what she was thinking, she knew he would leave her life forever. But John's husky voice broke her fantasy and brought her back to reality.

"Ah sweet Jenny," he said, "I knew it would be like this. You give me so much pleasure." She smiled into his eyes and realized it was only the second time she had ever made love. This time she was more relaxed knowing what to expect and she enjoyed the pleasure he gave her. "You are like a golden angel above me. You are so beautiful and whole. A goddess doesn't compare to your innocent beauty." Jenny shivered as he spoke love words to her. Never in her life had anyone ever spoken words of affection such as his. After they made love, John cradled her in his arms while he massaged her large abdomen. She reached for his hand bringing it to her lips and kissed the tips of his fingers. "That was wonderful," he said trailing his finger lightly over her abdomen. Jenny wondered how many women he bedded during the time he was gone. After all, he was handsome and devilish and had a way of getting what he wanted from people. He seemed a lot more experienced than Gregg had been and John knew just what to do to please her. The women of the past didn't matter to her now. She needed John and he was there. Nothing else mattered.

"Have you picked names yet?" he asked still massaging her skin. It felt warm beneath his touch and it made her feel sleepy.

"How about Joseph, John if one is a boy?" she asked. John's adoptive father's name was Joseph, but everyone called him Joe. John loved Joe and it pleased him that she would choose his name for her son.

"What if you have two boys?" He asked as he continued to massage her.

"Then we will name them Joseph and John." She smiled lazily. They lay together for a long while before Jenny was able to drift off to sleep. Thoughts of Gregg clouded her mind and saddened her heart. "Good night Gregg," she whispered as a single tear slid down the side of her cheek. "I love you." But John didn't hear. He was already locked into his own nightmarish dreams.

Chapter 15

Jenny was awakened in the early morning hours before the sound of the birds to the feel of dampness between her legs. It was not the same dampness created by the lovemaking of the night before. She looked at John as he slept on his side next to her. His arm was flung across her chest. She moved his arm and placed it gently back on the bed. As she climbed out of bed a gush of fluid came from her body. Then she knew her water had broken. She remembered her mother telling her that it was the surest sign that the baby was ready. Trying to remain calm, she went to the bathroom and put on her robe. She turned on the lamp and went to the opposite side of the bed to wake John.

"John! "John!" she shouted.

John sat up in bed with a start. He rubbed his eyes for a moment.

"What, what is it." He reached for her hand and tried to pull her back to bed with him.

"No, it's time."

"Time for what?"

"Time for the babies!"

"Oh my gosh!" Fully awake now, he jumped out of bed and reached for his pants.

"I thought you weren't due for another couple of weeks!" he shouted.

"I'm not," she replied nervously. "But my water broke and it won't be long now." John looked at the clock. It was four thirty. Jenny appeared frightened.

"Are you going in that?" he asked pointing to her robe.

"I'm not going to bother to get dressed. It's dark and I'll be slipping into a hospital gown anyway." He laughed at her ridiculous reasoning.

He was stunned that she would go out in just her robe, but he knew she was stubborn and didn't bother to argue with her. He pulled her by the hand and led her to the door. "Wait, I forgot my shirt." He ran back to the bedroom to retrieve his shirt, pulled it over his shoulders and ran out the door behind her. She got in his car and sat quietly while John drove her to the hospital. He drove recklessly for the few blocks they had to go.

"One would think you were the one having the babies," she giggled. He watched her double over in the seat beside him.

"What's the matter?"

Jenny didn't answer but breathed through the contraction until it was over.

"The hospital is one block ahead. Hang in there!" he said as he squeezed her hand. John wheeled the car in front of the emergency entrance. He got out and ran inside to get a wheel chair. Jenny opened her door and stepped out into the fresh air. She watched John and a nurse approach with a wheel chair. She smiled at John who had a sheepish grin on his face.

"I could have walked, but thanks for the ride."

"How far apart are your contractions?" The nurse asked.

"I've only had one strong one a minute ago. My water has broken though." The nurse wheeled her into a brightly lit room and instructed her to dress in a fresh gown and get into bed. John helped Jenny change and swung her feet up for her as she climbed in the bed. The sheets were bright white and crisp as she settled in. The nurse attached monitors so the babies' heart rate could be observed.

"Another one is coming," she announced remembering to breath properly. John took her hand as he stood by her bed. He stroked her forehead.

"I wish there was something I could do," he said planting a kiss on her head.

She looked at him with a serious grin. He could see the fear in her eyes. "Just stay with me John. Don't leave. Not even for a minute." She squeezed his hand tight. Within minutes another contraction forced her to cry out in pain.

"I'm scared," she cried through clenched teeth.

"Breathe deep, Jenny. That's it. Good girl," John said soothingly. The doctor studied the chart. After quickly strapping her legs to the table he leaned over the bed railing.

"I'm afraid your babies are in distress. I'm sure the cord is wrapped around the neck. We are going to get them out as soon as possible. You are dilating rapidly. A few more contractions and I will let you begin pushing. The first baby is already in the birth canal so we cannot do a cesarean."

Jenny breathed through more contractions and then the doctor told her to begin pushing. She screamed out in pain as John's expression went from one of happiness to fear. She squeezed his hand so tight it hurt. Her palms were sweaty and her long blonde hair was matted to her head. John took a cloth, moistened it and wiped her forehead. Within seconds, another contraction and then another wracked her body.

"I can see its head! Push hard on the next contraction Jenny." Jenny leaned forward as John supported her shoulders.

"Breathe," the doctor told her.

The pain was so intense Jenny thought that her crotch was being ripped apart. She felt punished for the one night of bliss she shared with a man she thought had loved her. She cried as she remembered the night with Gregg. The night that seemed so long ago and so wrong. Sweat ran down her face as John faithfully stood by her blotting her skin.

"Come on Jenny push hard for this last one," the doctor coached. Jenny leaned forward with all her strength screaming through gritted teeth. She felt a warm gush and leaned back on the bed exhausted. The silence in the room was frightening as she lay waiting for the sound of her child. She leaned up on her elbows as the doctor worked at the foot of the bed. Suddenly she felt deaf and became frightened of her surroundings. She was worn out and could only lean back on the bed to rest. The baby was put in an incubator and rushed off to the neonatal emergency room. John watched defiantly as the blue baby boy was rushed away.

"That is Joseph John," he told Jenny happily. He shook her shoulder.

"He's going to be all right," the doctor assured him. "His cord was around his neck and he is blue from lack of oxygen but he'll be fine. We got him out just in time." He patted Jenny's knee. "Good work," he said. "But we have a little further to go. Let's see if that little guy will have a brother or sister." Jenny barely heard the words as another contraction struck. She felt like she was in a bubble and everything that was happening was going on outside the bubble and was out of her control. With a scream and a push the second baby arrived in healthy condition.

"It's a girl!" John screamed in delight. "Jenny, we have a boy and a girl!" He bent down and kissed her sweaty forehead. He smiled into her exhausted face and began dancing around the room.

"You did it, Jenny. It's over."

"No it's not!" the doctor replied. John looked up in surprise.

"Give me one more gentle push for the afterbirth, then it's all over," the doctor laughed.

John laughed too and then the baby's cry could be heard. The nurse brought her to the bed wrapped in a warm blanket. She was all gooey and her hair was blond and damp. The drops that were put in her eyes immediately after her birth ran down her cheeks. Jenny spoke to her through tears as she clung the little child to her breast.

"You are so beautiful." John reached for the baby's hand and slipped his pinky into her tiny fist.

"She's so little. How much does she weigh?" he asked the nurse.

"That one weighs five pounds, four ounces. She's small but she's healthy. The boy is a little smaller. He weighs five pounds even. He is in the incubator and his temp is a little low. We will keep him there overnight. When you feel a little stronger you can go see him."

Jenny cried as she held the baby up to John. "Here, you hold her now." Jenny kissed her little girl before she passed her to John. All she wanted to do now was sleep. Tears filled John's eyes as he looked into the little girls face. He walked over to the recliner and sat down. He didn't take his eyes off the precious gift he was holding until she was asleep warm and safe in his lap. John looked over to Jenny and saw that she slept as well. He sat there content for an hour before giving the baby up to the nurse. The nurse put her in her cradle and took her to the nursery to be cleaned, diapered and fed.

John watched until the nurse disappeared around the corner with the baby. He checked on Jenny before going to the neonatal ward to see Joseph. On the way there he wondered what last name Jenny would chose for the babies. It bothered him to think she would chose their father's last name and the decision would need to be made soon. He reached the room where Joseph slept and watched through the window as a nurse took his temperature. She put a blue stocking cap on the boy's head and he was lying on his side turned away from the window. He was the only baby presently in the neonatal ward. John heard another woman scream down the hall earlier and he wondered how her delivery had gone. All was silent now. The nurse looked up and smiled, motioning for him to enter.

"You can wash over there," she said pointing to a sink. "And put this on too," she added handing him a yellow paper gown. John did as the nurse instructed and then turned toward the incubator.

"You can put your hands through the holes. Go ahead, touch him." John walked around to the other side of the incubator in order to look at the child's face. His color was still blue from the lack of oxygen and his head was shaped like a cone. John frowned at the child and wondered if he was going to be okay.

"His is coming along fine. In a few hours he should have good color. His temp is still too low though. He'll be kept incubated until he is in satisfactory condition." She looked over her shoulder as she charted his vital signs.

"What's his name?"

John smiled a wide grin. "His name is Joseph John," he said without hesitation. John couldn't imagine his life being any happier than it was right now. A tear slid down John's cheeks as he gently rubbed the boy's hand through the hole. "I can't wait to hold him."

The nurse smiled. "That will come soon enough. Why don't you go home and get some rest. Everything will be fine."

"I can't go home, I'm too excited," he said through tears of joy. "I've never been a father before." John knew he didn't have a claim on the babies yet he felt more like a father than anything. He thanked the nurse before he went back to Jenny's room. He sat down in the recliner and fell asleep. Four hours later Jenny awoke to the smell of steaming food. Her bottom hurt and she felt groggy and exhausted. She lifted her gown and looked down at her abdomen. It looked flat and Jenny smiled to herself. She sat up, put her legs on the floor and tried to stand up. She felt dizzy and weak. She sat down for a while and tried again. On the third try she managed to get to the bathroom. She stepped into the shower stall and put a towel on the seat provided. When she looked down this time her stomach no longer looked flat. The skin on her abdomen was wrinkled and sagged. She felt ugly. The steam filled the room as she sat on the blood soaked towel letting the hot water cleanse her body. After twenty minutes she got out feeling refreshed but still weak.

The early delivery came as quite a surprise to everyone. She knew now that the dull ache she had in her back yesterday was a sign. She thought about the act of love she shared with John and felt embarrassed by it now. Did he think she was sleazy? What would Gregg think if he ever found out? Did she care? She wondered why she led John to her bedroom. Perhaps she needed to feel loved. Perhaps it was to get even with Gregg for abandoning her. What ever her reason, she knew she didn't love John the way she loved Gregg. She wondered if her son would have died had she gone full term with the pregnancy.

When she arrived back in her room, John was still asleep in the chair. She took a blanket from her bed and laid it across his chest. She studied his dark hair, his nose, and his lips. She was grateful for his presence and the support he had given her through everything. She knew he must love her for taking responsibility for someone else's babies and someone else's girlfriend. She felt like used books. She thought about Gregg and wondered if she should notify him of the birth. Did he even know she was expecting twins? Had he even read her letters? Would he even care? The babies were here and nothing was going to change how he felt about John.

Jenny sat on the edge of the bed as the dinner cart was being wheeled down the hall. A middle-aged male kitchen aide came in and offered her lunch. Jenny denied it saying she was too exhausted to eat but he didn't care. He left the food and whistled on his way. She brushed her hair and walked down the hall to the neonatal ward. There were machines everywhere in the room. Cords hung from ceilings and the room was silent except for the whooshing sound of electric lungs coming from a room down the hall. She peered through the glass window and watched the sleeping baby. The nurse that helped deliver him went home and Kathy was on duty for the day to fill in for a sick call. Jenny felt a tap on her shoulder and when she turned around, Kathy was standing there with fresh flowers.

"Congratulations Jenny," She hugged her friend. "How are you feeling?"

Jenny couldn't answer but could only choke on tears at the sight of her baby boy. She was overwhelmed by the thought of having two children to care for and stunned by John's profession of love for her. It was all too much to handle. Kathy continued to hug Jenny giving her a supportive shoulder to cry on. "I'll put these in your room. Shhhh?"

"Everything is going to be okay. Your baby boy will be out of intensive care in a few hours. I will bring him to you then. Your children are beautiful Jenny. You can go in and touch him if you like. Preemies need lots of touching. Wash up over there and put on that yellow gown. I'll be in your room to talk over a few things in about an hour okay?"

Kathy squeezed her shoulder and walked away down the hall. Jenny dressed in the gown and stood at the side of the incubator. Her baby began to stir as she touched his small hand. He opened his eyes revealing bright blue eyes. The same blue eyes that Gregg had. She cried for her son and she cried for Gregg wishing he could see what a beautiful baby boy they created.

"I have named you Joseph John young man, but in my heart I will always know you as little Greggory." The baby began to cry and he opened his mouth wide releasing a tiny scream of hunger. He had light blonde hair and fair skin, much like her own. A haunting feeling came over her as she studied him. Gregg's features were there, staring her in the face. Another nurse approached her and stood quietly for a minute.

"It's about time this little guy has some lunch. Do you plan to breast feed?"

Jenny turned around in shock and looked at the nurse. She hadn't even given it a thought. She knew the cost of formula was extremely high and breastfeeding was going to be necessary.

"I'll give it a try. Can you show me?"

"Sure, sit down in that rocker over there. It's about time for him to come out of that incubator to meet his mother." The nurse opened the cover of the incubator and removed the fussing child. She carried him in loving arms. Jenny held out her arms awkwardly as the nurse placed him in her arms. She held him gently as though he was a piece of fragile glass. The nurse helped Jenny open her gown and positioned the baby's mouth on her breast. The baby continued to scream and refused her breast. Each time the nurse tried to fasten his mouth on his mother's breast, the baby would turn his head.

"What if he doesn't take it?" Jenny asked nervously.

"He will, it will just take a little time." The nurse touched the baby's cheek and he turned toward her finger. Then she placed the baby's head closer to Jenny's breast. Milk trickled out the side of the baby's mouth as he closed his mouth around her nipple. In a minute sucking motion began and the baby was content. Within a few minutes he was sound asleep.

"Newborns will do that for the first few weeks. They will want to drink and then fall asleep. Try to keep him awake until he is full if you can or you might be feeding him every half hour. It will come with practice. A nurse will contact you after you are home to see how things are going. Don't give up. You will both benefit if you can keep breastfeeding. It can be a wonderful experience for both you and the baby. When you get really good at it you will be able to feed them both at the same time." The nurse laughed as she massaged the baby's head.

"We will try again when he wakes. Someone will bring him to you. For now we should put him back into the incubator for a few more hours." The nurse took the baby from her and placed him back in the incubator. Then she handed Jenny a jar of salve.

"Your breasts are going to be sore for the first few weeks. Clean your breasts after each feeding and apply this salve. It will get better as you learn to position the baby and after they get a little stronger, they will be able to get a better hold. Tonight at seven o'clock there is a breastfeeding class in the room across the hall. There will be a video and a nurse will be available for any questions you may have. It is very important for you to attend," the nurse said thoughtfully, pitying the young girl before her.

Jenny walked nervously down to the nursery to view her baby girl. She hadn't decided on a name for her yet. Jenny put her hand on the glass as she watched the baby sleep in her cart. Kathy motioned excitedly for her to come into the room. In all, there were five babies in the nursery. Three were girls and two were boys. Jenny glanced at one that had a crop of thick black hair. She smiled as she tiptoed past the sleeping angel. She bent down close to her own sleeping daughter and peered into her tiny face. Her skin was a little darker but her hair was just as fair as Joseph's. It was long on top and the tops of her ears were covered with little tufts of downy hairs. Her face was tiny and her features were small much like her own. She touched her curled fingers lightly as she spoke softly to the baby.

"And you young lady, shall be called Rosalie Jeanine. After my mother and me."

"I'll write that on her card then," the nurse suggested. "We'll bring her to you when she wakes up. You should get some rest. Once those little ones perk up, they will keep you busy."

"Thanks, I will."

Jenny placed a kiss on the top of her daughter's head and backed quietly out of the doorway. She watched her for a moment before she turned and walked back to her room. It was time to notify her parents. The phone rang twice, three times then four before someone answered. It was Jason.

"Hi, Jason, it's me. Is mom home?"

"Yea, are you okay? You sound a little weird."

"I'm fine. You have a niece and nephew," she said choking back tears.

For a moment silence filled the other end. Then Jason's voice came in hurried excitement.

"Oh my gosh! This is cool. I'll get mom right away!" Jenny heard him bellow over the receiver.

"Mooooom, come quick! Jenny had the babies!" It seemed like five minutes passed before her mother finally answered.

"Hello! Jenny?"

"Hi mom." Jenny didn't get a chance to explain any details. Her mother wept profusely on the other end.

"Did everything go okay?" she asked through sobs.

"Joseph had a little trouble at first but he is doing fine. He will be out of incubation in about an hour or so." She smiled as his name spilled across her lips for the first time.

"Is there a problem?"

"No, mom. He is just a little small that's all."

"Dad and I will be there in a little while," she paused. "We love you."

"I love you too mom," she replied with a wavering voice.

Jenny waited for a few minutes to collect her thoughts and then dialed Gregg's number. Her hands shook as she waited for the phone to ring and for someone to answer. When Ruth answered, Jenny's shoulders slumped in disappointment. Jenny's lips quivered as she spoke.

"Ruth, it's Jenny. Is Gregg home?" Jenny hoped Ruth wouldn't hang up on her again, but Ruth sensed the urgency in Jenny's voice. There was silence for a long time and then Gregg's voice came low and quiet. He spoke into the phone without saying hello. His mother must have told him it was she that was calling.

"Have you scheduled the test?"

His sharp words hurt her and it took her a minute to compose her thoughts.

"I don't think a test is going to be necessary." She paused for a minute to try to control her tears.

"All you need to do is look at your son and you will know he is yours. He looks at the world with those same blue eyes that you share with your own father."

"A son?"

"Our daughter is doing fine."

"Daughter!" He shouted in horror. "We have two children?"

"I thought you ought to know. It's up to you whether you acknowledge them as yours or not. I have to go. I'm feeling a little dizzy." Jenny put down the receiver and hugged her pillow. Tears streamed down her cheeks as she sat rocking on the edge of her bed.

Chapter 16

Gregg rushed to the hospital like a maniac swerving around parked cars and speeding through a stop sign. He dashed into the building. The small pocket change jingled in his pocket to the rhythm of his pace. He inquired at the front desk, asking for Jenny's room number. A nurse motioned him to the maternity ward, which was just to the right of the nursery. He stopped at the nursery window and looked in through misty eyes. Most of the babies had dark hair. He spotted one blonde child and noticed the cart was labeled with a pink card. He studied the label. In bold black letters it read: Rosalie. All the other baby carts had last names on them.

He quickly entered the room and spoke with a nurse who inquired about his identity. When he satisfied her inquiries, he walked slowly toward the bassinet. The nurse stayed in the room with him as he studied the sleeping infant. The baby resembled Jenny a lot with her tiny features and thick blonde hair. The baby was extremely small and seemed content in her cart. After staring at the baby for several minutes, he thanked the nurse and walked to the neonatal ward. There were now two infants in the room. One had just been delivered. Kathy recognized Gregg immediately and greeted him with a warm smile.

"Congratulations! He's over there," she said pointing to one of the two babies with the same colored hair. All during Jenny's pregnancy, Kathy too had wondered if John was the father or if Gregg was. There was no more doubt after seeing the babies. "He'll be out of neonatal in a few minutes. You have a beautiful son." Gregg looked back at her as she busied herself in the room. He walked closer to the incubator as the baby yawned a big yawn. He opened his small glassy eyes not looking at anything in particular. His hands stretched apart as he yawned again waving his tiny arms in front of him. Gregg was astonished as his own features reflected in the baby's face. How foolish he felt now to think Jenny would lie about such a thing. He read the card attached to the outside of the incubator. The name Joseph John was scribbled over the card. Gregg grew furious as he read the name. It angered him to think she would name their child after a man that had taken his place. He stormed out of the neonatal room to find Jenny.

John left the hospital to retrieve requested personal items and had just returned with an armful of red roses. He displayed them on a bureau, which was built between the sink and the bathroom door. He set her bag of personal items on the opposing bed.

"How is my little mother doing?" he asked as he kissed her forehead.

"She is very exhausted. All I did was shower and walk around a bit and I feel like I worked all day."

"Do you want me to call your parents for you?"

"I already did. Mom said they would be here in a little while."

Just then Kathy knocked on the door.

"Excuse me," she said peeking her head in the door. "Jenny, we need to put a name on the birth certificate." She gazed at Jenny and then John. An uneasiness settled over her as his eyes narrowed on her. His eyes haunted her and she was sure she had seen him somewhere before meeting him at the clinic. She could not put her finger on it.

Gregg stopped outside of the room and listened as the voices wafted through the open door. A woman asked what name should be put on the birth certificate.

"Rosalie Jeanine and Joseph John," Jenny said smiling into John's face.

"What last name will the babies carry?"

Quietness filled the room while Gregg stood outside the door and listened carefully. When he heard the question he stormed into the room and stood among them with his hands on his hips. The door swung shut with a loud bang that made everyone jump.

"Johnson. The children shall bear the last name of Johnson." His steely eyes bore into Jenny's and a shiver of fear crept up her spine.

Jenny dropped the pen she was holding as Gregg presented himself. Her heart pounded with his handsome presence as he stared at her with steel blue eyes and clenched teeth.

"My children will not be known as bastards!" he growled at her.

Jenny's mouth dropped open at his derogatory statement. "I'll leave you three alone," Kathy muttered and quickly left the room.

"You have no right to claim them as your own!" John blurted out angrily, taking a step across the room toward Gregg. John grabbed

Gregg's shirt at the neck and shoved him against the closet door. The door which was slightly open went shut with a bang.

The two men stood glaring at each other, each breathing heavily.

"Yes! He does." Jenny interrupted. John released Gregg and turned to face her, astonished at her reply.

"What?"

"They are his biological children. Whether or not he claims them as his own, they deserve the right to bear their father's name."

John could not believe the words he was hearing. What had possessed her to allow the man who had abandoned her to stand there and demand that the children bear his name?

"Did nothing that happened last night mean anything to you?"

Jenny didn't answer but stared into John's bewildered eyes. She looked away as John strode angrily out of the room. He shoved a doctor against the wall as he stormed down the hall.

"Why didn't you tell me you were having twins?" Gregg demanded.

"I told you!" she cried. "I wrote to you every week. Didn't you read my letters?"

Gregg stared at the floor ashamed that he hadn't.

"No, I burned them."

"I told you everything in my letters! It was the only way. You refused to listen to me. You refused my calls." She cried hard as he strode across the room and sat down on the edge of her bed. He didn't know if he should hold her or scream out loud. He did neither. He turned and faced the window wondering what he should do next. After a long moment of silence he turned back to her and rested his hand on her knee. Her sad eyes met his as he spoke to her.

"I still have feelings for you, ya know."

Tears streamed down her cheeks as she listened to his words.

"You hurt me in a terrible way. Maybe you didn't mean to but when I saw you in that guy's arms I freaked out. I know I left in a jealous rage that night and still to this day whenever I close my eyes that's all I can see. It's none of my business what you two choose to do with your own lives and I hope you can forgive me for ignoring you these past months. I willingly fathered those two children and I don't intend to turn my back on them too." Jenny watched his lips through teary eyes. She examined the deep scar that remained under his left eye from the accident.

"I know they are my children and deep in my heart I knew when I first saw you at George's. I don't know what it was but something told me that was my child you were carrying, but I brushed it off because I was angry. I am sorry I ever doubted you."

Jenny sat quietly listening to Gregg. In her own heart she never stopped loving Gregg either. John became a very important part of her life and she once felt he was responsible for tearing her away from something that she knew was meant to be. She knew her babies needed a father and so far Gregg was saying he wanted to be part of their lives. She owed John so much and had grown to love his child-like heart and caring attitude. He was funny and exciting and fun to be with. His drug addiction worried her most, and she wondered if she could ever trust him fully. She knew that if she let Gregg be a part of her life again that John would rebel and reject her. She knew that Gregg could just as easily walk out the door and refuse to acknowledge the babies as his own. He hadn't done that. Where did that leave her?

"Are you saying that you are okay with my relationship with John?"

"I don't know what your relationship is with that man but I can tell you that he will never be a father to our children."

"And how will you feel if one day I marry John?" Jenny knew she was way off base but she figured it was the only way to get a feel for what Gregg's intentions were. Gregg clenched his teeth and looked away.

"Has he asked you?"

"He wants to be a family."

"And you said?"

"Nothing."

"Do you love him?"

Jenny looked down into her lap. Gregg moved closer and lifted her chin. Their eyes met.

"Yes, I love him."

Gregg dropped his hand from her chin and looked away. "But not the way I love you."

Gregg moved to the window and glimpsed out over the parking lot at nothing in particular.

"I don't know what to do next. I don't think it will ever be like it was. Too much has happened." Gregg thought for a while longer as he leaned against the windowsill.

"I'm willing to try to work things out but John is going to have to disappear." Gregg's words were like a stab wound to her heart. She owed John so much. How could she ever ban him from being a part of her life?

"Suppose John does leave and things don't work out with us. Where does that leave me and two babies?"

Gregg spun around to face her again. His face was tightly set in an angry grimace.

"I told you I wouldn't turn my back on those children!"

"Yes, but will you turn your back on me again?" The knife had been twisted and she could not stop herself from letting the words spill across her lips.

Gregg was stunned by her remark but he knew she was right. If things didn't work out between them, she was going to be the one who suffered. Gregg was being selfish and he knew it. He couldn't stand to see her with John any more than he could stand him being a father to his children. But if she did agree to his proposition it would prove one thing. It would prove whom she really loved. A light knock sounded on the door and they both turned to look. It was Kathy, smiling brightly as she wheeled the cart into the room. Rosalie lay nestled inside, gnawing on her fist. Another nurse followed behind with a cart that carried Joseph. Jenny wiped her tears as the babies were brought to her bedside. Gregg squeezed her shoulder before going to one of the carts. He reached in and gently removed Rosalie from her soft bed. He cradled her head in his hands as he held her in front of him and spoke softly to her.

"Hello Rosalie," he said glancing at Jenny to see if she approved of the way he pronounced her name. He moved his eyes back to Rosalie and studied her newborn perfection. She had every feature of her mothers except for the brightness of her blue eyes. A tear lay in the corner of her eye as he spoke to her. "It looks like you've been crying little girl."

"She's hungry," Kathy replied. She moved closer to the bed.

"Jenny are you ready to give this another try?" Jenny shook her head and reached for Rosalie as Gregg gently handed her to her mother. It was only the second time she held her baby and feelings of joy tingled in her heart as the warm bundle was placed in her arms. Kathy helped Jenny slide her robe over her shoulder and placed the infant near her breast. Gregg watched enthusiastically as the baby quickly learned to suckle at her mother's breast. Jenny smiled, delighted that it went more smoothly this time. Gregg stood back and watched mother and daughter bond. He knew Jenny would be a good mother and he hoped she would accept his proposal for the sake of the children.

He studied her face tracing her features as his eyes lowered to her bare breast. He was amazed at how large and swollen with milk her breasts had become and was thrilled about the miracle of the lives they created out of love. He rubbed Rosalie's head as she suckled and eventually she had her fill and drifted off to sleep. Gregg turned to the sound of a loud wailing cry as Joseph declared his hunger. Gregg took a step closer to Joseph's bassinet and lifted him to his chest. He took the baby's small fingers between his own and spoke to him trying to hush him until his mother could prepare to feed him. Kathy gently burped Rosalie and put her in the bassinet while Gregg soothed Joseph's cry for hunger.

"Now you will need to feed him at the other breast."

Jenny wiped her breast clean, careful to make sure it was dry like the nurse taught her. Gregg watched as she nervously cleaned her skin. Her fingers trembled, as she wiped, aware that she was under Gregg's scrutinizing stare. When she was finished, she held her hands up to accept her son into her arms. Gregg handed Joseph to her as he carefully supported his head. His fingers brushed against Jenny's as he slid the child into her arms. Their eyes met briefly as she turned the baby to face her exposed breast. Joseph continued to cry while Jenny touched his cheek like the nurse showed her. He turned his head toward her finger as she guided his mouth over her nipple. At first she felt pain as the baby struggled to grip her nipple. Jenny pulled the baby away uttering words of pain.

"If it is painful, then his mouth is not covering your breast properly," Kathy stated. "He must take in the whole nipple, not just the tip of it. Here, try again."

After several tries, Joseph was still crying and Jenny was still feeling pain. She broke down in tears as she held him out to Gregg.

"I can't do this!" she cried. "I'm never going to be able to do this!"

Gregg took Joseph and put his finger in his mouth to quiet his cries. He felt sorry for Jenny as she struggled to deal with new motherhood. He felt guilty himself for not being there for her all those months. It was a time he would never get back and stabs of jealousy pained him as he thought about John and his role in Jenny's life. Kathy sat down on the bed and put her arms around Jenny.

"It's going to take a lot of patience and a lot of practice. We can give him a bottle, but if you want to do this, you have to keep trying. I know it is painful at first but it will get better. I just want you to understand that if we do give him a bottle, it will be more difficult to get him to breast feed later on." Jenny watched Gregg coo at the baby as he held his finger in his mouth. It worked for a few minutes and then Joseph was wailing again.

"All right, I'll try again." She opened her robe once more and took the baby from Gregg.

"Relax a little. He can sense you are nervous."

Jenny took a deep breath and held Joseph to her breast. Kathy guided her breast into the baby's mouth this time making a good fit. Joseph was soon feeding happily. Jenny and Gregg watched with fascination as he sucked long and hard. Occasionally the baby would cough as though he were getting too much. Jenny winced and pulled her breast from his mouth.

"He's okay. He'll know when he's had too much." Kathy reassured her.

"But I feel like I'm shoving my breast down his throat. It's so big and he is so little." Gregg tried to hide his smile and turned his attention to Rosalie.

"Your breast is soft and conforms to the shape of his mouth. You're doing great."

Kathy stayed and reassured Jenny during the entire feeding. After twenty minutes, the baby fell asleep. Jenny handed Joseph to Gregg.

"Would you like to burp him while I clean up?"

Gregg smiled as he took the infant from her. He awkwardly put the child against his chest and patted his back. It made him feel good that Jenny asked him to help her.

"I remember doing this for my nephew. He won't spit up all over me will he?"

Kathy laughed. "Not until he gets a little older. For now it's just minor stuff."

Jenny watched as Gregg held his son. He looked calm and confident as he sat in the easy chair across the room. Joseph never did burp and eventually was put back in his bassinet and taken to the nursery.

"I have one more request if we are going to try to make this work." Gregg sounded cool and gruff. His eyes burned into hers once more.

Jenny looked into his steely blue eyes waiting for his request.

"I respect the name you have chosen for our daughter, but I will not have my son named after a man I despise." Gregg waited for a sign of emotion before continuing. "I want his middle name changed."

Jenny nodded as a single tear slid down her cheek. "You think about that. I'll be back tonight."

Without another word he stormed out of the hospital room and left Jenny frightened and confused. Jenny didn't like the terms he was throwing at her. How could she trust him not to turn his back on her after he did once already? She knew that she could handle being a single parent but what she was afraid of most was losing love. If she changed Joseph's name, John might understand. If she accepted Gregg's agreement, she would lose John for sure. If Gregg decided it wasn't going to work out between them, she would lose out again. She knew she could never survive another broken heart. She didn't have the strength or the courage. She sat on her bed and stared out over the parking lot. The spring trees swayed gracefully in the afternoon breeze. Gregg's words clung in the air like a bad odor. She recalled how he had referred to Rosalie as "their daughter" and it frightened her what

John might do. She not only had to worry about single parenting, but also the issue of joint custody. Surely Gregg was going to want visiting rights.

Chapter 17

"Hello, Mommy!" She was startled when her mother's voice broke the silence in the room. She turned to face her mother's smiling face. Her mother held her arms out to Jenny as she stood to greet them. She hugged them both before climbing back into her bed. Her mother sat down next to her as her father took a seat across the room in a more comfortable chair. Her father looked tired and his age seemed to be catching up with him.

"Jenny, I wish you would have called us earlier. I didn't want you to go through this alone."

"Mom, don't worry. It wasn't that bad. John was here for me."

Her mother looked surprised...and hurt. "Why did you call him and not us?"

"It's a long story and I don't feel up to it right now. He just happened to be in the right place at the right time for a change." Rose and Dave exchanged frowns.

"Tell us about things," Dave said in a concerned fatherly tone. "I see you have named them. You have made a beautiful choice. I'm glad you didn't name the boy after me. I had to put up with being called Davie all my childhood years. I hated it." Dave laughed and his face softened a little.

"You didn't mind it when I called you Davie," her mother chided.

Dave scratched his head. "Well, you see that was a little different. I was sweet on you. Speaking of being sweet, have you notified Gregg?" Dave knew he was being bold but he didn't know how to ask any other way. It bothered him that Jenny faced the possibility of raising two children all on her own. He knew she would refuse help from them and he wanted to make sure she was going to be all right.

"Gregg just left. He said he'd be back later tonight." Jenny looked down at her lap and fidgeted with her fingers.

"Are the roses from him?" her mother asked.

"No, John brought them," she answered too quickly. Rose brushed the hair back from her face tucking it routinely behind her ear.

"Oh, where is he?"

"He left."

"Will he be back?"

Jenny sighed. "Good grief, can we talk about something else?" It was Dave who spoke up.

"Jenny!" he said springing from his chair. "I don't think you know how serious of a situation you are in. You are a young woman, now a single mother with one income and you're trying to do it all alone. Parenting is a difficult thing when you have one child. But you have two. Two who are going to demand every ounce of your attention and energy every day of your life. It's not going to be easy." Jenny glared at her father.

"Don't you think I know that? I've been worried about it from the day I realized I was pregnant!" Jenny slid slowly off the edge of the bed. She swung her hands to her hips like she always did when she was angry. "I've been taking responsibility for my actions! I didn't think it was going to be easy but what else am I going to do Dad?"

"You can stop being stubborn and move back home with us where you belong!"

Jenny threw up her hands. "I can't!"

"Why not?" Her parents asked in unison. Jenny was quiet for a while before she looked up to her parents with tear-filled eyes.

"Because you and mom are ready to retire." Her voice was low as she struggled to tell them without losing control. "Because you will be moving into a retirement home after this fall's harvest. Because you deserve to be retired and not raising my kids!" Dave jumped up from his seat and shook his finger at her. It made her feel like a schoolgirl being scolded for pinching a boy in class.

"Jenny Jeanine Elerose! You are a stubborn, silly girl. If you think you are going to be able to handle this on your own you guess again! It's a tough job and I won't allow you to do it alone!"

She fidgeted with the tie of her robe. Keeping her head lowered she raised her eyes to her father. In a quiet voice she replied, "Gregg has accepted responsibility for our children." She knew it wasn't entirely true but she knew nothing else to tell her father to calm him. She was not ready for the questions asked to her now.

"What does that mean Jenny? Does he still want to marry you? Is he going to live with you and be there for you in the middle of the night? Is he going to be available to help bathe, diaper and feed those two youngsters?" He threw his hands up in the air and then rested them on his hips. "You tell us how you plan to do this."

Jenny tried to hold back the tears. She didn't have the answers her father wanted but she did know she had a responsibility and it was up to her to accept it. She knew it wasn't going to be easy and she knew she had to make it work with Gregg. She also knew she had to put John out of her life if she were to ever have a family life with Gregg. Gregg didn't give her any other choice. Her mother put her arms around her in a comforting gesture. Jenny wiped her tears and released her mother's hug.

"Thank you both for offering your support, but I can't move back home. I won't do it! I am going to try to work things out with Gregg. He says he still loves me and I love him. I never stopped."

"Where does that leave John?" Dave interrupted. "He loves you too. He told me several months ago." Rose glared at Dave unaware that he knew anything about John's feelings. If he did, he never shared them with Rose.

"You don't have to hide anything. I know he was with you last night and we know Gregg is the father of your babies. We know what's been going on. John has come back for you. I didn't realize it at first," he said scratching his head. "I should have seen it coming when he lived with us. It wasn't until John told me his feelings for you that I realized why he was here. I don't like the idea of you being personally involved with John. I think he is a troubled boy. We don't know what he has been doing for the last three years. So far every thing he has told us about Jeanine and his former jobs has been one big lie. The only thing I think he hasn't lied about is how he feels about you." Dave walked to the bed and sat down on the edge to face her. He took her chin in his hand and shook his head sadly.

"My little Peach. You sure know how to get yourself into a fix. You have some choices to make. When you need help, your mother and I will be here for you." He rubbed her chin with his thumb. "All I'm saying is be careful!"

Jenny smiled. "I will." She hugged him close and whispered in his ear. "I love you Dad."

"I love you too Peach," he whispered in return.

"What do you say we walk down and take a look at our new grand children," Rose interrupted.

Jenny took her father's hand and they walked as a threesome down the hall to the nursery. They stood outside the looking window contemplating which had more hair, which looked more like Jenny and which resembled their father. Every one agreed that Joseph looked like Gregg and that Rosalie's features paralleled Jenny's. Kathy appeared in the hallway and Jenny introduced everyone. Kathy suggested that they take the babies to a guest room so that Rose and Dave could hold their grandchildren for the first time.

Dave and Rose each wheeled a baby in a bassinet to a private guest room down the opposite hall. They stayed for two more hours talking to and holding the babies and watching Jenny struggle to breast-feed the children. Joseph proved to be the most difficult and Jenny figured it was due to his problems at birth. Kathy encouraged her to continue to try, and soon Jenny was feeling more at ease about feeding them. Dave and Rose smiled at each other when at last Jenny succeeded in the process. Tomorrow she would go home and a whole new set of obstacles would be waiting for her like bombs in a minefield.

John sat in his corvette overlooking a steep embankment. Below, the scene was beautiful with a deep pond surrounded by rows of blue spruce trees on one side and weeping willows on the other. He stared out over the ridge and watched the city that seemed like a far away fairyland. The distant sky was hazy as the sun began its descent into the western sky. All he would have to do to end his misery was put the car in neutral and let it roll down the embankment. Then his life of drugs, women and violence would be over. He wouldn't have to worry about being accepted by Jenny or her precious family or by Jeanine.

John wiped the remains of the coke powder from his nose as he leaned back in his corvette. For the first few minutes, feelings of anger and rage flooded his mind. He pictured a cozy scene with Jenny and the babies. They were each holding one and everyone was smiling. Then the face in the picture turned to Gregg's face. John was enraged as he put his hands to his head and tried to squeeze the image from his mind. Then the man in the picture was himself again and he felt happy and relieved. His mind reeled as pictures of his laughing parents burned an image in his mind. Blood streaked down their faces as they opened their mouths wide, laughing wickedly in his face. Then a loud gun blast brought him reeling back to the scene of the pine trees and the pond. John started the engine and backed away from the edge of the embankment. Putting the car in gear, he accessed the gravel road that led to the main highway and sped down the road leaving a trail of dust hanging thick in the evening air.

Gregg returned to the hospital that evening and found Jenny resting in her bed. He stood in the doorway and quietly watched her sleep thinking about all the things they had been through and all the things that lay ahead for them. He wondered what her decision would be about trying to work things out. He despised John for coming into their life and he cursed Jenny for having a heart that could love two men. He went to the nursery and requested to have the babies brought to her room. Gregg strolled happily back to her room and quietly sat down in the easy chair. Within a few minutes a nurse brought the babies in. Seeing Gregg put his finger to his lips, she left the room without a sound. Gregg lifted Rosalie from her bassinet in one scoop and then picked up Joseph with his other arm. With the two babies in his arms, he carried them to the easy chair and sank into it. He held them opposite each other studying their angelic faces.

"Hello," he whispered. "I'm your daddy. I'm going to help your mommy take very good care of you." He kissed the top of Rosalie's head and then did the same to Joseph.

"Your mother and I loved each other very much once. I know we can again," he said rubbing his cheek against Joseph's downy hair. "Your mommy went through a lot for you. She went through a lot without me. From this day forward I promise to be there for her and for you." He smiled into their tiny faces not realizing Jenny was awake and heard his words. She observed Gregg and the babies and realized that the picture before her was the way it was supposed to be. They were meant to be together as a family. What was it going to take to get to that point? What if it didn't work?

Jenny knew that if it were just herself, she would try working things out with Gregg. Now she had two children to worry about and she was having mixed feelings about his proposal. She made so many mistakes in her life and she needed to be even more cautious especially where her children were concerned. She wondered how the children would feel if they were old enough to understand what was going on. She wondered where John had gone. Was he using drugs? How could she ever trust him not to? She decided she must give in to Gregg's request if she knew what was best for everyone involved. Everyone that is, except for John. How was she going to tell him he could no longer be involved in her life? How would he react when she would tell him that she and the babies couldn't be a family with him? Perhaps he already knew. She continued to observe Gregg as he held the infants and spoke softly to them memorizing the moment as though it would be the last. He would be a good father.

"Would you be disappointed if we named our son Joseph Gregory?"

Gregg looked up from the faces of the babies to meet Jenny's weak smile. He carefully stood from the easy chair and carried them to the bed. He put Joseph in her arms.

"Joseph Gregory is a wonderful name and I would be honored to call him that." He looked into her eyes. "Does that mean you have accepted my proposal?" His breath was hot on her cheek and he smelled like fresh cinnamon.

"It means that I want us to be together. It's what I've always wanted Gregg, but it's more complicated than you think though." He watched her and listened carefully. "When you rejected me, John stepped into the picture. He took care of me. He became like a..." Gregg gritted his teeth.

"Like a husband?" he interrupted coldly.

"No, let me finish, please! He became a companion to me. He helped me through loneliness when there was no one else. He went to Lamaze classes with me. He even fixed up the nursery in my apartment."

"And did he share your bed?" Gregg's icy stare burned the flesh on her face.

Jenny looked down in embarrassment. "That's not the point here! The point is that John and I became very close while you were off pouting like a teenager!"

"And you're throwing this all in my face now? I know I should have been there! That was my mistake! For gosh sakes what was I supposed to think Jenny? How long are you going to punish me for this? I am here now! Isn't that enough for you?"

"It's always about what you want isn't it? All you care about is how you fit into all this. To hell with what everybody else's feelings are! I care about John a lot! All I am trying to say is that what you are asking me to do is very difficult. Don't expect it to happen over night! I need time to smooth things out with John! He deserves to know where he stands in all of this!" Gregg shook his head.

"Why do you have to do everything so right? Why does everything have to go by the book?"

"Because I don't want to intentionally hurt anybody. It's never been my style and it never will be." She turned her attention to her baby.

Joseph awakened, frightened by the shouting. His lower lip curled out and his eyes opened wide in fear. He let out a screeching squeal. Gregg put Rosalie into her bassinet. He turned to Jenny as she tried to comfort her son.

"The nurse at the desk told me you can go home tomorrow at two o'clock. I'll come for you then." He turned and strode out the door.

Jenny dressed in a light pair of sweat pants and sweat shirt that John so kindly brought for her the day before. It was much too warm for a sweatshirt but she appreciated having clothes that fit. She had gained so much weight during her pregnancy and she felt ugly. She pulled her long blond hair back in a single ponytail. When Gregg came for her the next day, she was ready to go home. She hugged Kathy who promised to visit. Then she climbed into the wheel chair. She gathered the roses that John brought her into her arms and Gregg pushed her to the entrance. Kathy walked along beside them, pushing the bundled up babies in a cart. Gregg turned to Kathy, shook her hand and thanked her for the wonderful care of Jenny and the babies. Together Gregg and Kathy put the babies into car seats that were rented from the hospital and secured the safety belts. Kathy watched as their car pulled away from the curb waving them on.

"I'll purchase seats of our own tomorrow," Gregg said sternly not looking at her. He drove the few blocks to her apartment and helped her bring the babies and their things inside. The apartment was stuffy and Gregg proceeded to open windows. They took the babies to the nursery and laid them in Jenny's old crib. Laying them on their side like Kathy had instructed, she covered them lightly with a soft cotton blanket. Jenny went to her room and closed the door. She opened her dresser and chose a white cotton v-neck t-shirt. She slipped it over her head and pulled her long hair out of the back of the shirt. The shirt looked too tight as it hung over her still large belly. She tucked it in as she came out of her bedroom. She looked down in disgust at the bulge on her stomach. She removed her shirt from the waistband for a minute then tucked it in again. Gregg chuckled as he watched her. The shirt was very snug fitting and he noticed she was not wearing a bra.

"You look beautiful no matter how you wear your shirt," he said in an emotionless breath.

Jenny blushed at his comment. "I'll go put something else on." She turned to leave as he caught her arm.

"No, you don't have to do it for me. I'll be leaving in a minute. Is there something I can do for you before I go?" She pulled her arm away and crossed them in front of her. Jenny wanted to make him stay. She wanted to tell him she missed him all those months. She wanted to feel him in her arms again like she used to. She wondered if this was how it would always be. She wondered if their relationship would always be cold and uncomfortable.

"Your mother will be coming this evening. I've asked her to stay with you for a few days while I get stuff taken care of."

Jenny opened her mouth to protest. She wanted to tell him she didn't need help. She wanted to ask him when he spoke with her mother. She wanted to know what "stuff" he had to take care of but she was too exhausted to fight anymore. He turned to leave.

"When will you be back?" she asked as she followed him to the door.

He looked at her in surprise. "I'll be back tomorrow night."

After Gregg left she rested on the sofa. She tried to sleep but thought of John and Gregg confused her mind. Gregg hadn't changed in all those months. He was still the mature guy she fell in love with. He was respectful and still very handsome. She fell asleep dreaming of a life with Gregg and her children.

Chapter 18

The first night home with the babies was frustrating and scary. First Joseph wanted to eat and then an hour later Rosalie wanted to eat. It went off and on like that every hour all night. The babies were on two-hour intervals but each baby ate at a different time. Her mother awoke each hour and helped her diaper the babies before sending Jenny back to bed for rest. By five a.m. Jenny was exhausted. She broke down in tears when her mother didn't awaken for the six o'clock feeding. Jenny diapered Rosalie and then fed her. She carried her back to the crib hoping this would be the last time for a while. When she turned to leave the room she heard a loud gurgling noise. Jenny opened her diaper to find it full again. She diapered Rosalie three more times.

Rose came into the nursery yawning. "Is she up again?"

"It appears she has the diarrhea or something. I changed her three times just now."

"Babies that are breast fed tend to do that. Try feeding them first and then changing them."

"I don't know if I made the right decision to breast feed. I'm not getting any rest," she said truthfully.

Rose squeezed her arm. She noticed the rings around Jenny's eyes and knew that the nights were going to get worse before they got better. If only her daughter would listen to their advice and move back home. Rose touched Jenny's arm. "The first days will be very difficult for you. Let's try to waken whoever is sleeping at the next feeding. Maybe we can get them on the same schedule."

"I never thought it was going to be this difficult," she said placing the baby in the crib once more. "I'm glad you're here."

Rose was concerned about her daughter's rest. She knew from experience what lay ahead for Jenny. "When is Gregg coming by?"

"He'll be here tonight mom. If you need to go I think I can handle it for a while." Rose knew that was a lie.

"Well, I'm sure you two have things to discuss. I can stay for as long as you like but maybe I will run home and check on things there while he is here."

When Gregg knocked on the apartment door, Rose answered. He carried a big box in his arms. He set it down inside the apartment and hurried back out to the car to bring in another large box. He set it down next to the first one.

"What is this, Christmas?"

"They're car seats. I promised Jenny I would buy seats of our own. I bought them down town. They will work well for a day chair too when the babies get a little older," Gregg said smiling as he ripped open one of the boxes. Rose studied him thinking he seemed like a child with a brand new bike. She prayed every night that Gregg and Jenny would work things out. Not just for Jenny's sake or the babies' sakes, but because she liked Gregg and over the period of his courtship with Jenny she had grown to love him like her own son. She too felt he was mature beyond his years and that quality alone would make him a good father. "Where is Jenny?"

Rose clasped her hands together. "I'm afraid she is resting. The babies didn't sleep well last night."

"Would it help if she breast fed one and bottle fed the other or both?" he said over his shoulder.

"It would but she is determined to breast feed both. We are trying to get them on a dual schedule. With patience it will work." She took his arm and pulled him to face her. "Gregg, I'm glad you came. I would like to talk to you about something."

Gregg looked at Rose in surprise. "Is everything all right Rose?"

"Come, sit down." Rose lowered her voice as Gregg sat down on the couch next to her.

"Look, we love Jenny very much. Whatever it is that happened between you two is none of my business, but as her mother I am concerned for Jenny's future. I need to know what your intentions are so I can put my mind at ease. I am not crazy about John being so involved in her life and to tell you the truth, I don't trust him very much."

Gregg leaned forward with his elbows on his knees, his hands clasped between them.

"Rest assured Rose, that I am going to do everything in my power to make us a family. Jenny is a strong willed girl and I also happen to love her very much. I always have." He paused for a moment before continuing.

"How does John fit into this picture?" Gregg raised a brow. "Who is he anyway?"

Rose told Gregg the story about John not leaving out any details.

"Dave and I feel he is pursuing her for the wrong reasons." Gregg shook his head.

"So did I have cause to worry when I saw them in her bedroom?" Rose remembered when he had come to the farm in a drunken stupor and told them what he saw. At the time, he seemed confused and Rose took his story lightly.

"I don't know what you saw that day," she said in a low voice.

"She was in his arms Rose, and her robe was wide open in front." Gregg's face flushed as he discussed the details with Rose. "He had his hands on her in a very personal manner. She said he was comforting her because he had just discovered she was pregnant and she was upset." Gregg recounted the details with Rose just as he had done that day he came to the farm.

"Did it look like he was forcing her?"

"She wasn't struggling but I didn't get a look at her face. She was just lying there letting him touch her." It was an ugly scene to describe and it sliced his heart every time he pictured it.

"Do you believe her?"

Gregg let out a deep sigh. "I didn't at first. But the more I learn about this guy, the more I feel like an idiot for wasting so many months in anger."

"Jenny loved you so much Gregg and I know she still does. Being young is so difficult. It's hard to know what you really want until it's taken away from you. She is going through a lot of changes right now. Difficult changes. She is going to need your help, support and stability. Can you give her that?"

"I can if she will let me," he replied with a shrug.

Rose patted his knee. "Give her time young man. She'll get her head on straight. I know she will." Can you stay for a while? I need to run home and check on things. Maybe wash a load of clothes or two." She smiled at him through deep wrinkled eyes.

"Sure," he replied. "Uh, Rose?" She turned to look at him. "Thanks, for listening." Rose quietly picked up her purse and headed for the door.

"I put two small bottles of pumped breast milk in the fridge. They shouldn't need to eat for another couple of hours. If she is too exhausted to get up, use them for their feedings. Make sure you warm them up first."

"I know, I remember from my nephew."

Rose took his hand and looked lovingly into his eyes. Her hands felt warm and soft and he could see moisture forming on the lids of her deep eyes. "Congratulations Gregg. And welcome back." She dropped his hand and hugged him. She turned and quickly left before he could see the tears falling from her eyes.

Gregg looked around the apartment and straightened up before making himself comfortable in her recliner. The apartment was decorated adorably but lacked abundant room for growing children. He relaxed in the recliner for a while and then dug through her cupboards for something to eat. He decided one could tell a person's personality by digging through their kitchens. He opened one cupboard and found dried fruit, raisins and canned fruit in natural juices. He opened another and found herbal tea and different types of pasta. He opened the refrigerator and found much of the same kind of stuff. Apples, oranges, celery and ground turkey were among the contents. No wonder she was always so skinny.

Joseph let out a squeal and Gregg hurried to the nursery to see who was awake. Both babies lay in the crib making grunting noises. The odor in the room was a clue that it was time for a diaper change. He located the diapers and the wipes and proceeded to clean the babies' bottoms. Their bottoms were so tiny and as he closed the tape on the diapers the two strips nearly overlapped in front. Without taking the time to hold them, he laid them back in their bed.

"Daddy has a surprise for you," he whispered. Gregg hurried out to his car and brought in a double stroller he bought at the same store as the car seats. The sales guy gave him a great deal for buying all three items. Gregg liked the old man that operated the store and remembered him from when he was a little kid. After a lot of chatter and congratulations, he drove away with the items in his car one hundred and seventy dollars poor.

Gregg strapped the babies in the stroller and wrapped them tightly in the cotton blanket. He locked the door and strolled downtown, enjoying the beautiful evening air. Birds were singing happily as new parents flew from lawn to tree with worms to feed hungry gaping mouths in nests perched in the tree tops. The air was fresh and smelled clean as he sucked it into his nostrils. Several people had to stop and peek at the sleeping babies and the trip took longer than he expected. He forgot to leave a note and he was sure Jenny would be upset. After picking up supplies for dinner and letting the checkout clerk ogle the babies, he was on his way.

When he arrived back at the apartment, it was still quiet. He parked the stroller in the living room and let the babies sleep while he prepared no-cook lasagna, creamy garlic toast and fresh green beans. The aroma in the kitchen wafted through the tiny apartment arousing Jenny from her sleep. She went to the nursery to find the crib empty. Realizing it was nearly eight o'clock she became frightened. She went to the living room and found the children asleep in the double stroller. She went to the kitchen where Gregg was busy cooking. The table was set for two and everything was almost ready. Jenny scanned the table. There was a mug at each place setting. One was filled with Root beer. The other was filled with milk. She smiled to herself for his thoughtfulness. A small candle burned in the center.

"What's all this?" she asked lazily.

He turned to face her. "I was wondering how long you would sleep. I hope you are hungry. Have a seat. Dinner is almost ready."

"I'm not very hungry."

"You must eat something other than dried fruit. The contents of your cupboards are pathetic. You are feeding two other mouths too so you need extra nutrients." After ordering her to be seated and filling the table with the beans, toast and lasagna, he sat down across from her. He put a serving of everything on her plate and then filled his own. She watched as he loaded his plate till it was heaping with lasagna.

"Are you going to eat all that?"

"Yep," he smiled. "You should eat too. It's getting cold."

"Have the babies been awake?"

"I changed their diapers and took them to the store in the stroller. They have been sleeping ever since." Gregg waited for her to get angry.

Jenny's eyes grew wide. "Do you know what that means? That means they've gone three and one half hours without eating." She crossed her arms over her chest; her messy hair fell around her shoulders like a silk robe. She let out a joyous sigh. "My chest could use the rest." She smiled with the same soft smile her mother had.

Gregg's eyes twinkled as she expressed her relief. "That's great! Your mother said you had a rough night."

"When is she coming back?"

"She's not. You have to put up with me for a while." The look on Jenny's face was a solemn one. He noticed her disappointment and then he smiled at her. "Is it so bad to put up with me?" Jenny toyed with her fork, and when she did not answer him, he spoke. "Actually, she asked me to call her when I'm ready to go. I'm not ready yet. Is that okay with you?" he asked sincerely.

Jenny set her fork down next to her plate. She had always been the type of person who needed organization in her daily life. She wanted to know what was going to happen ahead of time and it helped her feel in control of things. "Do you plan on just poking your head in from time to time? Is that how you plan on being a father."

Gregg finished chewing his food. "Is that what's bugging you? How I plan on spending my time?"

"Right now I have a strong need for some kind of schedule. My life has been tuned into an automatic alarm clock every hour. It seems like it happened over night. I just need to know what is going to happen around here. I need some kind of ..." Her voice trailed off and Gregg finished her sentence.

"Commitment?"

She lowered her eyes. In essence, that was exactly what she was looking for. Commitment. Gregg was about to speak again when the phone rang. She refused to let Gregg pick it up. She was in the middle of a very important conversation and she didn't want her concern to go unexpressed. Gregg scooted back his chair just as the answering machine picked up. There was a long silence after the beep and then

John's voice broke the silence. Jenny froze in the chair as John's voice echoed through her tiny apartment.

"Hi, Jenny. It's me. I heard you went home. Just wondering how you are? I really miss you and what we shared the other night. I'd like to come to see you and the babies. You know where to find me." There was a long pause and then he hung up. The apartment was silent as Jenny and Gregg finished their meal. A few minutes later the phone rang again. Jenny could hear the urgency in his voice and wondered if he was fighting the need for a hit. "Will you pick up the phone? Maybe you're busy. I'll call you later." Click.

Gregg looked at Jenny's red face. "If you want a commitment from me, you know what you have to do," he said, as he looked deep into her eyes. Gregg stood and pushed in his chair. "Why don't you go sit in the tub? I'll get the dishes." That was typical of Gregg. He had everything under control. He was thoughtful just as he always was but he seemed like a stranger to her now.

Jenny left the table without saying a word. She trudged to the bathroom and filled the tub with hot steamy water. She retrieved a candle from a cupboard and lit it, then unscrewed two of the four bulbs from the light fixture. She turned on the radio to soft music and when the tub was full of glistening bubbles, she sank into it with gratitude. Almost an hour later, she was awakened by a knock on the door. She jolted upright as the chilling water drained over her shoulders and down her aching breasts.

"What is it," she called as she reached for her towel.

"Is everything okay in there?"

"Yea, I'll be out in a minute." Jenny could hear the sound of infant cries and she knew the children must be hungry again. She motivated her exhausted body and climbed out of the tub. She dressed quickly in her robe and went to the living room where she found both children screaming for milk. Gregg was holding Rosalie and pacing the floor. He looked bewildered as he handed her the baby.

"Here, feed this one first. She's been crying the longest."

"I'm sorry it took so long. I fell asleep."

Gregg followed Jenny to her bedroom and watched her situate herself on the bed. She sat cross-legged on the bed, and put a pillow on her knee and lay Rosalie across it. Rosalie immediately formed a grip and began sucking strongly. She put another pillow on her other knee and motioned for Gregg to put Joseph there. Supporting his head, she helped him reach her nipple and soon both babies were suckling noisily. Gregg lay across the bottom of the bed and propped himself up on one elbow. He conscientiously observed as she successfully fed each infant. She looked up at him to see his satisfied smile.

"You are a clever one," he said raising his right brow.

"I tried it this morning once when mother was still asleep. It's going better now than it did before."

Her hair was wet and she had it tossed into a bun. She was even more beautiful as a mother. He studied her and noticed how her body changed, especially the size of her breasts. He wantonly studied them as the infants suckled there. He remembered how they felt to his touch and how the nipples became stiff when he massaged them. It seemed like so long ago since the time they made love and he wondered if they would ever again. His mind became aware of the bed he was resting on and he wondered if John had slept there. He squeezed his eyes tightly to block out the vision of the two of them romping in this very bed. Gregg stood and left the room with out saying anything. Twenty minutes later her mother entered her bedroom. Jenny looked up in surprise.

"Where is Gregg?"

"He said he didn't want to disturb you and that he would be back tomorrow, same time."

Jenny's shoulders slumped in disappointment.

"It looks like it is going better for you. What smells so good?"

"Gregg made lasagna and garlic toast."

Her mother chuckled. "Did the nurse's tell you to be careful of what you eat when you breast feed?"

Jenny's mouth fell open.

"Oh my gosh. They did and I forgot. What is going to happen?"

"It will probably create a lot of gas which makes for a very cranky baby."

Jenny looked at her mother with a grin.

"Make that, babies." They both burst into laughter until tears came to their eyes.

Chapter 19

For the next several weeks, Gregg and Jenny's mother and sister-in-law took turns staying with her and the babies. Gregg dropped in occasionally and always let her know when he was coming. John tried to call several times and Jenny didn't return any of his calls. It made her heart sink every time the phone rang. She loved hearing his voice and wondered how he was doing. She felt guilty for the decision she made and couldn't bring herself to tell him. He drove past her apartment several times and each time there was always someone there. He wanted to speak to her alone. His drug habit became uncontrollable and he couldn't make it for more than half a day without needing a hit. Most of the time he didn't know what day of the week it was and his days passed in a sea of mood swings and hallucinations.

It was a warm summer evening and the air was filled with song of birds and rustling leaves on the trees. Jenny and Gregg sat outside with the babies. Gregg spread a blanket for the two of them to sit on. Each held a baby as they talked. Jenny was telling Gregg that Rosalie had a fever and as she was speaking, she caught a glimpse of John's corvette rolling slowly down the narrow street. He drove by and waved to her through the open window. Jenny pretended to ignore him and played with Rosalie's fingers.

A few minutes later, the corvette pulled up to the curb. John approached them angrily as he watched Gregg and Jenny laugh together. They got to their feet before John reached them. She quickly put Rosalie in the stroller. John stomped over to Jenny and without warning he took her into his arms and kissed her firmly on the lips. It seemed like a minute went by before he released her. Gregg put Joseph in the stroller and folded his arms across his chest as he watched like an onlooker at a circus. Gregg could tell that it was difficult for her to ignore what John had just done. He knew her feelings went deeper for John than just a mutual friendship. Jenny's face reddened and she turned away. She went over to where the babies lay in the stroller and fussed with their blanket. Then John turned to Gregg despising the man who stood before him.

"I need to speak to Jenny, alone," John said in a snarled voice.

"I don't think you're wanted here. So leave, now," Gregg demanded as he motioned to the street where the corvette was parked.

"I'm not going anywhere until I speak to Jenny," John snarled through gritted teeth.

Jenny took a step closer so she could hear their conversation. "Gregg, it's okay. Really. I need to be alone with John for just a little while. Gregg looked at her through his deep blue eyes hating what she was asking. Jenny could see the pain it caused him.

"All right, I'm going to take the babies for a walk. I'll be back in a half hour. That's all you get. Then I want you gone!"

Without another word he pushed the stroller off the grass and down the sidewalk, not once looking back. John studied Jenny as she stood silently looking at everything except him. He could tell she wore no bra and he wondered if she did it for Gregg or the ease of feeding the children.

"Being a mother agrees with you," he teased as he looked approvingly at her figure. Then his voice took on a serious tone. "Why haven't you returned any of my calls?"

"I've been busy," she shrugged.

"I've missed you," he said stepping close for an embrace. She pushed his hands away from her arms. Still she ignored eye contact with him. "What's going on in your life Peanut?"

Jenny sighed. "Sit down John. We have to talk." John walked over to the blanket where she and Gregg sat earlier enjoying the evening air. He sat cross-legged facing her. He took her hand in his. They were warm and rough and she noticed how they trembled.

"I promised Gregg that I would try to make things work with him."

John clenched his teeth and dropped her hand.

"John, please listen. You are an important part of my life and I care about you deeply, but I have two babies who need a father."

"They have a father right here!" he said thrusting a finger into his chest. "I've been more like a father to them for the last few months than he will ever be in a lifetime!" John was quick tempered today and she guessed he must be high on something. Jenny understood his anger but she doubted John's harsh words.

"Where have you been the last few days?" She felt her heart sink and wished she wouldn't have asked him that. When he didn't answer she continued. "I owe it to Gregg and to the children. I've made a lot of mistakes and it's up to me to make them right."

"Even if it means hurting the hell out of me?"

She looked down into her lap. "Even if it means hurting you," she whispered in a trembling voice.

"Why did you make love with me that night?" he yelled. Jenny glanced around hoping no one heard John scream at her.

"Because it felt right. Because…I love you." Her voice trailed off as she stood and walked to a nearby tree. She saw old man Carter pass the kitchen window in the house behind her apartment. Old man Carter was her landlord. He was a kind old man who liked to spy on his neighbors when he thought they weren't looking. He must have thought no one could see him behind the window as he stared at what ever his neighbors were doing.

Chapter 20

John came up behind her and put his arms around her waist. Jenny trembled as she felt the warmth from his chest on her back. She did not want to push him away. His hands moved up the sides of her body to her soft eminent breasts. He cupped first one then the other as he whispered into her ear. He nuzzled her neck with his nose and swayed back and forth. She winced as he squeezed her sore nipples. "I want you and I know you want me too." A shiver went down her neck as she put her hands on top of his and removed them.

"We can't see each other ever again," she cried. He dropped his hands to her waist.

"It was good between us Jenny. It can be again," he said letting his hands roam back to her breasts this time even more roughly. She tried to push them away and he pulled her closer to him in a tight arm hold. "What's the matter, Peanut? Are you trying to tell me you don't want an abandoned bastard for a lover anymore?" He nibbled her neck biting into her skin. Jenny flinched at the pain and tried to break free from his hold. She could feel his erection hard against her back. Jenny felt afraid of him and feared that he would try forcing her to have sex with him. "What would your new boyfriend think if he caught us making love right here on the grass?" he said swinging her to the ground. Tears fell down her cheeks as she listened to his words.

"Stop John! You're hurting me! You don't want to do this!" Jenny crawled on the ground trying to escape his advance. He caught her leg and forced her onto her back. He forced himself on top of her. Jenny cried hard into his chest.

"Isn't this what you want?" John hadn't meant to hurt Jenny. He wanted her to accept him back into her life. Things were getting out of control and he couldn't stop. She reached up and sent a punch into his left cheek. He grabbed her hand and saw a glimpse of fear in her eyes. He stopped and looked at her. Tears filled his own eyes as he released her hand. He stayed on top of her laying his head on her chest and cried softly into her hair. "Oh Jenny, what have I done? I don't want to hurt you. I need you my sweet Jenny," he sobbed. Jenny cried with him.

"You're scaring me John. I can't have you in my life anymore." His body went limp and she pushed him off her. She left him lie on the grass and ran to her apartment and locked the door. Breathing heavily, John brushed the grass clippings from his pants and sat on the front steps of her apartment. His drug crazed mind whirled and he felt angry. Angry with himself for the life he led. Angry at Jenny for refusing him. Angry at Gregg for taking her away from him. He sat in silence waiting for Gregg to return.

"It's not over yet," he mumbled through clenched teeth. After fifteen minutes, John spotted Gregg strolling down the sidewalk. As Gregg approached, John crept toward him like a panther on the prowl as he yelled insulting accusations at Gregg.

"Who the hell are you to be dictating to her how she should live her life you son of a bitch?" John grabbed Gregg's shirt and pushed him away from the stroller. The babies were frightened by the commotion and began to cry.

"You deserted her when she needed you the most. How dare you come back and rule her life like a king?" Gregg stood with his fists prompted in front of him ready for a fight. He kept an eye on the stroller hoping John would leave without a confrontation.

"Things would have been just fine if you never would have come back. What do you really want from her?" Gregg asked.

"I want what's rightfully mine. I want her and the kids."

"She doesn't belong to you. She never has." Gregg ducked as a fist came from his left. Gregg backed away from the area where the babies lay crying. Jenny came running out of the apartment then. A blood curdling fear struck her as she ran toward the stroller. Everything seemed to be happening in slow motion as she watched John pull something out of his boot. What was it? When she reached the stroller she turned and realized it was a gun. Jenny tried to scream, to shout out to Gregg that John had a gun but nothing came out of her mouth. John waved a small pistol first at Gregg, then at Jenny. John stood before them unsure of what to do next. He wanted revenge but he didn't know how. Blasting sounds ricocheted through his mind like an echo in a valley as he stood waving the gun. Jenny's body seemed frozen until John's piercing cry echoed through the evening air.

"No one goes near that stroller or I'll shoot! Do you hear?" John bellowed. Jenny screamed in fright as John stood wild-eyed waving the gun at them. John backed up to the stroller and began to push it to his car. He didn't know what had over come him or what he planned to do with the babies. In John's drug filled mind he thought perhaps if there were no babies, there would be no need for Gregg in Jenny's life. That's what he would do. He would dispose of the babies.

Suddenly, police sirens could be heard in the distance. When John saw them approach he panicked and ran to his car leaving the stroller alone on the sidewalk. Gregg ran to the sidewalk and grabbed the babies out of the stroller their tiny heads bobbed freely as Gregg ran for safety. Jenny ran with him inside the apartment. Another police car approached from the opposite direction. An officer jumped out of the passenger side and apprehended John before he could put the car in gear.

Officer Shank opened the door of the corvette not realizing John had a gun. John aimed the small gun and pulled the trigger, hitting the officer in the shoulder. In deafening silence the officer fell to the street, a pool of blood surrounded his shoulder. Officer Jones approached the driver's side as John swung the gun around. John shot once more and missed his target. Officer Shank staggered to his feet and struck John on the head with his stick. The force of the blow knocked John unconscious before he fell to the ground again. Gregg witnessed the incident from the bathroom window and called an ambulance for the injured police officer as his partner tended to his wound.

Officer Shank lay on the ground breathing rapidly. All around him he could hear feet thundering across the ground.

"That's him," he mumbled to Officer Jones. He winced at the pain and continued with his message to Officer Jones. "That's the guy my wife told me about. I should have listened..." Officer Shank's eyes rolled back in his head and he passed into unconsciousness.

"Stay here with the babies. I am going to talk to the police," Gregg commanded.

"Please be careful," she cried as she closed the door behind him. She sat on the floor and cradled her babies in her lap. Jenny was in shock. The activities of the past half hour stunned her and she sat dumbfounded on the floor rocking the twins. She hummed a lullaby as they settled into her lap.

A policeman waiting outside observed Gregg approaching the scene.

"Put your hands above your head!" The policeman shouted.

Gregg did as he was told, staying away from the corvette and the ambulance. Officer Jones handcuffed Gregg and scanned his body for possible weapons. John awoke and looked around him. He climbed over the armrest keeping low in the car. He opened the passenger door. The door squeaked and proclaimed his intention of escaping to the officers near the car. John cussed aloud remembering too late, the sound of the squeaking door. Officer Jones ran after him and threw his nightstick at the back of John's legs with all his might. John stumbled and fell to the ground. The officer comprehended him just a few hundred feet away. He knew then that his mistake had just cost him his life. The officer handcuffed John and forced him to walk back to the scene of the shooting.

"Are you John Hawkins?" An officer asked. John spit on the sidewalk as he glared at Gregg. His teeth were clenched tightly.

"He is," John said motioning his head to Gregg. Gregg backed away.

"Check his I.D." Gregg shouted.

"Shut up!" One officer shouted. By now there were three other squad cars present. There were flashing lights and ambulance sirens everywhere. The officer checked John's pocket and found his wallet and a small bag of white powder. He held the contents up for Officer Jones to view. Then he opened the wallet and discovered his driver's license. It was issued by the state of Texas.

"Looks like this is our man," he said to Jones. Both officers studied the license.

"Check out the other guy," Jones said.

The officer frisked Gregg's body again.

"Nothing," he told Jones.

"My wallet is in my car over there. I'm Gregg Johnson. This guy tried to steal my children."

"Is that so," he sneered. "We'll find that out later." He turned to John.

"John Hawkins, or what ever your name is, you are under the arrest for the murder of Dan and Karen Olsen and the attempted murder of officer Shank."

"Look," Gregg continued. "Their mother is in the apartment with them right now. She witnessed the whole thing. Ask her!"

"Watch him," Officer Jones said to another policeman. Jones entered the apartment with his gun drawn carefully as he observed every inch of the apartment. He saw the woman on the floor and watched her as she covered her babies from harm. She was humming to them to keep them calm. Jones checked out the entire apartment before he knelt down by her and put his hand on her shoulder. She pulled away from him.

"It's all right miss, I'm not going to hurt you. We've been told that someone tried to steal your children. Is that true?" Jenny shook her head, still covering the children as though he would try to take them from her. "Is there someone you can call to stay with them? We need you to come to the station to make a statement." Jenny did not answer but continued to cover her children with her arms. Another backup officer entered the apartment. She listened to them exchange words about Officer Shank.

"Officer Shank is going to be okay. He left in the ambulance a minute ago," he told officer Jones. "What have we got here?" he said putting his gun back into his holster.

"The mother of the babies," officer Jones replied. "Stay with her, I'm going to see if she has any relatives that can stay with the children while she comes to the station."

Gregg was already in the squad car. He hoped that being in handcuffs was only routine and once at the station he would make his statement and be released. The events of the day replayed in his mind like a rerun movie. He closed his eyes trying to block out the events of the afternoon.

"Mr. Johnson, does the woman have someone she can call to take care of the babies?" Gregg gave the officer the name of her parents and their number. Officer Jones called them immediately and briefed them on what happened. Her parents arrived in fifteen minutes. Rose was ecstatic. Dave was furious. Jenny seemed to be in a state of shock. When Rose tried to take the babies, she clung to them.

"It's okay, Peach," her father said. "We'll be here for them. You go with officer Jones and everything will be all right." Officer Jones waited as Rose and Dave pried the children from her arms. Her shirt was dirty, wet and stained. Dave hugged her and then released her to the officer. Then she was put in a different squad car and driven to the station. During the ride Jenny stared out the window feeling numb. Nothing made any sense. A little over nine months ago, life was normal. She was getting married. She was in love with the most incredible, caring man in her world. She had a job and she was happy. She felt like she was walking through a storybook along with the characters living out someone else's life.

Chapter 21

Gregg sat in a tiny dark room that contained a desk with a chair behind it and two chairs opposite each other. He was the first one to be questioned. He was glad to have the handcuffs off and he rubbed his wrists where the cuffs scraped his skin. In a half hour the Sheriff came in and started the questions. Gregg answered them honestly and to the best of his ability.

"Is Jenny okay?" Gregg demanded. The sheriff ignored his question. Frankly, he did not know.

"What is your relationship to John Hawkins?" the sheriff asked stiffly.

"I have no relationship with John Hawkins. Jenny does. Is she okay?"

"Is Jenny the mother of the twins?" he asked ignoring him again.

"Yes."

"What is her relationship with this Hawkins guy?"

Gregg didn't know how to answer. Were they lovers, friends? He wasn't sure. "I believe they were very good friends, maybe lovers. I don't know," he shrugged. The painful thought of them being lovers, stabbed his heart again and again.

"What is your relationship to the mother?"

"She was my fiancé," he replied more coldly than he meant to. He was tired and hungry and wanted to be with Jenny and the babies. He wanted to hold them all in his arms and protect them forever.

"Was?" The sheriff looked at him over the top rim of his glasses. His thick red eyebrows stuck out over the tops of his glasses and his hair was matted from his cap. This was proving to be a very interesting case so far.

"We had a falling out a few months ago. We're working it out though."

"Who is the father of the babies?"

"I am," he replied proudly.

"What took place tonight Mr. Johnson." The sheriff shoved his chair back, put his hands behind his head and plopped his feet up on his desk simultaneously.

Gregg sighed and put his face in his hands. He rested his elbows on his knees.

"Jenny and I were sitting outside on the lawn with the babies. John came and made a pass at her. He said he wanted to talk to her so I took the babies and went for a walk. When I came back Jenny was inside and John was outside. He approached me and started to swing his fists. I left the stroller so the babies wouldn't get in the middle of a fight. We had words and then Jenny came out to get the babies away from us. That's when he pulled out a gun. He told us if we moved near the stroller he was going to shoot."

"Who was he going to shoot?"

"I don't know, he didn't say. He just waved the gun at us and the babies."

"Go on."

"He started to push the stroller to his car. Then the squad car showed up and he left the stroller and started to run. That's when I grabbed the babies and ran inside. A few minutes later, I heard a gun shot and saw officer Shank fall to the ground. I was watching through the bathroom window. When I came back out John was unconscious. Where is Jenny?" Gregg bounced his knee in a nervous gesture.

"She's in another room waiting to be questioned. She is shook up but she'll be all right," the sheriff answered, oblivious to her condition.

"When can we go home?"

"She has to be questioned before we can release her. You can wait outside."

John signed the statement and left the room to pick up his wallet. He sat down in the chair outside the questioning room and waited for Jenny.

Jenny sat with her arms around her body shivering in the same chair in the tiny room. The sheriff sat stiffly across from her with his notepad ready. He felt sorry for her.

"Please state your full name miss."

"Jennifer Jeanine Elerose."

"Now miss Elerose, can you tell me what your relationship is with John Hawkins?"

Jenny's lips trembled as she tried to form the words. "He is my friend."

"Were you lovers?"

Jenny's heart cringed at the personal questions he was asking of her. She wrung her fingers.

"Please answer the question miss."

"Yes, but only once," she stammered. "You see, he took care of me when Gregg left me." The sheriff rolled his eyes and held up his hand. "That's enough explanation. How old are you?"

"Twenty."

"Did you know John Hawkins had a drug problem?"

Jenny bit her lip.

"Yes, but he told me he was clean."

"Well, he's not. We found a bag of coke in his pocket. Have you ever seen the weapon before?"

"Weapon?"

"You know, the gun he used to shoot Officer Shank."

Jenny's eyes grew wide with fear. Her hands flew to her mouth. "Oh my gosh! He shot Officer Shank?" The sheriff held up his hands. Jenny had no idea he shot anyone and she wondered if Kathy had been notified of her husband's shooting.

"Officer Shank is going to be fine. The bullet went through his left shoulder. He'll make it, calm down." The sheriff studied her disheveled hair and the black under her eyes where her makeup had run.

Jenny cried and put her arms around her body, rocking in her chair.

"Tell me the details from the beginning when you were sitting outside with Mr. Johnson."

Through trembling lips Jenny explained how John approached her and kissed her and then demanded to be alone with her. She explained how Gregg took the babies for a walk and after telling John it was over between them she went inside. She left out the part where he forced her to the ground in an attempt to rape her. "I thought he left. I wanted to be alone because I was upset. I didn't know he was still outside. I didn't hear any gun shot. I was afraid. I wanted to protect my babies."

"Why do you think John wanted to take the babies?"

"I don't know."

The sheriff studied her over the rim of his glasses. "You are lucky that you have a nosey neighbor that cares about you. He may have saved the life of you and your babies today."

Jenny gave the sheriff a questioning look wiping tears from her sweat stained face.

"Who do you mean?

"Mr. Carter called the police miss. He witnessed the whole thing from his kitchen window. I know about the struggle miss. It's called attempted rape. It's up to you if you want to press charges or not. I can't tell you what to do, but Mr. Hawkins is in one hell of a lot of trouble. He is a dangerous man. I don't think you know Mr. Hawkins as well as you think you do. It will help to put him away for good and keep him from hurting you or your children." The sheriff preoccupied himself with the paperwork on his desk. "One more thing, miss. Do you know anyone by the name of Dan or Karen Olsen?"

"No, why?"

"Never mind. You can go home." The sheriff didn't want to weigh her burden by telling her that John was a suspect in the killing of Dan and Karen Olsen several months earlier in Texas. A bulletin went out for his arrest, early last fall and police were searching for him since then.

"What is going to happen to John?"

The sheriff looked at her, flabbergasted that she even cared. He took in the sight of her dirty clothes, the absence of a bra under her light cotton shirt. He scratched a wiry eyebrow. "He will be charged with attempted murder of officer Shank and if you press charges, he will be charged with attempted kidnapping and assault."

Jenny sank in her chair. She was happy that her children weren't harmed but she knew she could never press charges against John. Whatever the reason he did what he did today, she knew she could one day forgive him.

Kathy paced impatiently in the waiting room while her husband underwent surgery to repair the damaged tissues in his shoulder. She was terrified about the condition of her husband as she watched pictures of John Hawkins flash all over the television screen. News of the incident interrupted regularly scheduled programs. Kathy knew she had seen a picture of John somewhere and told her husband offhandedly about her suspicion. She couldn't remember where she had seen him until today. She had seen him on a wanted bulletin that she found in her husband's briefcase. It was among a hundred others and the face stuck with her as she leafed through them. It wasn't until today that Officer Shank put his wife's concern with a picture from his briefcase.

Gregg met Jenny outside of the tiny office. He stood to greet her and took her into his arms. He held her for a long time before they walked together out into the late evening moonlight. Jenny worried that her children were hungry and her heavy breasts were already leaking. She hoped her mother found the excess milk she pumped earlier in the day to feed her babies. They walked exhaustedly, hand in hand up the walkway to her apartment. Neither one spoke as they entered the apartment. Her parents opened the door and greeted them anxiously, waiting to hear first hand about what happened.

"How are the children? Have they eaten?" she asked her mother. She was concerned only for her children's well being.

"I found milk in the refrigerator but I didn't know if it was fresh so I sent dad down to the store to get some ready mixed formula. It didn't go over so well, but they are satisfied enough to go to sleep. I suspect they will be waking shortly. I heard some stirring a little while ago."

Gregg and Jenny sat down in the living room and recounted the events that led to the shooting. Dave and Rose were speechless as they listened to their horrifying story. Her mother sat next to her and hugged her until she calmed down. The babies stirred and let everyone know they wanted their mother's breast milk. Dave studied Gregg and motioned him outside with a tilt of his head. Gregg followed Dave out the door. His face held a ghostly expression in the light of the bright yellow moon.

Dave put his hand on Gregg's shoulder. "The arresting officer told me that they have been looking for John for several months. It turns out that he is a suspect in the shooting of Dan and Karen Olsen."

"The sheriff asked me if I knew them," Gregg interrupted. "Who are they?"

"They are John's birth parents."

Gregg's shoulders slumped. "Oh dear god."

"Does Jenny know?" Dave asked.

"She didn't say anything," Gregg answered with a horrifying look. "Rose doesn't know either. Did you press charges?"

"Not yet. What happens next?" Gregg asked quietly so the women couldn't hear from inside.

"I suspect we will all have to be witnesses in a trial. Eventually he will be extradited to Texas to stand trial for the murder of his parents."

Gregg shook his head. "Why would he do such a thing?"

"We'll never know. Maybe Jenny knows better than any of us. I don't want to upset her any more tonight. I've never seen such a horrified look on her face before. Is she all right?"

"I think so. I will stay with her tonight, Dave."

Dave patted him on the back. "Thank you Gregg." The two men shook hands and went back into the apartment. After long hours of talking and comforting, Jenny fell asleep on the couch. Gregg followed her parents to the door.

"Take care of her," Rose said. Gregg and Dave shook hands again.

"If you need anything, call right away," Dave added.

"I will. Good night."

He closed the door and locked it behind him. Gregg went back to the living room and checked on Jenny. She was snoring lightly on the couch. He picked her up and carried her to her bedroom. He laid her on top of the spread and reached for a blanket from a nearby chair. He covered her and sat down in the chair next to her. As he watched her sleep he thought about the events of the day and how close they all came to death. He wondered what would have happened if Mr. Carter was not a nosey neighbor. He knew he must speak to the man in the morning and thank him for what he did.

Gregg wondered how he would have ever lived with his guilt if the babies were harmed. He knew Jenny would not have been able to survive another heartbreak like that. He felt guilty for the way he treated her. John was right about one thing. He did abandon her. He wondered if things would have been different if he would have let Jenny explain about the night he found them together in her room. He knew he must get her out of this apartment. The incident would haunt her forever if she remained living there.

Gregg heard a knock on the door and he woke up stiff, realizing he slept all night in the chair next to Jenny's bed. Jenny remained sleeping where he laid her. He went into the living room realizing it was only six o'clock in the morning. The babies were sleeping for four and one half hours by then. Gregg opened the door to two pair of frightened eyes. It was Shari whom he hadn't seen in several months.

"Oh my gosh, we heard what happened here? Are the babies all right?" Shari asked pulling Gregg to her in a hug.

"Where is Jenny?" Shari asked.

Gregg held up his hands. "Everything is fine. Jenny is resting and I'm sure the babies will be waking soon. It's been a while since their last feeding. Come in."

Gregg was barefoot and his button up shirt was hanging out of his pants. He realized his long hair was a mess and he combed his hands through it.

"Uh, can I offer you some tea? I think she keeps a lot of it on hand."

"No, I just wondered if there was anything I could do."

"Actually, there is. Can you spend the day with her? I have some spraying I need to get done in the field that can't wait another day. It's been a wet field and the thistles have taken over. With this weather, the corn will be too high to do anything with. I can't afford to let the weeds take control, yet I don't want her to be alone. Not yet. If the police need me I'll be in the field south of the farm."

"I'll be happy to." Shari said squeezing his shoulder. Suddenly he looked so old to her. He had always reminded her of a little boy, but not today. Today he was a man, a man who had his hands full of responsibility. Gregg felt guilty for leaving Jenny this way, but he knew she would be okay as long as Shari was with her.

"The babies ate last around one this morning. Rose bought some formula in case Jenny is too exhausted to get up. There's breast milk in there too. It's from yesterday. I don't know how long it keeps fresh." Gregg tiptoed to the nursery to check on the babies. Joseph was awake and waving his arms in the air. Gregg picked him up and carried him to the living room.

"He's soaked too."

"Don't worry. I'll take good care of him."

"I think there is a load of laundry too."

Shari motioned to the door.

"You go do your farmin'. Everything will be taken care of."

Gregg smiled sincerely. "Thanks, I'll be back tonight."

Later on that day, as Jenny sat in numb silence, she learned from a news broadcast that John's arrest led to the cracking of a murder case in Texas. She was horrified when she learned that he was a major suspect in the shooting deaths of his parents. Jenny held her hand to her mouth and screamed at the top of her lungs as the news broadcaster delivered the astonishing news to the world. Shari held her as she cried in horror.

"Why did he do this? Why? Oh god, I should have known! Why did I believe him?" she said as she fell back into her reclining chair. Jenny sat with her arms around her knees, her head buried in her knees crying.

"Believe him about what?" Shari asked.

"He told me he came back to Minnesota for me. He said he loved me. He didn't. All this time he was running from the police! He told me he was clean! The police found a bag of coke in his pocket! I almost agreed to marry him! I slept with him! Oh god, I slept with a killer!" Jenny screamed in horror. Shari held her and tried to calm her.

"Look Jenny, what ever he did, it wasn't your fault. The important thing is that he is put away.

He won't ever be able to hurt you or your babies again. Texas has the death penalty. If he is found guilty he'll..."

"Stop! Don't say it! Please don't say it." Jenny got up and ran to the door. She stumbled out into the bright sunny morning. She ran into the backyard and collapsed onto the cool green grass under a large oak tree. Mr. Carter was pacing in front of his kitchen window all morning. He saw Jenny storm out of the apartment. He waited a minute for her to calm down and then he went out to talk to her.

He cleared his throat to make his presence known. She looked up at him. Her eyes were red and very swollen. "I just wanted to remind you that your rent was due a few days ago." He felt like an ass but he knew no other way to break the ice.

"Oh, I'm sorry Mr. Carter. So much has been going on here lately, I forgot." She wiped her eyes with the back of her hand.

"I know it's a bad time and all. He bent down close to her. Actually I just wanted to know how you are?"

Jenny reached up to take his hand. She held tight as he pulled her to her feet.

"I want to thank you for calling the police when you did. You saved my life and the life of my children. I don't know how to repay you for that." She squinted as she looked up at him. The morning sun was already peeking over the treetops. It was going to be a hot, steamy day.

"There's no need to thank me. I'm just glad I happened to be looking out the window. I couldn't bear to see anything happen to you and those babies of yours. How did you ever get mixed up with a fella like that, anyway?" He shoved his hands into his pockets.

"It's a long story Mr. Carter."

"I see," he said looking down at the ground.

"You know I had a child once," he said in an emotional voice. "Had a wife too. That was a long time ago, but it seemed like just yesterday. They were killed when a tornado struck our farm. Buried them beneath the house. That was almost forty years ago now. There was nothing I could do to save them. I was working in the field when the storm struck. Just had to get the darn thing ploughed. Nothing was more important to me than my family. I feel like I paid my tribute to my lovely wife by doing what I did last night. Those babies of yours are mighty fine and I wish you the best." Jenny took Mr. Carter's hand.

"Thank you for everything. I'll be bringing your check by later today." Jenny tried to let go of Mr. Carter's hand but he held on to it shaking it slowly. She reached over and hugged him briefly. He released her and turned back to his own empty house. Jenny walked down to the police station. She entered the cold dark place and met the sheriff at the desk. He looked up at her in surprise, letting out a lengthy sigh that meant he was up all night too.

"You know, it's not a good idea that you're here. Mr. Hawkins is going to be turned over to the state of Texas today."

"I know. I just wanted to say good bye." He jingled the key in his hands for a moment, noticing her beautiful fresh appearance this morning.

"All right, come this way." He opened a door that led to a room full of cells. "You have fifteen minutes."

Jenny's heart sank. Fifteen minutes didn't seem like much time to say goodbye for a lifetime. She fidgeted with her fingers as she walked close to the cell where John slept on the bunk. The room was cool and damp and every noise echoed when she took a step forward. There was a cell on each side of a narrow walkway. John scooted off the bed and came to the bars. He reached through them for her but she hesitated a few feet away.

"Jenny, I'm glad you're here. I'm scared," he said in a little boy's voice. Jenny studied his features one last time. She observed his thick jet-black hair, his dark-brown eyes, long lashes and long narrow nose. His thin lips were parted before perfectly straight white teeth. He was so handsome she thought. She looked at him memorizing every thing about him. When she spoke it was barely above a whisper.

"Why did you do it? Why did you tell me you came back for me?"

His eyes fell to the floor as he leaned his head against the bars. Holding a bar in each hand his voice came deep and rough.

"I did come back for you but not before I got my revenge. I couldn't let them live like that after what they did to me. They left me alone in a dirty filthy home and went to Texas after they inherited a bundle of money from my grandmother. My mother was a whore! Best yet, my father was her pimp when she had me! They got married after they left me in that filthy place they called a house. It wasn't even a fit home for a louse. Marrying that whore was the only way my father could get his hands on my mother's inheritance. They lived high on the hog for years and not once did they care if I lived or died. They tried to make me happy with money and gifts when I found them. I hated them for what they did to me! They deserved it! It makes me sick to think about it," he said spitting on the floor. "I shot them in cold blood. I can still feel their blood on my hands." He held them up and looked at them. His eyes held a faraway look.

"You were the only one that had ever been good to me. You were the only one that cared about me. You were good and pure," he said pointing to his heart.

"You made me feel loved and I loved you for that in return. You're lucky they caught me because Gregg was going to be next," John said un-remorsefully. "I wanted him out of our lives so we could be together. I wanted to show you how good a father I could be to those babies."

Tears streamed down her cheeks as she listened to his confession.

"No! Stop!" she screamed as she put her hands to her ears.

"I can't believe this is happening! I can't believe you killed any body! I loved you so much. What has happened to you? You're not the same John I knew." She stepped closer to him.

"I know you have a good heart," she pleaded. "I have seen it. You have shown me for the last few months." She reached through the bars and touched his cheek. "John, please tell me it isn't true."

John only nodded.

"You only thought you knew me. Good bye, Jenny," he whispered.

He reached for her fingers, taking them to his lips and kissed them. His hands felt as cold as the stone walls that surrounded his cell.

"Thank you for loving me. It was always my dream to know what it would be like to make love with you. Thank you for giving me that much. I am ready to die." He kissed her fingertips before dropping her hand.

"I'm sorry, Peanut." John turned and went back to his cot. He stood with his back to Jenny. With a numb heart and tears enough for a lifetime, she turned and left the cell. She ran all the way back to her apartment and took a shower. She stood for a long time letting the scalding water run over her body. She wanted to clean her body, to cleanse all of John's touch from her skin. She thought about the night they made love, how gentle he was then and she wondered where the monster was hiding that he now confessed to be.

For the next few weeks Jenny grieved for John's life on earth. She understood why he did what he did. She vowed she would be a good mother to her children, the kind of mother she knew John always wanted. She vowed to love her children always and to forgive their mistakes. She prayed for the repose of John's soul as though he were already dead. She wiped her tears dry of him and promised she would never look back on that day.

Chapter 22

A few weeks later, Jenny answered a light knock on her door. She just finished three loads of laundry and changed two runny diapers. The children were sick with the flu and she felt exhausted. At night her dreams were filled with horror as memories of John's actions replayed in her mind over and over again. The ponytail she put in her hair earlier in the day had fallen and stray hairs escaped, forming a frame around her face. She wiped the sweat from her forehead and opened the door to find her parents standing there with smiling faces.

"Mom, Dad, I wasn't expecting you. The place is a mess, but come in." She motioned into her tiny apartment. She seemed exhausted.

"Your father has been working on something special for you for a long time. He has finally completed it," Rose exclaimed with pride as Dave reached around the corner and presented a double wooden high chair. It was made of beautiful dark oak with a tray in the middle and a chair on each side of it. It was conveniently built on six sturdy wheels. The seat had grooves that would fit the stocky figure of a child and safety straps were fastened to the inside. The tabletops lifted for easy entrance and cleanup. Two bibs were fastened to the backrests. One read: Grandpa's Future Fishin' Buddy. The other read: Grandma's Little Angel. Jenny became emotional as she watched her dad proudly hold Joseph up as though the baby should understand that it was a gift for him. Jenny wheeled the high chair into the kitchen area. The chair seemed large in the tiny apartment.

"Wait, there's more." Dave handed Joseph to his mother.

"I'll be right back," he said with a twinkle in his eyes. He was having more fun than he had in a long time, Jenny thought. Dave went out to the truck and unloaded the crib piece by piece and brought it into the apartment. He put the pieces in the nursery. Jenny watched in awe until the final piece was brought inside. He went to work assembling the crib and after what seemed like a long time, he put the mattress in place. Her mother retrieved the package she brought with her. Jenny opened the bag and found a white mattress pad and set of sheets with animal figures on it for the crib. Her fingers trembled as she unfolded them and put them on the bed. She took Joseph from one crib and put him into the new crib.

"It's beautiful Dad. Thank you so much." She hugged him then. Jenny put Rosalie next to Joseph in their new bed. Everyone laughed as the two babies lay in the new crib waving their arms and playing with their toes.

"Jenny you look exhausted," her mother said as she observed the dark circles around her daughter's eyes.

"The babies have been sick for a week now. I had them to the doctor yesterday and it's something that just has to run its course."

"Have you considered bottle feeding?" Rose asked.

Jenny let out a sigh. "Why, I have more than enough milk. The doctor says the babies combined consume as much as one average infant. He says I have more than enough milk. I even dump most of what I pump because I produce so much."

Rose listened carefully as Jenny explained about her milk production. Sometimes Jenny could be so naïve about things in life. "I meant that if it's getting to be too much for you, I think you should consider switching to formula. You look so worn out."

Jenny understood her mother's concern, but Jenny had a concern of her own too. Money. So far Gregg had not offered to support her financially but did spend money on the children where it was needed. He bought the stroller and the car seats and on occasion he would supply diapers. She didn't expect him to support her financially and being as stubborn as she was she would probably refuse if he tried.

For several weeks, Gregg stayed away during the day and returned to Jenny's small apartment at night. Each night, he made himself a place on the rollaway bed she kept folded up in the corner. Most of the time, she was already asleep when he returned. Most of the time she was too exhausted to even open her eyes. Jenny loved having Gregg around on the weekends and sometimes when he came sneaking in during the night, she would wake up and talk to him for a while before going back to her own bed. He would tell her about his day on the farm and she in turn would tell him about her day with the children. She was excited to tell him that they had slept through the night for the third time that week.

Gregg slept through the middle of the night feedings and was gone by the time she rose in the morning. The babies were on a steady schedule every five hours and each night was getting easier. They were responding more and more each day. On Sunday's Gregg would come back in the late morning and spend time with her and the twins until late afternoon. Jenny loved being a mother and a lot of people stopped her on the street to peek at the babies as she pushed them in the stroller. She tried to avoid most of them who only wanted to criticize her for her involvement in the John Hawkin's case.

In only a few more days, Jenny would need to return to work. The babies were already three months old and she had reluctantly agreed to let her parents take care of them during the day. She was frightened to let a stranger take care of them and still had anxiety about someone trying to steal them. Gregg tried to convince Jenny to move in with him on several occasions but each time he mentioned it the topic led to an argument. He was concerned about the safety of his children and it would make things easier on him. Between trying to run a farm and worrying about her all alone, he was exhausted too. "You know," he said to her one night. "It's about time we baptize the twins."

And so the next day they visited the catholic priest and discussed the baptismal rites with him. It was agreed that they would baptize the children after Jenny and Gregg completed a three-hour class on the rites of baptism. It was a small celebration with Jenny's parents, Scott, Shari and Gregg's parents. Scott and Shari were the Godparents. It had been awkward to meet Gregg's parents again but after seeing the babies, they warmed to her and the children.

Gregg's mother hugged Jenny which left her feeling stunned. There was never any warm gestures from Ruth before now. Jenny dressed simply in a pink cotton dress with lacy sleeves. She braided her hair in a French style braid and wore a pink ribbon tied to the bottom of it. Gregg, dressed in tan khaki pants and a white button up shirt, stood next to Jenny. His skin was deeply tanned and showed off nicely against his white shirt. He held Rosalie in his arms as the priest asked, "What name do you give this child?"

"Rosalie Jeanine Johnson," Gregg replied with a smile.

The priest poured water over her forehead and said, "Rosalie Jeanine Johnson, I baptize you in the name of the Father, the Son and the Holy Spirit." When Rosalie was baptized, Jenny stepped forward holding Joseph.

"What name do you give this child?" the priest asked.

Jenny and Gregg looked at each other. Jenny was the first to speak up.

"Joseph Gregory Johnson," she replied. Gregg stared at her happily as the priest baptized Joseph. At least we are on the right path to being a family he thought. He knew that each small step was a step in the right direction. He wished it wasn't so difficult for Jenny to accept the fact that he wanted her and the children to live with him as a family. Gregg's thoughts drowned out the part where the parents and godparents took a vow to teach the children about God and to bring them up in Christian faith. Everyone was invited to the farm for a celebration of the baptism afterward. When the celebration ended, Jenny and Gregg left the farm with the children. On the way back to her apartment, Gregg turned off a dirt road that led to his grandparents' farm.

"Where are we going?" she asked.

"I want to show you something," He drove in silence to the farm and pulled into the driveway. He opened the garage door and parked the car in the garage.

"Let's bring the babies in," he said calmly.

Jenny unstrapped one of the babies and Gregg did the same. She followed him to the door that led into an entryway. The house was cool and the entry was dark as he led her through a hall and into the kitchen. Jenny looked in awe at the beautiful empty home.

"Where are your grandparents?" she asked.

"They moved to town a few months back. Haven't you heard? They bought the old Thompson house. This is ours now."

"Ours?"

He spread a blanket down on the floor and laid Joseph there. He took Rosalie from her arms and laid her next to Joseph. "These two will be fine for a little while." He took her by the hand and led her through the house. The rooms were large and the carpet was ripped out of most of them. The house smelled like fresh paint.

"The painters were here most of this week. They are coming back tomorrow to finish up. The carpet is due next week. Each room down here will have the same color." He pulled her around the house proudly, showing off the work he had put into the old house. They walked into the living room where a patio door had been roughed in.

"Some day there will be a deck out here." Jenny looked around taking in the sight of the house. It was huge and airy and would be beautiful when it was finished. The smell of fresh wood and paint intoxicated her. He led her to the top of the stairs that led to the bedrooms. They stood side by side at the window at the top of the landing, looking out over the beautiful countryside. He led her further into the rooms. The first room on the right was a large bathroom, which had been completely remodeled. The old claw tub had been removed and replaced with a whirlpool tub big enough for both of them. The carpeted floor had been replaced with peach ceramic tile.

"I thought you might like this color for a bathroom," he said. Jenny didn't respond but continued to look through the house. He led her to the three bedrooms that remained on the upper floor. He opened the doors to each room. They were completely finished with fresh paint and polished hardwood floors. The shades that Grandmother Johnson had hung remained.

"Gregg, this home is beautiful," she said holding her hand to her chest.

"The carpenters have been busy since the week after Grandpa and Grandma moved out. In a few more weeks, it will be complete."

"I've never seen such a beautiful home, but what do you mean it's ours?"

He turned to face her, taking her hands into his. He looked into her pale blue eyes.

"I want you and the kids to live here with me."

She looked into his eyes for a brief moment and then pulled away. "I appreciate your offer but I don't think that's a good idea. After all, we're not married or anything."

"I thought you might worry about that. You could have this room here," he said pointing to the largest room with cream-colored walls.

"The kids can share one for now in there," he said pointing to a room across the hall. It was white with a cornflower border across the top. "I'll take the one down there." It was the smallest of the three but large enough for a bed, dressers and a chair or two. Jenny was speechless. In all the months that had passed, he hadn't mentioned the idea of being a family. He hadn't made any effort to touch her in a romantic sort of way. Occasionally he would peck her on the cheek before he left in the early morning hours before he thought she was awake. It would be a difficult situation to adjust to and a dangerous one indeed.

"I think we better wait for a while," she suggested trying to convince him that living together without romantic ties wasn't going to work for her.

Gregg crossed his arms, prepared for her rebuttal. "The babies are growing bigger and your apartment is too small for all their things. They are going to need more room."

"The answer is no!" She stormed down the stairs. She picked up Joseph and began walking to the back entrance. Gregg followed close behind with Rosalie. They fastened the children into the seats in silence.

"Will you at least think about it?"

"I have, and the answer is still no."

He drove in silence angered by her rejection. He thought he was doing what was right for the babies. He helped her carry everything into the apartment and put the children down for a nap. He wasn't going to let her weasel her way out of this conversation till it was completely over. He followed her into the living room.

"Why won't you move in with me? It is the best thing for the babies."

"I can't. I have a life too. I need to return to work tomorrow. It would be too much of a change right now."

"Okay then, we will wait until you are comfortable with your work routine."

"No!" she shouted. "You don't understand." She was shaking now, surprised by her own anger.

Oh how he missed her. He wished she could just put all her silliness aside and listen to him for once. "Do you understand this?"

He reached behind her head and pulled her to his lips. He kissed her roughly at first and then gently. She didn't protest but melted into his arms like she used to so long ago. He probed her mouth with his tongue tasting her lips with his own. He planted kisses down her neck and at the top of her milk-swollen breasts. She leaned backward as he hungrily tasted her skin as he held her close to his body. He set her away from him and angrily strode to the door. "Women!" he grumbled as he slammed it shut behind him. Jenny stood in the middle of the living room, shaken by the whole experience of feeling him in her arms again. It felt so good to her. She wondered if he would return later. When at last the children were put to bed for the night, she prepared her clothes for the workday that lay ahead of her. When Gregg didn't return late that evening, she locked the door, turned out the light and went to bed. Visions of John's death penalty whirred through her mind. She wondered where he was and if he thought of her. She dreamed that she saw him running with a noose around his neck. It dangled behind him as he fled. It was three a.m. when she last looked at the clock.

    The morning was hectic as she rushed to get the babies fed. She had alternated between breast and bottle feedings so Rose wouldn't have such a difficult time to feed them during the hours she was gone. At last, a knock came at the door. Her mother arrived in time to change two dirty diapers. Jenny cried as she left the children with her mother. The first day she came home during her lunch break to check on them. She breast-fed Rosalie while Joseph lay on the floor sucking his thumb as he peacefully slept. She cried again as she parted with the babies for the afternoon. Rose encouraged her not to worry. Jenny missed them dearly and was happy at the end of the day when she could return to her apartment. That night she collapsed into her chair after the children were asleep. Her legs ached from being on her feet all day and she thought about Rachael and wondered where she was tonight. She longed for her carefree days and knew they would never come again.

    In another month, the work on Gregg's home was completed. The beige Berber carpet had been laid throughout the lower level of the house. The trim work was complete and he began to collect pieces of furniture for the house. The living room furniture consisted of a reclining lazy boy chair and a sectional couch. He purchased them new at the local furniture store. With the purchase, he received a free wooden rocking chair, which he thought would fit nicely for Jenny. He removed all the drapes and sent them to the dry cleaners. Most of them looked like they hadn't been cleaned in several years but were in good enough condition to use another few years. He spent hours washing windows and making the house comfortable before Jenny and the babies came to live there. She still hadn't agreed that she would, and he figured she needed more time to adjust to being back to work. He told Jenny that he wouldn't be able to spend nights with her during the fall harvest, which was just around the corner.

    He made his bed at the farm and lay down for the first peaceful night he had had in a long time. He was grateful that he didn't have to sleep in the room next to Jenny, yet he knew he would miss her presence. It was difficult to lie on the cot in her apartment and try to sleep wondering what she was wearing, what she was dreaming and what it felt like to wake up next to her. He wondered what it felt like to feel her head on his bare chest and to feel her silky hair next to his skin. If he had things his way, it wouldn't be long until he found out. It didn't take long for him to realize that no matter where he slept, he couldn't shake the thoughts of her. He glanced at his watch. Ten thirty. He flung back the covers and padded down the stairs to the empty living room. Rose had offered to stay with Jenny at night until harvest was over but she strongly refused saying it was time she learned to be on her own. He knew he could use that as an excuse to call her. He picked up the phone and dialed her number. The phone rang six times before the answering machine picked up. He began to listen to the message when Jenny's voice broke through.

    "Hello," she said in a groggy voice. She had already gone to bed for the night. Gregg cleared his throat.

    "Hi, it's me. I just wanted to say goodnight." Jenny smiled to herself.

    "That's sweet. I was already in bed," she said softly.

    "I thought so. I was just wondering if everything was okay."

    Jenny hesitated, wishing he were there instead of on the phone. "Everything is fine." Silence fell on the line as she stood in her pajamas.

"Well, good night then," he said.

"Good night Gregg," she said and put the phone back in the cradle before she heard Gregg's last words.

"I love you," he said in a soft whisper. He heard a click on the other end. He wondered if she heard him at all. He climbed the quiet stairs and lay back down for a sleepless night. By four a.m. he would be up and ready to begin work in the field.

Chapter 23

Jenny missed Gregg and she often prepared dinner and took it to him when he worked in the field. He enjoyed seeing her and she would bring the babies along so he could see how they had grown. His face looked like a raccoon and the dust from the field covered his entire body. The only white on his skin was the white of his eyes. He would pick up the babies in his dirty hands and hold one while he ate his sandwich. At first they were frightened but when he spoke softly to them, they would recognize his voice and be silent. When he was through, he would kiss them and hold each one for a while. His hands left dirty marks on their tiny faces and their clothes would be black where he had touched them. They were growing strong and in another month or so, they would be able to sit on their own. He wished he wouldn't have to let go. He wanted to hold them forever. They seemed to be growing far too fast and he missed seeing them every day.

Sometimes it was difficult for Jenny to keep up with their drooling faces and dirty diapers but she felt like she was handling things fairly well. The babies were sleeping through the night and so far they hadn't had any serious illnesses. She had lost all of the weight she had gained during her pregnancy and was still pumping her breast milk for feedings during the day. It was always inconvenient to try and schedule time to pump at work, and her breaks were consumed with the tedious responsibility.

One Sunday during harvest season, Jenny invited Gregg for noon lunch. She knew it was a lot to ask of him to abandon his fieldwork but she missed him. After all, it would only be a few hours until he could return to the fields. She fried chicken and prepared mashed potatoes and gravy. She loved having him visit her apartment and looked forward to the time when harvest would be finished. Gregg knocked on the door and waited for Jenny to answer. Since he started seeing her again, he always respected her privacy and never just walked in on her and the babies except at night. She came to the door in blue jeans he hadn't seen in a while. They fit snugly against her body. She wore a red pullover blouse that revealed a hint of cleavage. She had her hair pulled back in a French braid that made her look like a young teenager. In his arms he carried a jug of Root beer. He looked handsome standing there in her doorway. The apartment smelled wonderful and he smiled to himself knowing she felt proud of her cooking. He lifted Joseph from his infant seat and swung him into his arms for a hug.

"Look, mommy. I think our little boy is growing a mustache," he teased. He set Joseph back in his seat and lifted Rosalie to his chest.

"I don't think you are going to be doing any dating until you are older than your mother young lady." Rosalie smiled.

"Look, she understands what I said," he exclaimed.

"I think it's just gas," Jenny suggested from the kitchen. She smiled at his pleasant humor. She worried he might be angry with her for taking him away from his work. She was relieved that he wasn't.

"You have a beautiful smile Rosalie. Just like your mother." Jenny smiled to herself as she busied herself in the kitchen. When dinner was ready she dished it to his plate. They sat together at the table enjoying each other's company. They made small talk through dinner like they had always done, both avoiding what was really on their minds. When the children were put down for their afternoon naps the apartment grew silent.

Jenny felt suddenly uncomfortable being alone with him and sensed something was on his mind. The tension between them had been growing far too long. She refused to move in with him for that reason mostly. She knew she could never rest knowing Gregg was sleeping in the room next to her. It would be awkward sharing personal living space with the attraction that existed between them and lately small things began to bother her. Things like sitting together on the couch, touching hands and making eye contact. She could see his messages there and it scared her. She wasn't about to make any more mistakes but her heart was weakening.

She thought a lot about the times they shared together and the feelings she once had for him grew stronger with every visit. She envied him for being strong about the terms of their relationship and she wondered if he knew she pretended to be un-attracted to him. It wasn't that she was not attracted to him. She just wasn't ready for another relationship with anyone, physically or emotionally. The delivery left her feeling fat and ugly and bluish stretch marks covered her stomach and thighs. Her breasts had never been so huge and they felt disproportionate to the rest of her body. She knew everyone noticed, especially Gregg. She would catch him staring as his eyes moved from her chest to meet hers in an approving grin.

"Motherhood agrees with you," he said as the last of the dishes had been put away.

"Why thank you," she replied uncomfortably. She blushed a little and was relieved when Gregg went into the living room and sat down in the recliner. Jenny took a load of laundry across the hall before joining him in the living room. He surfed through the channels pretending to be interested in star wars at one point. He was trying to work up the courage to ask Jenny again to move in with him. He was afraid of the rejection he knew she would give him and he didn't look forward to starting a fight. Jenny watched the screen. She knew he hated star wars. He turned off the television and joined her on the couch. Her heart pounded in her chest at his nearness. He reached for her hand and laced his fingers through hers. She glanced at him through the corner of her eyes. His face was red and he continued to stare straight ahead. She tightened her grip enjoying the warmth of his hand in hers. After a few moments of silence, he turned to her.

"Jenny, we need to do something about this relationship. I need you and it gets more difficult every day to turn my back and walk out of here. I want you to be more than just a mother to my kids. I want to be with you and the children so much," he stuttered. Jenny melted at his words and she felt a rush of heat flash across her body. He reached for her and took her into his arms, his lips crushed against hers. He gently laid her back on the couch and kissed her lips. She knew heaven was just around the corner as she returned his passionate kisses. His lips roamed down her neck. He moved slowly lower planting more kisses until he moved to the tops of her breasts. Her body responded against her will as her hips arched upward and ground into his. Her mind rejected every thought that told her to stop, that it wasn't what she wanted at all. They lay on the couch together, touching and panting eager to fulfill the other's needs with their own.

"Move in with me Jenny," he prodded as his hands slid down her waist to the button on her jeans. Jenny froze in his arms disappointed at his request. She had hoped he would ask her to marry him like they were meant to be long ago. Now she knew what she had feared all along, was true. She wasn't good enough to be his wife. He just wanted her for his whore. Not once since the birth of the babies had he told her he loved her. She waited for so long to hear those words from him, and when she didn't she knew he must not love her the way he used to. She pushed him off her and scrambled to her feet. Her chest heaved heavily as she stood glaring at him.

"Listen you creep! There's a lot of things I've done wrong in my life and I've done a lot of things I never thought I would! But one thing I refuse to be is your whore! Get out!" she shouted pointing to the door. Gregg glared at her wild eyes seeing a side of her he had never seen before.

"Jenny, I just think it would be best..."

"I know! It would be best for you! Then you could come into my room any time of the night you wanted and take advantage of me! Get out!" She picked up a pillow and threw it at him. He dodged the pillow knowing it was best if he left. There was no mistaking that her answer was no, but he still didn't understand what she wanted from him.

"Women," he mumbled as he opened the door and slammed it behind him.

"And don't come back unless you call first," were the last words he heard.

It was early November when Gregg finished the harvest. He put his machinery away just in time for the first few flakes of snow. He was happy about the high yields of grain that his fields produced and he had plenty money in his pocket after all the bills were paid. He walked into the empty house and turned up the furnace to take the chill out of the room. He sat down in the new recliner he bought and turned on the television. Nothing interested him. He shut it off and sat there in silence. He wondered what Jenny and the babies were doing.

She had been so cool to him since the last time he asked her to move in with him and he felt like he was not welcome in her apartment any longer. It bothered him to have to make an appointment every time he wanted to see the babies. He wanted them to be a part of his entire life. Not just when it suited her. It shouldn't be that way he thought.

I should be able to see my children whenever I feel like it. He wondered how she really felt about him and just when he thought they were making progress, she snapped and screamed at him like a maniac. Gregg was nuts about her. He always had been. He ran upstairs to his room and began to rummage through his dresser drawer. After shuffling around the contents, he lifted out a tiny blue box. He studied the tiny box and noticed the scrape in the velvety material. He recalled how he had thrown the box at the wall the night he found John in her room. He gently lifted the lid as a smile formed on his lips. His heart beat rapidly as the tiny diamond glittered in the dark room. He snapped the box shut and stuffed it back in his drawer. He went downstairs and dialed Jenny's number.

"Hi, Jenny."

"Hi," she sounded cold on the other end.

"How are the kids?"

"They are sleeping right now. Joseph had a runny nose all week. Rosalie is fine." Talking about the kids had become a common ground for communication and Jenny felt comfortable talking to Gregg about them.

An awkward silence fell over the line.

"Well, I was wondering. Are you free tomorrow night?"

"Why?"

"I was wondering if you and the kids would come for dinner. I am planning a special meal and would love to have you and the kids over. I know it's hard for you to pack everything up but I can come around four when the babies are through with their nap to help you."

Jenny wondered what he was up to this time. "What is the occasion?" He couldn't help but notice the snobbishness in her voice and it hurt him.

Did he dare tell her? "Well, the house is finished and I thought you might like to see it." He sat in the recliner with his fingers crossed.

Oh the house thing again, she thought. But knowing how proud he was of the remodeling, she agreed.

"Okay, I'll see you at four, but the answer is still no," she replied softening her tone.

The next day Gregg bought enough groceries to feed any army. He picked up a few fresh roses and salmon steak. He realized he didn't have a vase so he stuck the flowers in a Root beer mug. He took out the vanilla candle that he purchased and placed it next to the roses. He held up the wine and studied it. He wondered whether he should purchase it, but he did. It was now in the refrigerator to chill. He didn't know if Jenny would be able to have any since she still breastfed. He didn't think one glass on a special occasion would hurt the babies. When everything was in place he showered and put on khaki pants and a white shirt. His heart raced as he drove to the apartment. He arrived at four like he said he would. Jenny just finished feeding the babies when he knocked.

"Hi," he said with a devilish smile. She knew he was up to something as he presented her with one of the red roses from the bunch he had bought. She sniffed the rose, closing her eyes to breath in the lovely scent.

"Thank you. Come in." She was dressed in tight dark green cotton jeans and a long sleeved button up beige shirt. Her hair was braided and wrapped around the top of her head neatly. The babies' eyes lit up when they saw their daddy enter the room. He picked each one up separately and bounced them on his hip. Rosalie was dressed in a pink dress and tights with little ballet booties. Joseph was dressed in denim overalls and tennis shoes.

"New outfits?" he asked raising a brow.

"Your mother sent them. They haven't fit until now."

She finished packing their diaper bag and flung it over her shoulder.

"It looks like your beautiful mommy is ready to go," he said as he looked approvingly at Jenny.

"I'm ready when you are," she said with a smile.

She put a cap on each child and put a heavy quilt over each infant seat. The weather wasn't quite cold enough for a snowsuit but chilly enough to need to cover the children. They each took a child and loaded them in the car. During the drive they talked about the bountiful harvest and her job and the babies' runny noses. When they arrived at the farmhouse, Gregg took the babies inside first and set them on the floor in the spacious but empty living room. Then he led Jenny into the house.

"Close your eyes now. I want to surprise you." As they entered the house, Jenny could smell a light scent of fresh glue or paint or both. She took small steps as he pulled her through the hall into the kitchen.

"Ta da! You can open them now," he said proudly.

Jenny held her hand to her chest. The kitchen was breathtakingly beautiful. It would be every cook's dream come true. The cupboards were light colored oak and hung low from the ceilings. No step stools were needed to reach those high cupboards. Above the cupboards there was a spoke railing, which decorated the border of the wood. A ceiling fan hung above the table, which Gregg demonstrated.

"And a dimmer switch for those late night romantic dinners when the children are in bed," he said winking at Jenny. Her heart fell at his last comment. He just doesn't give up, she thought to herself.

"It really is beautiful Gregg," she crooned. "So this is where you've been spending all your free time," she said with a little more vengeance than she wanted. She wished she had caught her words before they slipped over her tongue. She hadn't seen much of Gregg lately and she was feeling bitter about it. She thought he was still angry with her for their last disagreement until she realized what he was doing instead. She felt a fight brewing and she knew that the only reason she was here was so he could try to convince her that she belonged here with him under the same roof. Gregg noticed her tone and chose to ignore her words. Instead he pulled her by the hand and led her into the laundry room. She scanned the room noticing that it was made to perfection.

The washer and dryer sat side by side and a hanging rod was affixed above it. A washtub complete with a separate faucet sat next to the washer and a counter top ran the entire length of the opposite wall. There was room for laundry soap and supplies underneath. An ironing board was mounted in a cupboard on the wall, which folded up for space and convenience. Next he led her to the bathroom, which was enlarged to encompass a double sink vanity and a large walk in storage closet on one end and a shower on the other. It had another door, which led into the master bedroom.

"Wasn't this was a dining room last time I was here?" she asked taking in the view that over looked a grove of trees. Two glass French doors would eventually lead to a private patio.

"This room isn't finished yet," he said flipping on the light.

"See this step?" he asked pointing with his foot.

"I am going to have a step down Jacuzzi here. The carpenters have work to do in the basement before it can be completed. The tub should be here next week." He took a brochure off a chair and showed her a picture of it. It looked extravagant and left her speechless. He turned out the light and led her to the family room where the children were busy amusing themselves with their shoes.

"This is my favorite room. The fireplace is the original built back when my great-grandparents first lived here. I like the rustic look, don't you?" Jenny ignored his question but continued to look in amazement.

The fireplace took up one whole wall at the end of the room. It was encompassed in brick, which flowed from floor to ceiling.

"I put marble here to keep the carpet clean," he said pointing to the spot in front of the firebase. Two ceiling fans were installed on each end of the room, which were also equipped with dimmer switches. On the opposite end of the room was a large patio door.

"Someday there will be a deck out there," he said. "Right now I'm about out of extra cash. He stuck his hands in his pockets. This has been a big project for me. The carpenters have really been wonderful. They've done everything to my specification."

"It's beautiful Gregg. It is hard to believe it's the same house. Not that it wasn't nice before. It was. It's just that I never dreamed this house could look like this."

"You like it then?" he asked cocking his head to the side.

"Any one would be a fool not to," she said hoping this wasn't going to lead to the ultimate conversation about her moving in again.

"I haven't shown you the upstairs yet. Come," he said pulling her by the hand.

The enclosed stair well had been opened up on one side and was encased in a beautiful light oak railing from floor to ceiling. The bottom two steps veered to the left opening up into the family room. At the top of the stairs was a window, which overlooked a field of un-ploughed cornstalks. To the left there was a bathroom and a bedroom, which looked the same as the first time he brought her there. To the right was a hall with a railing like the one on the stair well. Two bedrooms remained on that wing both of which were unchanged. The bathroom was large with plenty of storage. The peach whirlpool tub in the center was a lighter shade than the tile. A shower encased in glass which stood in the corner, had been added since her last visit. He led her to a window.

"Look," he said pointing to the ground.

Jenny looked down to the ground searching the backyard. A wooden swing set was erected in the middle with a sandbox to one side.

"Oh Gregg, you shouldn't have," she said holding her hand to her mouth.

"I didn't. My grandparents did. The sandbox used to be my dad's. They bought the swing set. They said they want their grandchildren to remember them when they play. I thought it would be nice for when the kids come to visit." He rested his hand on her shoulder.

"That is, if you intend to bring them here from time to time to see their dad." He raised his brow to her and waited for her reply. A shy smile formed on his lips.

"Of course they can come here," she said sadly turning to stare out the window. It wasn't what she was hoping to hear from him. How long would they continue their relationship this way? The babies needed a full time father and she needed him more than just popping in from time to time. She wished they could be a real family like they were meant to be. He stood behind her and put his arms gently around her waist. When she didn't protest, he stepped closer and put his nose in her soft hair. It smelled fresh like strawberries. She leaned back against him letting herself relax into his chest. She put her arms on top of his. She was exhausted from constantly fighting him and being a single mom. She kept reminding herself that it was her decision but regretted it at times.

"All this can be yours," he whispered into her ear. "I did this for you." That was the start of it. She squeezed her eyes closed trying to block out what he was asking her again. She knew she must change the subject before a quarrel began.

"I can hear Rosalie crying," she said turning to him.

"I can't hear anything," he replied.

"I'm telling you she is crying! I have to get down there!" She nearly knocked him over on her way out of the room. When she reached the family room, Rosalie was fussing only a little. Jenny pretended to check her diaper.

"I need to change her," she said knowing she wasn't really wet.

"I can do it," he offered.

"No, I got it," she replied curtly. She wanted to show him that she could handle all the responsibility.

"I'll go start dinner then." She was relieved when Gregg finally left the room. She took her daughter on her lap and looked around the beautiful room. It felt cozy to her and she knew it would be a wonderful place to raise the children. If only Gregg loved her. Then she would be willing to say yes to him. She knew she could never live with a man who didn't love her.

Gregg stuck his hand in his pocket feeling for the little gold ring. It was still safely in place. He pulled pans from the cupboard and removed the salmon from the refrigerator. He prepared the salmon for the broiler and green beans for the stovetop. His mother hadn't told him how long to bake the salmon so he put it under the broiler thinking he would check it in about fifteen minutes. He went to the refrigerator and brought out the ready-made cheesecake dessert he bought at the store earlier that day. When the salmon was in the oven he went to the family room to check on Jenny and the kids. Jenny was on the floor talking to the babies and making them laugh. They rolled around and played with their feet. He stood in the doorway and watched. She was a good mother and he wished she were here under his roof with the babies all the time. He felt the gold ring again.

Tonight, he thought he would ask her to be his bride once and for all. He knelt down on the floor and joined in the fun. He lay on his back and held Rosalie in the air doing gentle airplane spins. She would giggle a little holding her mouth wide open. Her eyes grew wide as she waved her arms in the air spilling drool on her daddy's chest. She behaved as though all her trust lay in her daddy's arms. Gregg laughed and then brought her down to his chest for a hug. She snuggled her head up to his chin and lay there as though to hug him back.

Jenny sniffed. "What's burning?"

Gregg handed Rosalie to Jenny and jumped to his feet. By the time he got to the kitchen, the air was filled with smoke. It was too late. The fish had already burned. Jenny came bounding in behind him waving her arms in the air and coughing.

"Open some windows," he said reaching in for the burning salmon.

He removed it from the oven and tossed it onto the top of the stove. He took off his oven mitts and threw them on the counter. He rubbed the back of his neck with his hand.

"Well, there goes dinner. I hope you weren't too hungry. All I have left is beans and cheesecake dessert." Gregg felt disappointed. His perfect plan wasn't going so well.

"It's all right," she said seeing the disappointment in his eyes. "Got any sandwiches?"

"Nope," he said sheepishly. "I have popcorn though," he said with a seductive smile.

Jenny laughed. "I've made a meal of popcorn a time or two."

"No," he shook his head. "This was important to me. It's ruined."

He went to the phone and dialed. When Rose answered she asked if everything was all right. Jenny listened intently as he asked her if she could baby sit.

"We'll be there in fifteen minutes," he told her.

"Rose agreed to baby sit. I'm taking you out to dinner tonight."

"That's not really necessary. I can eat at home. I'm really tired anyway. We really should be going. The children's naps were pretty short today."

"Nonsense! I insist. Let's get the babies ready." Jenny didn't protest. Maybe he did have something important to tell her. Maybe he was finally going to tell her he loved her.

When they arrived at the farm, Rose already had the playpen setup. Dave was the first to come to the door. He took Joseph into his arms and spoke gently to him. He lifted him up in the air a few times and danced in a circle with him. Dave was very happy to see the children.

"This one is getting beefy. What are you feeding him Peach?"

Jenny blushed as she instructed her mother about their feeding schedule and placed two bottles of pumped breast milk in the refrigerator. "This should be all they need for tonight."

"You two have a wonderful time," Rose said as she hugged Rosalie.

"I just love the smell of babies. You two go on now," she said flicking her hand in the direction of the door. "We are going to have lots of fun tonight."

"We'll be back before midnight," Gregg assured them.

Chapter 24

Gregg took Jenny to the Red Hen restaurant. It was one of the first places he had taken Jenny when they were in high school. The place hadn't changed a bit. It wasn't the most romantic place in the world he thought as he looked around, but it was the closest within a sixty-mile radius. They were led to a table in the center of the restaurant. It was the same one they sat at the first time they visited there. Jenny ordered fried chicken with hash browns and root beer and Gregg ordered the same. He sat nervously across from Jenny, stealing looks at her when ever possible. They made small talk, mostly about the babies.

Gregg acted foolishly repeating himself and asking questions more than once. He wanted to ask Jenny to marry him. He wanted the time to be right. He had planned to do it during dinner but the restaurant was full of noisy chatter and didn't seem very romantic. After dinner he took her dancing across town to an old ballroom. The music was new style rock and didn't fit the occasion either. They didn't even get a chance to slow dance. They stayed for a half hour sipping on a glass of wine at the bar. He grabbed her hand and led her through the crowd. Gregg seemed uneasy and she sensed it. He was acting strangely.

"What's wrong with you tonight?" she asked as he pulled her across the parking lot.

"I thought there would be different music in there. I don't like that loud base stuff. It gets on my nerves that's all."

Jenny knew it had to be more than that. She could feel him staring at her and when she looked at him he quickly looked away.

"If you're worried about burning dinner forget it. I've done that lots of times. It gets frustrating when the babies are demanding. Now I've learned to shut everything off before I tend to their needs."

The moon had risen huge and bright and the flurries that lingered during the afternoon hours dissipated.

"Now what would you like to do?" he said staring at her again.

"I guess I'd be ready to go home now. Thank you for the lovely dinner. It felt good to get out of the apartment." Whew, she thought. The evening was almost over and they made it that far without arguing about her choice of living arrangements for herself and their children. Gregg looked at his watch.

"It's only nine thirty. I'm sure your parents are enjoying their time with the children. Let's give them a little more time shall we?"

Gregg drove around in the country explaining what he was going to do with next year's fields. He continued to drive making comments about certain pieces of land that Jenny squinted to see in the moonlight. He drove down a gravel road that led to a place where they used to visit when they were dating. Jenny's heart skipped in her chest, beating faster as they got closer. It was the place where they had made love the one and only time. It was the place where Rosalie and Joseph were conceived. It was the place where Gregg had kissed her for the first time. He pulled the car up the slope that led to the waterfalls.

"It's a beautiful night for a walk," he said clearing his throat. "Won't you join me?"

Jenny got out on the passenger side as Gregg came around to meet her. He took her hand and led her to the spot where the water fell to the pool below. The gushing water could be heard from a fair distance away. The full moon shined down brightly casting golden highlights on the flowing water and the surrounding banks. Little diamonds of light danced on the water as it gushed quickly down river. The ground was damp from the snow showers that had occurred earlier in the day. They stood silently on the edge of the bank listening to the sound of the gushing water. The damp wind blew gently forcing Jenny to huddle close to Gregg. He slipped his arm around her and pulled her close guarding her from the chilly wind.

"Is that better?" he asked slipping his left arm around the front of her body.

Jenny shook her head. "Why are we here?" she asked in a trembling voice.

He released her and stepped around to face her unable to stop his throbbing heart. His heart beat like a drum in his ears and it drowned out the sound of the rushing water as they walked.

"You are beautiful. Did I ever tell you that?" He said stopping to turn to her.

"It's been a while, but you have," she smiled.

"Do you remember this spot?" he asked his breath ragged.

"I do," she said turning away. "How could I forget? But that was a long time ago," she added calling over her shoulder.

"I know," he said stepping up behind her. "A lot has happened since then." He reached and put his hands on her shoulders.

"You have been the only one since then," he said cautiously.

Jenny knew she couldn't say the same and so she avoided his statement. She squeezed her eyes closed as flashbacks of their one night together danced in her mind. She remembered how confident she had been that night. She thought she had the world figured out. She was confident that everything was going according to her dream. She felt like a queen in his arms. She felt safe like she was in some kind of bubble, protected from the wrongs in the world. But somewhere along the line the bubble popped and everything went wrong. This was the spot where Gregg had made so many promises. Promises that were forgotten when he turned his back and ran out of her room. She remembered how they had joked about using protection and then went without it in the end. Neither of them was prepared for that day in late fall when Gregg brought her to this place to show her that he could walk on his own. The same joyous day Gregg first asked her to marry him and the same fateful day the twins were conceived. It was also the same day they had agreed to save their love for their wedding night. And now, here they were again a year later with so much pain and anger between them. They could never go back to where they were. How would they ever close the gap in their relationship so they could move forward?

She thought about John and how safe she once felt in his arms. She thought about all the promises he had made to her and the promises he had broken before they fell across his lips. She wondered if he was afraid of dying once his sentence was determined. She wondered if he thought of her and the babies. She was glad that he had been arrested before he could have harmed Gregg or the children. She wondered if he would have come back if he hadn't found his real parents. She wondered if they had ever come face to face with their murderer or knew the consequences that prompted John to act so viscously. She realized now that John led two lives. One life that had been supportive, loving and fun. Another that was dark and violent and driven by drugs. Gregg put his arms around her waist again. She opened her eyes as tears streamed down them.

"I want to try again," he said hoarsely.

"What?"

"I want you and the babies in my life all the time," he whispered into her hair. "I want all of us to live under the same roof. I want their father and mother together. They deserve that much and so do we." He kissed her gently at first then his lips became demanding. "I won't give up until you say yes," he whispered. She leaned backward away from him and opened her mouth ready to reject what she thought he was asking. She would refuse to live under the same roof with a man she wasn't married to. He pulled her back to him. His lips were inches away from hers. She opened her mouth to protest but he interrupted her.

"Will you marry me?" he blurted. She didn't get a chance to answer before he met her lips with his own again. He picked her up and carried her to a large boulder and set her down. He placed his hands on each side of her and looked directly into her eyes in the moonlight.

"I have to know tonight," he said pushing her hair away from her face. "I love you and I can't stand another night without you and the babies." Jenny was silent as she stared into his eyes. His words rang in her mind over and over. The only words she heard was, I love you. After a long silence she pushed him gently away.

"Why don't you visit us much any more?"

He came to her then and put his hand around the back of her neck. He rested his forehead on the top of her head.

"Because it's too hard to leave. The more often I do it the more difficult it gets. When I stayed with you those nights, all I could think of was you in the next room, sleeping by yourself. You don't know how many nights I almost crawled in next to you and how many nights I stayed awake watching you sleep. Each time I say goodbye means each time I'll be going home to an empty house. You belong with me. The babies belong with us. It was meant to be this way. We just got a little mixed up along the way."

Jenny remembered the nights he stayed with her and how she lay in her bed tracing his actions in her mind as he walked through the apartment locking the door, turning out the lights and then listening to the awkward silence. Each night she lay awake listening for his footsteps as he checked on the babies and made sure the doors and windows were secure. In the morning she would wake up and he'd be gone. Gregg didn't know that Jenny felt the same way. She missed his late night visits and his companionship.

He massaged her cheek with his thumb. "Please say yes," he pleaded. "I want a second chance to make your dreams come true," he added. Jenny wasn't sure but she thought she saw a glimmer of a teardrop in his eyes.

"Do you really love me?" she asked sincerely.

"Yes, I love you," he told her boldly. "How can you not know that?"

"You never told me. Do you know how long I've waited for you to tell me that? You always asked me to live with you, yet you never told me that you loved me. Don't you understand? How could I live with a man that didn't love me?"

"But I do love you! Can't you see that? I can hardly make it through one day without you. It kills me when I can't see you and sometimes I have to force myself not to because I'm afraid of pushing you further away from me. You've been so adamant about not moving in with me. I don't know what to do or say that won't make you angry anymore." She stared at him directly. His chest was heaving heavily as he spoke to her in a louder voice than he needed to.

She crossed her arms in front of her. "How can I be sure?" she inquired innocently.

Gregg released her and dug in his pocket for the tiny gold ring. He reached for her left hand and slipped the ring onto her finger. He slowly bent his head and kissed her soft hand.

"Accept this ring as a sign of my love," he said in a deep voice. Jenny felt the ring on her finger. It was a thin band with a tiny diamond attached. She slid off the boulder to stand before him. He knelt down on the damp ground and put his arms around her legs. Then he looked up at her and took her hand in his.

"Jenny Jeanine Elerose, will you do the honor and be my wife from now till death parts us?"

A tear slid down her cheeks as she wiped it away with a shaky hand. She stood there crying and shaking. Gregg thought she was going to refuse him again. He stood to face her.

"I'm sorry for everything I have done to hurt you. I regret the mistakes I've made. I regret the time I lost with you during your pregnancy and I want to make it up to you. I was jealous when I saw you with… John and it just about killed me." He struggled to say the man's name. John. John's name rang in his ears like an echo. He cursed the man who was the cause of both their heartaches. Gregg hoped the bastard would rot in hell. "I'm sorry I didn't listen to you. Just allow me to be your husband and let me show you how much I love you. Let me be the father I was meant to be. I don't want to make an appointment to come and see you and the babies. I want us to live together as a family in the house I made perfect for you. I want us to fill the house with more babies…" She put a finger to his lips.

"No more babies. I have my hands full right now," she said smiling. She took his face in her hands. His skin felt smooth and she could smell the hint of aftershave that she loved. She strung her arms around his neck and pulled herself close to him. She sighed a deep satisfying sigh.

"Gregory Johnson, I'd love to be your wife… till death parts us."

He picked her up and swung her around twice before setting her down for a long leisurely kiss. Jenny couldn't believe it was for real. She felt like she was watching herself in a movie and soon enough it would be over. All this time, she had hoped Gregg wanted the same for her and the babies. Now one of her dreams was coming true. His tongue tasted her lips and her neck as he planted kisses on her skin. His hands roamed up and down her back, as he tasted her sweetness. His hands lowered to her buttocks squeezing and massaging as he held her. She could feel his desire for her against her body as he held her tight.

"Jenny, I want you," he mumbled between kisses. His hands were warm wherever he touched her sending a thrilling sensation to all parts of her body. Her breasts tingled wanting to feel him touch her.

"No," she breathed between kisses. "Not this way."

He released her and stood back in confusion.

"What is it? Have you changed your mind already?" he asked angrily.

"Do you remember the vow we made to each other after the first time we made love?"

"I remember," he said softly this time.

Jenny thought he looked like the devil himself, standing before her as the moonlight cast a shadow across his face.

"I want to wait until we are married to make love again. I want to do this right, like we agreed to a long time ago," she stammered.

Gregg put his hands in his pocket. She was certainly a strong willed woman.

"You really plan on making me prove my love for you don't you?"

"Yes, I do," she replied keenly.

"You always were one to go by the book. I guess I can survive one more day." he shrugged. He picked her up and spun her in a circle.

"One more day?"

"Do you still have your heart set on a big wedding?"

Jenny rolled her eyes uncertain of what his intentions were.

"It's not that important to me anymore."

"Good, then it's settled. We'll elope. Come on." He said putting her down and pulled her by the hand. "You need to get a good night's rest. Tomorrow you will become my wife."

She laughed a giddy laugh. Everything was happening so soon. She chattered nonstop during the drive back to her parent's home asking him questions about their wedding. He wouldn't tell her any more than she needed to know. "What if I don't have a dress to wear?" They both knew she did and Gregg just laughed.

"Then come in jeans," he suggested with a hearty laugh. "Come in your bath robe if you like. I'll take you any way I can get you!"

It was eleven o'clock when Jenny quietly tiptoed into her parent's house. Rose met her coming around the corner and each woman jumped with fright.

"I thought everyone was sleeping," Jenny said fidgeting with her sleeve.

"Is everything all right Jenny?"

"Every thing is fine mom."

"Did you and Gregg have a good time?"

Jenny knew her mother could see right through her giddiness.

"Yes, we had the time of our lives," she giggled spinning in a half circle.

"You're acting goosey. Have you been drinking? You don't act like that unless you are up to something."

Jenny threw herself into her mother's arms. Rose was shocked but hugged her daughter in return.

"Gregg has asked me to marry him," she said excitedly.

Rose's eyes grew wide as Gregg rounded the corner and saw them embracing. He smiled broadly as Rose reached for him and included him in the embrace.

"I have to wake your dad," she said running to the bedroom.

Rosalie had awakened and got up on her hands and knees to see what was happening. Jenny went to her and picked her up. She smiled and her eyes lit up to see her mother. With wet fingers Rosalie grabbed Jenny's nose and squeezed. Jenny hugged her daughter and lay her back down in the playpen next to where Joseph slept. He looked angelic as he lay sleeping with his tiny fists curled around his face. They were finally going to be a family. Dave came into the living room in his striped pajamas. Jenny laughed as he stood there rubbing his eyes.

"What's all the fuss about?" he asked looking to Gregg for an answer.

Gregg scratched his head, feeling intoxicated by the events of the evening. "—Uh, I would like to have your daughter's hand in marriage. Will you give us your blessing?"

Dave slapped Gregg on the back. "By golly boy I thought you'd never ask," he said laughing.

"This calls for a celebration. Sit down here. Rose have we got any of that home made wine down stairs?" Jenny laughed aloud. The only time the homemade wine was served was at Christmas time or special occasions. This was certainly one of them.

It was Gregg who interrupted.

"Let's skip the wine until we get back. Jenny needs to get some rest before the wedding."

"Get back from where?" Dave questioned.

"We're going to elope... tomorrow," he said putting his arms around Jenny. He looked down at her and winked. "We figured the babies have been without a family for too long and we're not going to wait any longer," he said nudging Jenny's hips. Dave's eyes darted to Rose and their jaws dropped in awe.

"So soon?"

"Actually, your daughter refuses to sleep with me unless we are married. I can't wait another day," he added laughing. Jenny flushed, embarrassed that Gregg would even suggest such a thing in front of her parents.

"Well," Dave added. "I knew she had good sense about her," he said scratching his head.

"Can you sit for the kids while we're gone?" Gregg asked.

"Of course! How long will you be gone?" Rose and Dave chimed in unison.

"Just tomorrow night. We'll be back on Monday morning. Jenny do you think you can get off work Monday?"

Jenny had forgotten all about work. It was not her weekend to work so Monday would be her normal scheduled day. "I'll call one of the girls for a replacement. I'm sure I can find someone."

"It's settled then. We'll see you tomorrow." Jenny and Gregg each took a bundled up baby and scurried out the door. Dave winked at Rose and pulled her behind him to the bedroom.

Chapter 25

Gregg made several calls to different people late that night and made as many last minute plans that he could. His uncle, who would perform the ceremony, would help him with the rest. The house still smelled of burned salmon and he opened his bedroom window to let in some fresh air. He noticed the full moon and smiled to himself. Yes, he thought, this is right. He always wanted to give her the moon for her wedding. Now was the perfect time. He smiled at the moon and climbed into bed.

Jenny was able to reschedule her workweek, thankful that Kari, a new young technician was happy to have the extra hours. Jenny was tired when she rose to the babies' loud squeals for breakfast. The night had proved to be a long sleepless one. She tossed and turned seeing Gregg's face and then John's face. John was laughing at her with those perfect white teeth threatening to hurt the babies if she didn't marry him. Gregg was standing behind John pleading for her to marry him instead. Every time she closed her eyes, the dream seemed to start again. By the time she got to sleep, it was time to get up.

By nine o'clock, she bundled up the babies and pumped breast milk for their stay at the farm. She dressed in a simple purple dress with three quarter length sleeves and a low cut v in front. The waistline was tailored to fit snugly and was offset by tiny buttons from the waistline to the bottom of the v. The bottom of the jacket scalloped over the top of the attached skirt. The skirt portion was straight cut with a deep slit up the back. She wore black net nylons that she had to run down town to purchase before the trip. She packed the babies' things like she was going to be away for a week. When everything was ready, she sat patiently on the couch and waited for Gregg while the babies played on the floor. Joseph got too warm in his snug suit and began to fuss. Rosalie must have thought it was her turn too, because soon both babies were crying. She unwrapped them from their snowsuits and soon both simmered down again. Finally, Gregg knocked on the door. His arms were full of fresh cut red roses. Jenny had never seen so many before.

He smiled his devilish smile at her. She was a sight to behold. Her hair was braided and put atop her head like a crown.

"These are for you," he said as his eyes roamed her body. The deep v in the front of her dress showed off plump breasts and he couldn't wait until after the ceremony. Gregg was dressed in a black suit with a white short collared button up shirt. He left the top button open exposing a hint of chest hair. His hair was shorter than it was the night before. He had it cut short on top with longer strands in back. It was getting long enough to curl around his neck.

"I like your hair cut," she said turning to the kitchen.

"You look stunning in that dress," he commented wryly studying the slit in the back of the dress as she walked to the kitchen.

"She curtsied," thank you sire. "I shall repay you for your kind words," she said giggling.

"You shall in deed," he said groaning to himself.

"Are you ready to become Mrs. Johnson?" he questioned over his shoulder.

She put the roses in water and came to him. She was relaxed now and moved into his arms easily. He held her tight.

"More ready than I've ever been?" He kept her in his arms and kissed her deeply. He stuck his finger down the front of her dress. "I can't wait until tonight. Are you sure we can't slip into your bedroom for a little while," he teased. His deep blue eyes sparkled as he gave her breast a quick squeeze. She squirmed and pushed him gently away from her.

"Well, if you're in such a hurry to be married we better get going." She bent down to re-bundle the children in their snowsuits. He squeezed her buttocks before bending next to her and helping with the babies.

After the babies were safely delivered to the Johnson's, Gregg and Jenny set off for Baldwin. It was a tiny little chapel with candles burning near the altar. Vases of white carnations were scattered around the altar, which were probably left over from someone's funeral. Gregg had called ahead and made arrangements for the ceremony. The celebrant was Fr. Michael Johnson. He was an elderly man who was kind and also happened to be Gregg's uncle. Fr. Michael greeted them warmly. They sat in a pew while Fr. Michael busied himself at the altar. Gregg continued to look at his watch nervously.

"What are we waiting for?" she asked impatiently.

"Shhhh," he said putting his finger to her lips.

She became frustrated with him as she paced impatiently. Fr. Michael looked at Gregg and nodded several times.

"Would you tell me what is going on here?" she said loudly embarrassing Gregg as Fr. Michael looked up at them. Fr. Michael smiled and continued to busy himself at the altar.

The back door squeaked open and first Scott entered, and then Shari. They proceeded to the altar and whispered with Fr. Michael for a long time. After several nods and gestures, Scott and Shari greeted Gregg and Jenny. Scott bent down and whispered into Gregg's ear. Gregg listened intently and then nodded in return. Jenny clenched her fists and gritted her teeth.

"Will somebody tell me what is going on here?" she said out loud.

Gregg leaned over to her. "There has been a short delay. We will be able to begin in about fifteen minutes." He reached for her hand to reassure her. He winked at her. "Scott and Shari are our witnesses. Have you forgotten that we need them to get married?" Indeed she did.

"Oh Gregg, thank goodness you remembered." She hugged Scott and then Shari. "Thanks you guys. I never dreamed you would come for this."

"Hey, I wouldn't miss it for the world," Scott told her, gently punching her shoulder.

The back door creaked open and a spool of sunshine filled the dim room. Dave stepped inside. He was carrying Joseph. Dave held the door open for Rose. She carried Rosalie proudly into the room. After a moment, the door opened again and Ruth and Jim appeared in the doorway. Jenny held her hands to her cheeks. Ruth carried an armful of peach gladiolus. She brought them to Jenny and placed them in her arms.

"I called every floral shop this side of the Mississippi for these," she said hugging Jenny's shoulder. "Welcome to our family." Ruth quickly took a seat in the tiny chapel. Ruth had come to accept Jenny, but she wondered how long this marriage would last. She was thankful that the awful John Hawkins had finally been charged with murder. Jenny turned to Gregg with wonder in her eyes.

"How did you do all this?" She looked at Fr. Michael who had come to stand before them. Gregg held out his arm to her. Gregg wondered the same thing to himself. He was exhausted and slept little the night before. Jenny would never know how much planning and calling he did in the few short hours of the morning. A nice soft bed would feel great about now, with my wife beside me, he thought with a smile.

He leaned close to her. "I only wish I would have had time to invite everyone. Shall we get married now?" She smiled a teary smile as he led her to the altar. Scott and Shari took their places on each side of them. During the ceremony, the babies babbled and cooed and made everyone laugh. Gregg was the first to speak his vows and he shocked everyone with the beautiful words he spoke to her. He held her hands firmly and he could feel them tremble. He looked directly into her pale blue eyes as he spoke.

"Jenny, Jeanine, Elerose," he said softly. "I have waited for you for so long that I cannot wake to another day without you beside me. Together we created two beautiful human beings who love us and need us to teach them and guide them through life. But most importantly, I need you to guide me, to love me for whom I am now and always. I have hurt you and I promise to replace the pain I have caused with many happy memories beginning with this day. Thank you for waiting for me while I lay in a coma. I knew you were there for me. I felt your presence. I thank God every day for you and for your patience. Without you I never would have been able to open my eyes and see your beauty again. You have the most beautiful heart than any woman I have ever met. You are strong where I am weak, you can see that which I am blind to and you have been a wonderful mother to our children. But now the time has come for me to become strong and for me to see that which I have missed for so long. It is time for me to become the father I was meant to be and the husband you always wanted. I promise to take care of you, to love you and to support you from this day forward."

Sobs could be heard behind him and when Gregg was finished Jenny was trembling with tears and emotion. Jenny had a much more difficult time with her vows. Her lips trembled and she could not speak clearly through sobs. She turned to Fr. Michael who was waiting patiently for her to finish.

"I do," she said tearfully. "But I, I can't finish the words." Shari handed her a hankie. She dabbed her tears and blew her nose. Fr. Michael looked at Gregg who nodded in approval.

"Fine," Fr. Michael said in agreement. "I now pronounce you husband and wife. You may kiss the bride."

Gregg reached for Jenny pulling her gently to him. He crushed her lips beneath his own as everyone applauded and whistled. Rosalie squealed in fright as the noise escalated in the room. After a moment, Gregg and Jenny turned to the small group holding hands. Fr. Michael stepped around beside them and said, "I introduce to you, Mr. and Mrs. Gregg Johnson. Congratulations," he said as he hugged his nephew. He reached for Jenny and did the same.

"You have a fine young man here," Fr. Michael said. "I wish you all the happiness in the world."

"Thank you," she whispered to him. Gregg slipped him a small envelope for his services. Then he reached for his bride and pulled her close to his side.

"There is going to be a reception at the Hyatt Regency Select for all of us. Thank you all for being here. I know it was last minute and I," he turned to Jenny, "we appreciate your support," he said squeezing her hand. After hugs and kisses from everyone, they were joined at the Hyatt Regency Select for drinks and a steak dinner. Everyone took turns holding the babies and then they were put in their infant seats during the meal. The babies fussed during dinner, which made Jenny feel nervous, but Shari and Rose and Ruth tended to their needs for attention.

After the meal, Gregg quickly announced their departure and led Jenny to the honeymoon suite he had reserved that morning. He opened the door and a scent of musk escaped. The room was dimly lit and a candle burned on the table by the bed. In the center of the room a hot tub was noisily gushing water in circles creating bubbles galore. A flask of wine sat in a chilling basket next to the tub. Gregg took off his suit coat and casually unzipped the back of Jenny's dress. He planted kisses on her neck as he slid the dress off her shoulders and down her waist. He unhooked her bra and let it drop to the floor. He gently massaged her full breasts between his fingertips. Gregg stood back and watched as she removed her panty hose and placed them on the ledge of the tub. All thoughts of wanting to climb into bed and sleep for ten hours diminished. He laughed at her noticing how perfectly she placed her things aside.

"Come," he said, taking her by the hand. He led her to the window and slipped his fingers inside the drapes and gently held them apart. "See that?" He pointed to the beautiful orange moon hanging low in the Eastern sky. I've always wanted to give you the moon. There it is. I'm going to give you everything you've always wanted...and more," he said bending down to kiss her neck. Jenny felt happier than she had in her life and she knew she had made the right decision. She was now Gregg's wife. It was what she always dreamed of.

"You are the most wonderful man I've ever met. Do you know that?" she said staring at the full golden ball. I love you," she said, knowing that he meant what he told her. He picked her up and carried her to the tub. Fully naked she climbed into the tub and submerged her nervous body into the bubbles. Her eyes never left her husband's.

Gregg quickly dodged his clothes and climbed in the tub next to her. He lowered himself to the seat under the bubbles and pulled her to face him. She straddled his lap feeling the hardness of him rub against her thigh. They kissed, searching and acquainting each other's body with their lips and hands. A smile formed her lips as she watched him gently make love to her. She closed her eyes feeling him and needing him. Memories of her ugly past flashed through her mind and it was several minutes before she was able to completely relax. And when she did, her passion mounted and she was able to give him complete satisfaction. She felt him shudder and when she finally opened her eyes, he was still smiling at her.

"Ah! At last you are fully mine, my little wife," he said kissing her wet nose. "How does it feel to be married?"

"It feels wonderful," she said relaxing into his arms. To Jenny, it felt like months of struggle had just been removed from her life. She finally had Gregg back in her life and she knew this time she was going to hang on for dear life.

An hour later the newlyweds emerged from the tub and shared a glass of wine. They lay snuggled side by side on the bed and drifted off to sleep on top of the covers. Before daybreak, Jenny stirred feeling the weight of Gregg's legs on top of hers. She ran her hand down his outer thigh and nudged him off her. She sat up thinking she would be able to shower before they began their trip home. As she slipped off the edge of the bed, Gregg caught her around the waist. Without a word he pulled her back down and made love to her once more. This time it was slow and tender and he took the time to satisfy her needs before his own. Two hours later, they climbed into the hot tub once more and faced each other as man and wife. His hands and lips roamed her body taking full possession of her entire being. Her body shivered from his touch as he excited her all over again.

She smiled at him as she thought about the things he did to her body. It was the most erotic thing she had ever shared with anyone. It wasn't nasty or dirty like she was taught in parochial school when she was a kid. She knew it was what her mother and aunts talked about in hushed voices around the coffee table and when Jenny would make her presence known, the ladies would speak louder changing the subject. Her mother had told her about men and babies but she never told her how joyful and pleasurable a man could make a woman feel. She broke into laughter sinking low into the bubbles and teased him beneath the water.

"What?" he asked as she grinned at him.

"I would never have thought love making could be like this."

"I hope you don't believe in romance stories where the guy does it four times a day." He teased. Jenny laughed a naughty laugh.

"You mean it's not true?" she chortled. She tickled his toes in the depth of the water. Gregg threw his head back in laughter. "Shall we find out?" He teased standing to reach for his towel. He climbed out of the hot tub and headed for the shower. Jenny chased after him. She caught him around the waist and stumbled with him to the bed. He held her close to him speaking sincerely into her ear.

"I hate to disappoint you this early in our marriage, but Superman, I am not. Can you wait until tonight?" As she lay back exhausted, he made love to her with only his hands and his lips until her passion was finally spent.

"How was that for a start?" he asked seductively.

"That was the most beautiful beginning to anything I've ever experienced," she said turning onto her side. She backed up to him, and snuggled against the curve of his body.

As they lay together finally as man and wife, Jenny squeezed her arms tightly around his. "I can't wait to get home and start my life as Mrs. Gregory Johnson," she sighed.

"And I look forward to many more of these kind of beginnings in our very own house...I love you Gregg," she whispered. Those were the most beautiful words he had ever heard her say.

"I know," he whispered softly. Now they had their entire lives ahead of them together. They were finally a team and their mountains already seemed smaller than yesterday. John's trial lay ahead of them and he hated to see Jenny go through hell again, but this time it would be different. He would be there, supporting her just like he promised. He knew there was a possibility that John Hawkins could escape from prison and Gregg was fearful that he might come back to kill them both or their children. It was a reality that he could not ignore. After the trial, he planned to take her on a secret vacation to Hawaii. He could already feel the sun-warmed sand below his feet and he envisioned Jenny beside him, her freckles deepening in the southern sun. He listened to her melodious snoring, as he lay awake behind her. A sound he welcomed just to have her near.

He covered her body with his arm in a protective gesture thinking about how he almost lost her because of his own jealousy. He knew she loved him by the way she made love to him, giving him her body and soul as though it were a gift. He, too, loved her with a passion as deep as the ocean, opening his heart for the love she had to give him. He thought about the shadows that had come over their friendship and how the shadows had been lifted by a strong love for each other. They were shadows that darkened their lives, like a single cloud passing in the blue sky on a beautiful sunny day. Before he went to sleep, he thanked God for their blessings, for giving him a woman with an enormous heart and for two beautiful children to love and cherish every day of their lives.